But even a boy
knows that a man
never runs...

If I cry, his blood will be my tears.

Daquan crept up behind the Caddy and pulled out his nine. He cocked it back, took a deep breath, and smashed the driver's side window completely, making Black's alarm go crazy. He quickly dropped and rolled under the car, feeling the heat of the transmission on his face.

"What the fuck?! Hey!" Black came out of the motel room shouting, clad only in his boxers.

The sound of his own breathing was heavy in Daquan's ears, and it felt like his heartbeat was pulsing through the fingers that he had poised on the trigger. He could hear Black's bare feet hitting the pavement, coming closer and closer until his toes were directly beside Daquan's shoulder. Daquan closed his eyes for a second, then reopened them as he slid his torso from under the car, raised the gun, and fired twice into Black's stomach as he leaned in the car window to see if anything had been taken.

The girl, wrapped in a dingy white sheet, was only a few feet away from Black when the shots cracked the silence, and she let out a piercing scream as Black staggered back. Daquan came out from under the car and fired again, hitting Black in the chest. As Black fell back on the concrete, Daquan stood over him and hissed, "Charge *this* to the game, nigguh," then fired twice into Black's skull, opening it up like a cracked egg.

Advance praise for DEATH AROUND THE CORNER

"Just like his music, C. Miller paints a picture with words and rhythm that'll have you nodding your head from cover to cover. If you've never experienced N'awlins, you will after reading *Death Around the Corner*."

—Kwame Teague, author of *The Adventures of Ghetto Sam* and *The Glory of My Demise*

"C-Murder keeps it TRU his first time out the gate!"

—K'wan, bestselling author of *Gangsta*

death around the corner

A Novel by

C-MURDER

VIBE STREET LIT
is a division of VIBE MEDIA GROUP, LLC.
215 Lexington Avenue
New York, NY 10016
Rob Kenner, Editorial Director
Theodore A. Hatwood, Jr., Director, VIBE Enterprises

KENSINGTON BOOKS are published by

Kensington Publishing Corp.
850 Third Avenue
New York, NY 10022

All Kensington titles, imprints and distributed lines are available at special quantity discounts for bulk purchases for sales promotion, premi-
ums, fund-raising, educational or institutional use.

Special book excerpts or customized printings can also be created to fit
specific needs. For details, write or phone the Kensington Special Sales
Manager: Kensington Publishing Corp., 850 Third Avenue, New York,
NY 10022. Attn. Special Sales Department. Phone: 1-800-221-2647.

Kensington Books and the K logo Reg. U.S. Pat. & TM Off.

ISBN 1-60183-000-9

First Kensington Trade Paperback Printing: January 2007
10 9 8 7 6 5 4 3 2 1

Printed in the United States of America

ACKNOWLEDGMENTS

I dedicate this book to my lovely daughters, Chelsea, Courtney and Chanelle Miller. They inspire me to keep moving and never give up. To my grandmother, Big Mama, who raised me and has always been in my corner. And to my brother, Kevin Miller, may he rest in peace.

Special thanks to my family for all their help and support. Janelle, Keli, and Dee for their typing skills. Bre, Barbara, Lupe, Aish, and Rick for all their tireless groundwork. To Rob, Teddy, Manie, Danyel, Ari, Eric, and the whole VIBE Media Group, thanks for believing. To Steven, Laurie, and the whole Kensington Publishing team—can't knock your hustle.

Much love to my sister Germany, my brother Silkk, my nephew Lil' Kevin, Rev. Best, Moses, Montez, Momz, 2Saint, Karnell, Melinda, Ron and Gay, the whole CP3, Jimmy Watson, G-Money, Lil' One, DJ Spin, Go, 9 Fingers, Young Trump, Irvin, Jahbo, Mac and Renae, Ludacris, Kwame and Lashonda Teague, Blunt, Picture Man, Shak, Suave Bob, Will Horton, Hassan, Arman, Kiva, Malika, Marie, Nakita, Sherman, Noony, Ronnie, Mama Net, Uncle Marvin and Anthony, Aunt Joan and Ray and the whole fam. Stay Tru!!!

Most of all, thanks to everyone that purchases this book and to all my homies on lock: Walk by Faith . . .

1

"Macy! Macy! Can we go to the fair?"

"Daquan, for the last time, I'll take you to the fair! Now shut the hell up, boy!"

Daquan stared at the TV screen, wide-eyed with excitement and anticipation after hearing his mother's confirmation. Never mind her tone, or the fact that his last birthday, he never got the big wheel she promised; still, she was Mommy, and her words filled him with happiness.

The World's Fair of '84 was the biggest thing he had seen in his life. The commercial showed all the happy faces, shiny gadgets, fun rides, and delicious food, things he'd never experienced in his five-year-old world. All he knew was the Magnolia Projects. One of the roughest, most drug-infested housing projects in New Orleans, Magnolia was a world in and of itself. Despite its squalid conditions, there were plenty of other kids and large, grassy areas to play every game imaginable. The surrounding recreational parks had basketball hoops for the older cats, but at his age, Thomas Lafont Elementary was Daquan's very own amusement park, complete with monkey bars and seesaws and located right in the heart of the 'Nolia. Many a day he had gotten his ass tore up for going to Lafont without Macy's permission. Daquan wasn't a bad child, just a poor one, which meant he had to make do with whatever he had. And when it came to fun, Lafont was all he had. But now that the World's Fair was coming, it was like an early Christmas, and Daquan couldn't wait.

"Yeahh, yeahh," he squealed like a mini Lil Jon. "I'm goin' to the fair!"

He hopped down off of the clean but worn down plastic-covered couch and crossed the living room, entering the kitchen. "I hope my daddy can come with us," he said to himself, as he opened the refrigerator looking for Kool-Aid. "He works too much," he added as an afterthought.

His father Daryl worked at Gambino's Bakery, sometimes pulling a double shift just to keep the bills paid in their one-bedroom apartment. He wouldn't let Macy work because he was raised believing it was the man's responsibility to provide for his family. But in the era of Reaganomics, it was becoming next to impossible to do that alone. Still, he did the best he could, and Daquan loved him for it.

Daquan balanced the half-full pitcher of Kool-Aid between his chin and hands as he carried it to the table. He looked in the refrigerator and could basically figure out what his next meal would be. Inside was a pot of leftover red beans and rice, a hard block of commodity cheese, a box of corn flakes, and a box of powdered milk, so he knew it would be red beans and rice, unless his daddy brought home some eggs so Macy could make his favorite, scrambled eggs and rice.

He looked around for a clean glass or a mayo jar to drink from, but he couldn't find one. So he ran to his parents' bedroom door and yelled, "Macy! I need a glass."

"Boy, if you don't get away from my damn door!"

Daquan stepped back from the door. He knew she wasn't in the room alone. Teddy, his father's cousin, was in there, like he was almost every day at this time. He often wondered what they did in there. But since Teddy and Daryl weren't only cousins, they were also friends, Daquan didn't see anything wrong in his five-year-old mind. He forgot about the Kool-Aid and walked away from the door, ready to take a nap and dream about the upcoming fair.

Inside the bedroom, Teddy remained jittery since Daquan had come to the door.

"Macy, you know I don't like coming to your house, bringing you this stuff," he told her, sliding his works into a small leather pouch.

He was a petty hustler, homely looking and stupid, but Macy depended on him to keep the monkey off her back. As her heroin habit grew, it got harder and harder to hide from Daryl that she was getting high again. Besides, money was tight, and right about now the only thing tighter was her pussy, which she had recently started offering Teddy in return for the dope.

"Teddy, stop bitchin'! The boy don't know nothin'. He ain't but five," she replied, feeling the china white slowly coat her mind with that serene nothingness. *I'm feelin' good, and this clown blowin' my high*, she thought, eyelids at half-staff.

Still worried, he asked, "Why can't we meet somewhere else? Shit, Daquan might say the wrong thing. Man, look . . ." His voice trailed off.

Macy knew how to shut him up. She began to undress, revealing a petite but curvaceous frame. She watched Teddy's eyes fill with lust at her chocolate femininity.

"Daryl don't get home till eight and it ain't but four," she said. "Now, do you want some pussy or not? 'Cause I know a lot of nigguhs who would love to be in your shoes."

He watched her slowly massage her face and breasts, something she did routinely after getting hit with her fix, and it never failed to turn Teddy on. She laid back on the bed and spread her long, dark legs invitingly. She was feeling good and she wanted to pay Teddy before her high went down and the reality of her betrayal came raining down on her.

At the sight of her naked wetness, Teddy's heart began to

beat a rhythm through his erection. He knew this was wrong. She was Daryl's wife. Daryl was his cousin. But he had never had a woman so beautiful, and if it wasn't for her addiction, he never would again.

"You are beautiful, baby—I just can't get enough of you," he whispered as he mounted Macy and entered her. "Girl, you got some good pussy. This the best I done had yet . . . But how come you never let me kiss them pretty lips, or change positions?"

She eyed him coldly. "Just fuck me, and when you cum, don't make a lot of noise. My baby in the other room."

Her mind wandered away from the man on top of her to the man she had betrayed. The guilt of knowing how much Daryl loved her made her hate herself for being so weak. Macy was ashamed of her need for the drug that had taken so much from her, and always threatened to take more. At her lowest moments, she contemplated suicide. The thought of taking her own life had begun eight years ago, after losing her daughter, Diana, at birth. Macy knew it was because of her drug use during pregnancy, and she vowed to Daryl and herself that she'd stay clean—a promise she couldn't keep. Whenever Macy got high and thought of Diana, the tears would flow constantly and uncontrollably like clockwork.

"Girl, why you always cryin' while we fuckin'?" Teddy asked between humps, but received no answer. "Ain't it good to you, baby?"

His words fell on deaf ears because Macy was in her own world. A world where happiness would never come, where she convicted herself a murderer of her own flesh and blood, and betrayed her only love.

Her thoughts were suddenly interrupted by a slight noise coming from the living room. *Was that the door?* she asked herself, quickly glancing at the clock. She held her breath, listening intently, until she mentally dismissed the sound as either the TV or Daquan.

* * *

Daryl looked at the stitches in his hand and chuckled to himself lightly as he got off the bus in front of the 'Nolia.

He had been at work washing dishes when he accidentally cut his hand on a knife.

"Hell of a way to get the day off," he said to himself.

The cut wasn't serious, but it did require stitches. He was sent to Charity Hospital and then allowed to go home for the rest of the day. A little family time was a welcome idea, being that he worked so hard.

Every morning he was up at four in order to make the two-hour bus ride to Metairie, some thirty miles west of New Orleans, where Gambino's Bakery was located. In a car, it would only take thirty minutes, but that was a luxury Daryl could not afford.

Regardless, he wasn't fazed or frustrated by his current situation, because at age twenty-five, he already had a plan. He wanted to own his own bakery one day, then build and expand. He had already learned the proper functioning of the business, so he told himself that with hard work and patience, he knew he'd achieve his dream.

Daryl grew up hard. He had even done three years as a juvenile at Scotland Correctional Institute in Eastern Louisiana. But he vowed to himself that he'd get his family out of the 'Nolia and into a better quality of life. Daryl had already seen what ghetto life had done to his young wife, but he stuck by her, in hopes that love could conquer all.

He slid his hand into his pocket and winced from the pain of the still-tender cut, which was nothing compared to the pain he'd soon face inside his own home. He opened the door, entered, and then quietly closed it behind him. This was the sound Macy heard that put her senses on alert. Cartoons played quietly on the TV as Daquan lay on the couch in a peaceful sleep. Daryl sat down next to Daquan and gently kissed his slumbering son on the forehead. He admired his features, focusing on the thick eyebrows they both shared. The boy had Macy's nose and a mixture of his caramel complexion and Macy's Hershey hue.

His contemplative mood was suddenly interrupted by noises coming from the bedroom. There was a thud, and his instincts intensified his hearing, turning the noises into a man's voice and then the unthinkable . . .

The sexual sounds of a man being pleased.

Before his mind had fully grasped the situation, his body reacted and took the initiative to rush the door.

Locked.

With all of his six-foot, two-hundred-twenty-pound frame, he coiled his leg and aimed for the right side of the doorknob, kicking the flimsy door off of its top hinge. He didn't want to believe his eyes. He *wished* he didn't have to witness something like this, but what he saw could not be denied. Teddy leaped from between Macy's legs and stared at Daryl with total fear in his eyes.

"D-Daryl, man, look," Teddy stuttered.

But all Daryl could say was, "I got cut." The rage inside was building like a runaway locomotive. "You fuckin' bitch, I got *cut*," he screamed at his wife. He was the only one who knew the full significance of the statement.

Macy was frantic, screaming apologies while Teddy tried to cover his shamed nakedness.

"You dirty bitch, I *bled* for you," Daryl hissed.

Macy looked into her husband's eyes and saw a look she'd never seen before. It was like only a shell was there, his soul totally void. He moved in a zombie-like state as he turned his gaze to the doorless closet space a few feet away. Macy saw him, sensed his intentions, and yelled, "No, no, no, Daryl . . . I'm sorry . . . I *swear* I'm sorry!" But it was too late.

Daryl dug through the piled-up clothes and found the shoebox containing the .38 his father had given him. In an instant, the gun was in his hand. Teddy had no room to get out, so when he saw the gun, all he could do was back into the corner.

"Daryl, I swear to God, man—please, just listen," Teddy pleaded. But Daryl's heart couldn't be reached, nor could his mind comprehend.

Teddy released his bowels as Daryl pointed the gun at him—then, without hesitation, began to fire . . . and fire . . . and fire, until the revolver was spent and Teddy's chest was riddled. His body jerked violently as each hollow tip impacted on his flesh. Teddy's torso seemed to inflate to twice its size, like a balloon filling with air, then quickly deflated to normal size. His body slid down the wall, lifeless, staring at nothing.

Daryl was snapped out of his trance by Macy's screams and Daquan's crying. His son had witnessed it all from the doorway.

"Daddy, please stop! Please, I'm scared."

At the sound of his son's voice, Daryl dropped the gun and turned to the crying child.

"Come here, Daddy," Daquan sobbed. "Pick me up."

Daryl picked up Daquan, cradling him in his arms, and walked into the living room. Never once did he look at Macy or acknowledge her whimpers.

"Daryl . . ." she kept repeating. "Daryl, I'm sorry."

He sat on the couch with Daquan on his lap. He knew he was on borrowed time.

There would be no running for Daryl. No hiding. He was a man raised to be a man, and had done nothing that any other man in his position wouldn't do. Now, all that was left were these last few words he had for his son, from the deepness of his heart.

"Baby boy, you know your daddy loves you. I'm sorry about everything you saw. Daddy didn't mean to scare you. I love you. Don't ever forget that, okay?"

They were both crying now. Daquan's tears were the tears

of a child losing his world, and Daryl's the tears of a man being destroyed.

"I love you, too, Daddy," Daquan answered.

"Now, they're gonna take me away for a long time, so I need you to be a little man and do the right thing."

"*Nooo*, Daddy! We can go away. We can run."

Daryl silenced his son. "No, a man *never* runs, you hear me? A man never runs."

These were words Daquan would never forget. Daryl hugged his son tightly and continued, making the most of the little time they had left. "I'll always be here for you. I'll write you letters and talk to you on the phone. You can even come see me, okay?"

It seemed to Daquan's young mind that the police were kicking in the door the very next moment. They rushed in, slamming his father to the ground.

"Get off my daddy!" Daquan yelled with all the manliness he could muster.

"Calm down, Daquan, I'm okay," Daryl assured him, face-down on the floor.

But it wasn't okay to Daquan.

Macy, shameful and shaken, called Daryl's mother to come get Daquan. He would never see Macy again. The boy sat alone outside, amongst throngs of nosy neighbors and flashing police lights. All he could think about was how the cops took his daddy away, and a new emotion sprang into his young heart.

Hate.

It was making him see everything in a different light.

"Daquan!"

Daquan looked around and felt relieved to see Grandma Mama coming toward him with a young girl beside her. She was lanky and pretty with a caramel hue, her hair in pigtails. He had never seen the girl before, but she still looked familiar to him. Grandma Mama scooped him up in her arms, kissed him, and asked, "Are you okay, baby?"

All he could do was sob into her shoulder as she cried on his. She had lost a son, but gained a grandson to raise.

Daquan looked around for the little girl, but she was gone.

"Grandma Mama, who was that girl?"

"What girl, baby?"

He started to answer, but his attention was drawn to a policeman walking by. Daquan eyed him coldly as Grandma Mama toted the boy away from the place he had always called home. Away from a father being taken away and a mother who was running away. Theirs was a family forever scattered by the winds of change.

2

I hate you! I hate you for taking my daddy! Daddy, don't go, please don't go, daddy! But it's not a police car they put my daddy in. It's a long black car that looks like a station wagon, only bigger. Like when Macy's mama went away and the people came with all the pretty colors and horns and stuff. They were marching down the streets and Macy was crying and said that her mama was gettin' her wings. The car was like that. And my daddy got into a big wooden box in the back of the car . . . Where is my daddy going?

Then I jump up and chase the car. I'm runnin' 'cause I wanna see where they are takin' my daddy. But my legs are hurtin', and I fall . . . I fall real hard and when I get up, the car is gone and all the people are gone. It's just me . . . I put my head down on my knee so nobody could see me cry. I feel somebody touch my shoulder and I look up and it's the girl. The girl with Grandma Mama. She is reaching out her hand to me . . .

"Daquan, Daquan, time to get up, baby," he heard Grandma Mama say, bringing him out of the dream.

Daquan looked around the tiny bedroom, feeling the morning sun on his face. He rubbed his eyes as he sat up.

"I'm up, Grandma Mama."

"Good," she replied, kissing him on the forehead, 'cause Mama made you a big ol' breakfast. Go on and wash your face."

Daquan slid off the edge of the bed in his Incredible Hulk Underoos and ran off to the bathroom. He tried the knob but it was locked.

"I'm in here," said a woman's voice from inside.

Daquan began to hop around, doing the pee dance. "I gotta go," he urged her.

"Lissa! Is you still in there?" Grandma Mama yelled from the kitchen. "Chile, it's three other folk in here need to go too, now."

Moments later, the toilet flushed and Melissa came out of the bathroom. Daquan recognized her as his daddy's older sister, but he didn't stop to say good morning as he pushed past her and closed the door.

"Dang, say excuse me next time. Ol' mannish self," she quipped, heading for her room to get dressed.

Once Daquan pissed and washed his face, he followed his nose to the kitchen. The aroma alone had his stomach growling. He found Grandma Mama bent over the stove, finishing up the grits, scrambled eggs, and sausage patties. Daquan stood at the door, unsure of his place in the new surroundings. He studied Grandma Mama, hearing her hum a morning melody. Her flowered robe was slightly soiled, but still vivid in splashes of rose colors. She was a short woman, and a little wide. Her salt-and-pepper hair was pulled back in a bun, and when she spoke, her gold tooth winked at you. All warm and friendly, Grandma Mama had a heart of gold, but a fist full of fire at the same time. Daquan always loved to visit her, but now, living with her, he felt awkward.

"Well," Grandma Mama said without turning to him, "you gonna just stand there or you want something to eat?"

"Yes, please," he replied, trying to be on his best behavior, remembering his father's words.

She turned to him, wiping her hands on a dishrag. "Well, sit on down then."

She watched Daquan shyly cross the kitchen floor. She worried about the effects the situation would have on his young mind frame. Grandma Mama didn't know how much he had seen, but she knew he had been there.

Daquan lifted himself up into the chair while she put his plate in front of him. He was so short, he had to sit on his knees to reach table level. She watched him grab his fork and dig in before stopping him. "*Ut*-uh. What do we do 'fore we eat, Daquan?"

Daquan sheepishly returned her gaze, then put his hands together, and said, "Amen," as he shoved a forkful of food into his mouth.

Grandma Mama chuckled. "Boy, that there got to be the shortest prayer I never heard."

He only smiled slightly in response.

"How are you, baby?"

"Okay," he mumbled.

She started to tell him she was going to see his daddy in the county jail, but since Daquan wouldn't be going this time, she thought it better not to. Just then, Melissa stepped into the kitchen, putting her left earring in her ear. At thirty-five, it was hard to tell her age, or that she had a fifteen-year-old son. She had the same complexion as Daryl, but she was short with a thick frame and a small waist.

"Mama, you ain't even dressed. I told you I got stuff to do," she huffed, picking up one of the biscuits on the stove and buttering it lightly.

"Chile, I know you ain't rushing me," Grandma Mama shot right back, but in a relaxed drawl. "That's the problem now, always runnin' 'round like a chicken wit' the head cut off. And where is Jerome?" she asked, referring to Melissa's son.

"Where you think?" Melissa answered between bites. "Still in the bed."

"Jerome . . . *Jerome*! Boy, get yo' tail in here now!" Grandma Mama called out, filling the small apartment with her command. Daquan just took it all in as he ate himself into a full stomach. He knew Jerome was his big cousin, but he was seldom there when Daquan came to visit. Jerome half-staggered into the kitchen, one hand in his pants and the other rubbing his eyes.

"Dang, Grandma, it's summer. What I gotta get up fo'?" his sleepy voice cracked.

"Don't dang me, boy," Grandma Mama replied, getting up from her seat. "Summer time all the more reason to be up. Need to be workin' . . . least, cuttin' folks' grass, 'stead of layin' 'round heah wit' yo' lazy self."

Jerome had heard this speech a thousand times, so he yawned, letting the words go through one ear and out the other. Then he noticed Daquan. "Sup, lil' cuz? Heard you stayin' wit' us, huh? Welcome to the CP3," Jerome said with a grin, playfully punching Daquan on his arm. CP3 was street code for Calliope Projects, Third Ward.

Grandma Mama sucked her teeth.

"This ain't no CP3, or whatever you call it. Don't be teachin' that boy no foolishness while I'm gone, 'cause you fin' to watch him."

Jerome sighed hard as he fixed his plate and sat down. Grandma Mama leaned over and kissed Daquan on the cheek.

"You be good now, Daquan, and Grandma'll be home soon."

"Yes, ma'am."

No sooner were Melissa and Grandma Mama out the door, when Jerome pulled out a crinkled pack of Camels and lit up a cigarette.

"Damn," he cussed when he realized it had a rip in it. He placed his finger over the rip, took another draw, then said, "Yeah, I heard Uncle Daryl got him one," as he blew out the smoke. "I always knew he was a crazy muhfucka."

Daquan dropped his fork. "My daddy ain't crazy! And I'm tellin' Grandma Mama you smokin'."

Jerome leaned his elbows on the table. "And I'ma whoop yo' lil' ass. Look heah, we gon' get this straight. Ain't gon' be no tellin' if me and you gon' be cool. Don't you wanna be cool wit' me?"

Daquan just looked at him, still mad because he called his daddy crazy.

"Dig, lil' cuz, I ain't mean it like that. I just meant yo' daddy ain't no punk. You know, he don't take no shit. Ain't nothing wrong wit' being crazy like that, ya dig?"

Daquan drank his milk. He knew what a punk was, so if being crazy meant Daryl wasn't one, he was okay with that.

"But like I said, ain't no tellin', ya dig? If we cool, I'll make sure you have a lot of fun," Jerome offered.

"Will you take me to the fair?" Daquan inquired hopefully.

Jerome sat back and chuckled. "Fuck the fair. This heah da Calliope. Believe me, it's better than the fair. Come on, let's go get dressed and I'll show you."

An hour later, Daquan and Jerome stepped out of their building and into the sun. Daquan looked wide-eyed at his new surroundings. If the 'Nolia had been his world, the Calliope could easily be a child's universe. Sitting "backatown," it was the largest housing project in the N.O. Rows and rows of brick buildings, consisting of hundreds of individual apartments, were all evenly spaced and landscaped with a wide stretch of grass parallel to each row of buildings. They were perfect for a child to play football or any outdoor game, because the only interference was the trees that lined the sidewalks.

Jerome lit another cigarette, then hit PLAY on his boom box. Suddenly, the world came to life for Daquan.

Party People, Party People can y'all get funky?
Soulsonic Force, can y'all get funky?
The Zulu Nation, can y'all get funky?
Yeahhh, just hit me.

The sounds of Afrika Bambaataa's "Planet Rock" blasted from Jerome's box into Daquan's ears and all over his body. It was right then that he first fell in love with hip-hop.

"You like that, huh, lil' cuz?" Jerome yelled over the music when he saw the slight uncoordinated bop of a child in Daquan. "Come on."

Jerome slow-bopped down the sidewalk with Daquan right by his side; he was just the right height to be ear level with the speaker of Jerome's box. Daquan looked around at all the new faces going about their daily business. Women were inside cleaning up, with music of their own blasting through open windows. Proud men were outside washing and shining their cars, and little kids were running around making games out of anything. When Daquan saw the playground, he tugged at Jerome's pants, pointed to the playground, and shouted, "I wanna go over there!"

Jerome turned the music down a notch and answered, "Hol' up, lil' cuz. I got you. I just gotta handle somethin' right quick."

Daquan grudgingly trucked on, ready at an instant to remind Jerome if they got too far from the playground.

Jerome went to the next building, cut off the radio, and stepped inside. He knocked on the first door and waited. The sounds of "Love and Happiness" by Al Green could be heard seeping into the hallway. Moments later, a heavyset woman in pink rollers and an oversized T-shirt came to the door. She looked to be in her forties, and although Jerome was only fifteen, she eyed his lanky frame.

"Hello, Jerome," she greeted him. "What you doin' comin' to my house this early?"

"Uh, sorry, Ms. Baylor," Jerome stuttered, because her gaze always made him nervous. "Is Pepper home?"

She opened the door a little wider. "If he ain't, he need to be."

The door was open just wide enough for him to squeeze inside, but just tight enough where he felt her breast brush up against his back. Pepper was his man, but he hated coming to his house because of his mom. He knew what time it was, but he couldn't see fuckin' his best friend's mother and he didn't know how to tell Pepper, so he tried to avoid her.

Daquan followed Jerome in the back, to the last door. He knocked.

"Yo," was the response from inside.

"It's me, nigguh," Jerome replied, then entered the room.

Inside the small, cluttered bedroom sat Pepper, dressed only in a pair of cut-off shorts and talking on the phone. Clothes and toys were scattered everywhere, so Jerome cleared a spot on the other bed, while Daquan sat on the floor and began playing with a toy fire truck.

"So what's up?" Pepper spoke into the phone. "You gonna gimme that pussy or what? A nigguh got needs."

"Who dat?" Jerome asked.

Tamika, Pepper mouthed silently. "Yeah, I'm here," he said into the phone, then sighed hard. "Look, I'll call you back when you get off that bullshit." Then he hung up.

"Nigguh, Mika ain't fuckin'. All she do is dick tease," Jerome told him, as if he had firsthand knowledge.

"Man, fuck that bitch. Gimme a cigarette."

Jerome tossed him the pack.

"You think yo' mama got some weed, whody? That shit had me high as a muhfucka." Jerome grinned.

"Shit," Pepper toned, blowing out smoke. "We gotta wait till she leave so I can look. Might be a roach or two." Pepper's eyes fell on Daquan. "Who dis is?"

"My lil' cuz, Daquan. He live wit' us now 'cause his pops in jail."

"Fo' what?"

"Killin' a nigguh 'cause he was bangin' his ol' lady."

Pepper nodded. "That's some cold shit, man. He ain't do nothin' wrong. I'll kill a nigguh myself fo' that shit."

Daquan never looked up from the fire truck, but he heard every word, and what he heard made him more proud of his daddy. Everyone seemed to think what he did was right. They said he wasn't no punk, so in his young mind, it was starting to seem like killing a man wasn't wrong.

"Pepper, Mama want you," said Pepper's six-year-old brother Nut, as he came in the room. He was half asleep, but when he saw Daquan playing with his toy, he woke up.

"Gimme my *truck*!" he yelled, then swooped down on Daquan, snatching it out of his hand and pushing him.

Daquan fell back, then scrambled to his feet and got between Jerome's legs.

Pepper chuckled, but Jerome wasn't having it. "Quan! You better not let that lil' nigguh handle you like that. Take it back."

Daquan didn't move.

"Man, you couldn't pour your cousin on Nut right now, scared as he is," Pepper commented proudly.

"Oh, *hell*, no," Jerome spat, turning Daquan to face him. "Ain't gon' be no sucka shit. Now, whoop his ass fo' I whoop yours."

He spun Daquan back around and gave him a slight shove from between his legs. Nut was slightly taller, but Daquan was bigger. They eyed each other like two young pits.

"Give it back," Daquan ordered.

"It's mine," Nut hissed.

"Tear his ass up, Nut," Pepper urged, and Nut went into action.

He swatted Daquan's face hard. Daquan tried to grab him, but Nut dug his little fingers into his neck, making Daquan howl with pain. Nut fell on top of him with a thud.

"What's going on in there?" his mother's voice boomed from the living room. "Pepper, you hear me calling you, boy!"

Jerome broke up the tussle and pulled a crying Daquan off the floor.

"Crybaby, crybaby," teased Nut, then he ran out the room.

Pepper followed him out to see what his mother wanted. Jerome wiped Daquan's tears with the ends of his shirt. "Stop that cryin', boy. Stop. You okay, just can't fight. But the important thing is you *did* fight. Win or lose, don't let nobody take nothin' from you, you hear me?"

Daquan nodded.

"You want some candy?"

Daquan nodded harder.

"Alright, come on. Don't worry, I'ma teach you how to fight, so next time you gonna whoop Nut ass."

They went a few buildings down to Ms. Betty's, the neighborhood candy lady. She sold all the ice cream and sweets to the kids and most of the numbers and cigarettes to the adults. Jerome bought Daquan a bag of Mary Janes, some bubble gum, and Now and Laters. Ms. Betty even gave him a bag of pinwheel cookies because she knew who he was and what had happened, although she didn't say a word. News travels fast in the Calliope, especially with Ms. Betty.

Daquan was feeling his cousin more and more. He loved his music, the way he walked, and the cool stuff he did with cigarette smoke. But what made him love him even more was what he said when the police pulled up on a group of older dudes and began to harass them just because they could. Jerome narrowed his eyes through the cigarette smoke and spat, "Fuckin' police. I hate them motherfuckas."

Daquan didn't know what the word "hate" meant, but he knew what it felt like. He felt the same way. That statement alone made him love his cousin Jerome.

3

Daquan didn't cry, even though he wanted to. Life was teaching him the uselessness of tears. So at age five, he learned not to cry, regardless of how he felt inside. This was a dangerous decision, because when you don't cry, your heart hardens like stone in a parched, waterless desert.

Daquan rode back from visiting his father in the county jail without shedding one tear. He had been with Grandma Mama two weeks when he was finally able to see Daryl. He came out in his orange prison jumpsuit, chained and shackled like a beast instead of a man. He had lost weight because of the small portions of food served in county jail, and he had no money to buy anything from commissary. Grandma Mama offered to give him a few dollars, but he knew she needed it more than him, so he declined, not out of pride but out of priority.

He sat behind the two-inch-thick Plexiglas and spoke to them on the phone. At first he made small talk, then his eyes got serious as he spoke to Daquan.

"You bein' good for Mama?" Daryl inquired.

Daquan just nodded, holding the phone with both hands.

"Boy, speak up."

"Yes, Daddy."

"Okay," Daryl answered. "Look . . ." His words trailed off

because he didn't know what to say. "Daquan, I'm not a bad man. I killed a man, but I'm not sorry. I only regret that it had to happen. But I'm not a bad man. I'm not a good man, either. I'm just a man, a man that made a choice, and I want you to understand—it ain't enough to be good, Daquan. Just look at me. I worked, I had a family, I stayed away from foolishness, but *look* at me."

Daryl pinched his eyes to fight the tears that he, too, was finding useless. "What I'm trying to say is, them streets is poison, death waiting around every corner, and you got to be more than good to escape it. Just 'cause you ain't in 'em, don't mean you can't be a victim of 'em, you hear me?"

"Yes, Daddy," Daquan said. He would never forget these words, even though he had yet to comprehend them.

"You got to be more than good, Daquan, you got to be smart. And not just in school. Be *smart*, son . . . be smart."

"I love you, Daddy," Daquan vowed.

Daryl smiled with glassy eyes and held his hand up to the window. Daquan did the same. Palm to palm, separated by two inches of injustice, his hands were a smaller replica of his father's.

Once he got home, Daquan went straight to his bed and slept. He dozed all day, waking only to force himself into a deeper sleep. He wanted to disappear. He wanted to hide. But most of all, he didn't want to *feel*. Then he started to dream . . .

The sounds of booming bass filled the space. It was dark and he could hear people talking and laughing, but he couldn't see anyone. All he could make out was the boom, the bap, the boom-bap.

Suddenly, a light came on and he could see people lying around everywhere. End to end, overlapping, or on top of one another. Piles of human bodies in all shapes, ages, and hues. They were all black people, though—from Creole red to Mississippi black, Harlem brown to California caramel—all just lying there. The music was still loud and so were the voices, but he didn't know where it was coming from.

All of a sudden he saw her. The little girl with pigtails.

"What's wrong with them?" he asked. "Are they asleep?"

She shook her head. "No, they're dead."

"Where did they die?"

"Around the corner," she replied in a deadpan monotone.

He admired her complexion, because it matched his own. He admired her eyes because they reminded him of Macy's when she smiled.

"What's your name?" he asked.

She hesitated, then pointed off to the left. When he looked, he saw a small headstone, but he was too young to decipher the words engraved there.

"I can't read," he told her. "What does it say?"

"Look again."

He inched closer, laughter and voices and pounding drums all around, a wall of sound assaulting his eardrums. Daquan peered at the letters one by one, trying to memorize their shapes and curves.

When he turned around, she was gone.

As soon as Daquan awoke, he wrote each word down carefully, making sure every curve and line was exactly how he remembered it. When he showed it to Grandma Mama, she was shocked because she knew he couldn't read or write. But the words were clearly in a child's handwriting.

"Who wrote this?" she asked.

"I did," he replied proudly.

She looked at him. "Do you know what it says?"

He shook his head slowly, never losing eye contact.

"Do you want to know?"

The next time Daquan saw the word was in Providence

Cemetery, right there on the same headstone he had seen in his dream. Grandma Mama took him on a long bus ride out to the old graveyard that same day. Daquan held her hand tightly as they walked along the rows of headstones, small and large. Some were well kept, displaying flowers, newly taken pictures, and even candles, while others were just bare, cold, gray stones. The only flowers on those graves were the occasional yellows of wild dandelions.

They approached a headstone that Daquan recognized. It read:

Diana Watson
1976–1976
Rest in Peace

He looked at the words etched into the stone, then up into his grandmother's eyes. With a slight nod of her head, she loosened the grip on his hand. Slowly, tentatively, he walked closer to the stone. Daquan ran his fingers along the letters in her name, and when he was sure, he turned to Grandma Mama for confirmation. "It's the same one, Mama." He was making a statement, but the tone made it come off like a question. "Is she here too?"

Grandma Mama took a few steps forward. "Yes, she is, baby," she said calmly. "Do you know who she is? That's your sister."

He furrowed his brow. "Sister? I don't got no sister."

"Don't *have*, Daquan, not don't got. And you did, once. Her name was Diana. See? D-I-A-N-A," she spelled the letters out, holding his piece of paper up on the stone so he could see the similarities. "It spells Diana. She would've been your big sister."

Daquan looked at the grave as Grandma Mama continued.

"Your mama was bad off on that stuff . . . drugs. Even when she got pregnant, she kept right on with her wicked ways.

Your daddy tried, but he couldn't stop her until Diana was born and died on the same day."

"Died?" Daquan questioned. "I thought when people died they got their wings and went away."

Grandma Mama chuckled. "Not everyone, chile. And even the ones that do, sometimes they come back and see folks."

"Why?"

She shrugged. "They miss 'em, I reckon. Then sometimes they come back to look out for them. Like a guardian angel."

Her smile warmed Daquan and told him everything was okay. He looked at the headstone again. "Diana," he said, speaking her name for the first time.

"Daquan," Grandma Mama said, turning him to face her. "Listen to me, baby, like you never listened before. Them drugs is bad. Very bad. They took yo' sister, yo' mama, and yo' daddy, my son, from you." The tears rolled down her cheeks. "And don't you ever forget, you heah? Never."

Daquan nodded his head, his young brain soaking in more words that he didn't yet understand, but he was sure he'd never forget.

A few weeks later, Daryl was given a life sentence. Grandma Mama and Melissa cried in the courtroom like he had died. Even Jerome shed a tear. But Daquan remained dry-eyed as he watched the police take his daddy away for the second time. He wished all the police would die right there, but not get their wings. He vowed to himself to get Daryl out one day so they could be a family again.

After the trial, Daquan sat on the porch watching the people move to and fro through the Calliope. All he could think of was his daddy and how to get him out. Jerome came outside, blasting Run-DMC's "30 Days," but even the music couldn't snap Daquan out of his zone. Jerome shut the radio off, sat down next to Daquan, and asked, "What's happening, lil' whody?"

Daquan just shrugged.

Jerome knew his little cousin was taking his daddy's ordeal hard, and he hated it for him. Especially being so young.

"Lil' whody, you know what a soldier is?"

"Like in the army," Daquan replied.

"Naw, fuck the army. I'm talking about real soldiers. Nigguhs in these streets goin' to war ere' day with the police. Being broke, being mad wit' themselves, too," Jerome spat, looking out at all the people. To him, they scurried like roaches in a roach motel, either trying to get high, trying to get by, or trying to get over so the hood didn't take them under. He just shook his head in disgust.

"Lil' cuz, nigguhs die ere'day. Go to jail ere'day, too. One day it could be me, one day it could be you. But we gots to stand up . . . like your daddy did. I know you miss him, but he did what he had to do. That's a soldier, lil' cuz. Yo' daddy is a soldier."

Jerome lit a cigarette, then checked his watch. "You wanna go to Ms. Betty's real quick fo' I go? I'll buy you some cookies, okay?"

Daquan agreed, but not because of the cookies. He just wanted to be with Jerome. As they approached Ms. Betty's building, they saw Pepper coming up the sidewalk with Nut. As soon as Daquan saw Nut, his eyes locked on him, remembering when he called him a crybaby.

Jerome saw Daquan looking at Nut and smiled. "There he go, lil' cuz. You ready to tear his ass up?"

The look on Daquan's face said it all. When they got close enough, Jerome said to Pepper, "Nigguh, bag of weed say Quan tear Nut ass up."

Pepper, an avid gambler and all-around wild nigguh, had no problem accepting the challenge. "Nut, you want some ice cream? Beat him up and I'll get you *two* Popsicles."

That's all Nut had to hear. He looked at Daquan and ran at him, ready to grab him and push him to the ground. But

Daquan had other plans. Jerome had been teaching him how to punch. Not wild like a windmill, but straight, calculated blows. When Nut ran up, flailing his arms, Daquan shot out two clean jabs that caught him in his chin and shoulder. Nut managed to scratch Daquan across the face, but Daquan remained unfazed and hit him again, this time dead in the nose.

"Oh *hell* naw, nigguh!" Pepper exclaimed. "You been teaching that lil' nigguh!"

Jerome laughed. "A bet's a bet, yo!"

An older teenaged chick came by, shouting, "Y'all nigguhs is crazy! Stop them boys from fighting!"

Pepper hollered back, "The CP3 raise soldiers, bitch. The way that nigguh be whooping your ass, somebody shoulda trained you!" Pepper saw Daquan on top of a crying Nut, punching his little heart out, and commanded, "Nut, get yo' ass up!"

Jerome picked Daquan up by his belt loop, then set him on his feet. "That's enough, lil' whody. He won't be bothering you no mo'."

Daquan stood, huffing and puffing as Nut bawled like a baby. "I'ma tell my mama," he threatened.

Daquan felt like a burden had been lifted from his back. Like he could *breathe*. With every punch thrown or taken, all the frustrations he didn't have the words to describe were released and communicated to the world represented by Nut's little body.

The cookies Jerome bought him didn't even matter, because he had found something sweeter: his outlet.

When Jerome brought him through the door, Grandma Mama took one look at Daquan's reddened and slightly bruised face and asked, "Jerome, what happened to that boy?"

Jerome kissed her on the cheek, one foot out the door, and replied, "He okay, Mama. He had a little accident on the playground. See ya later."

Grandma Mama knew he was lying. Anybody with eyes

could see that Daquan had been fighting. The fighting wasn't the problem. She knew boys would be boys. Her concern was Jerome. Grandma Mama didn't like the man he was becoming, and she knew, without another male figure around, Daquan would follow him. She just prayed that Jerome wouldn't lead him the wrong way.

4

As Daquan stepped out of Crocker Elementary, he could just feel Grandma Mama's strap on his ass. She stood beside him, but he was scared to look at her. This had been the third time in as many months that he had been suspended from school. He was supposed to be expelled by now, but Grandma Mama knew the principal, Mr. Dupree. She had practically raised him up as a child. Their families had gone to the same church for years, so on the strength of that, he asked her to come in for a meeting. "Mama Watson, Daquan is uncontrollable," he told her. It's like he doesn't care. Every time I turn around, he's in my office, disrespecting teachers, bullying other students, and fighting. If it wasn't for the fact that I knew you, I'd wash my hands of the whole situation, just send him over to A.D. Cross school, and be done with it."

Grandma Mama looked at Daquan, who had his head down. All she could think of was what would she whoop him with.

"Daquan."

"Ma'am?"

"Look at me, chile."

Daquan looked up.

"Is that what you want? To be sent away to reform school?"

"No, ma'am," he answered.

"Then what are you going to do?" she asked.

He shrugged. "Be good," he answered.

The principal leaned forward and spoke over tented hands. He hated to see so many young black faces heading down a road he knew all too well. Both of his sons were locked up. One for murder, the other for armed robbery. Neither was even twenty-one. He sighed.

"Quan, you say that every time. Listen, I *know* you can do it. I see your grades. I see what you are capable of. You have the abilities, son, why the he—" he had to catch himself. "Why won't you use them?"

"But, I didn't start it this time, the boy—"

The principal held up his hand.

"I'm not talking about this time, or who did what. I'm talking about *you*. When are you going to see?" he asked, then sighed deeply. "I'm sorry, Mama Watson, but I'm going to have to suspend Daquan for three days, and if he's in my office one more time . . . I'll expel him for the rest of the year."

Grandma Mama nodded solemnly. "I understand." She positioned her cane to support her weight as she stood up. "Come on, boy."

Daquan followed her out, feeling like a sheep going to slaughter.

"You hungry?" Grandma Mama asked as they got off the bus, much to Daquan's surprise. "Well, I am," she continued, answering her own question. "We goin' to Williams."

Williams Soul Food was a spot near the Calliope that served the best cooking this side of grandmother's kitchen. Grandma Mama loved their gizzards and Daquan did, too. But he didn't expect to be fed so good after he'd been so bad.

The two sat in the booth looking out at the passing cars while they waited on their order.

"I'd better get Melissa something to eat, because I ain't doin' no cookin' today," she said, more to herself than to Daquan. "These ol' bones need some rest."

Daquan kept his eyes on the salt shaker, because he was too scared to look at her. This wasn't the way he was used to things going. Usually, they rode home in silence whenever she had to go to his school. The only words she spoke were, "Go get my belt," once they got home. Then right before she lashed him, she'd say, "Lord, please don't let me kill this chile." Then she beat him damn near to it.

He could handle that. But sitting in Williams eating gizzards had him scared to death, because he didn't know what was coming.

"Daquan . . . what do you think I should do?" she asked, as the waitress brought them their order. "S'cuse me, sweetie. Can I get a chicken dinner to go, please? Thank you," she told the waitress, then returned to her question. "Well?"

Daquan looked at the golden brown morsels, stomach growling, but too scared to eat or speak.

"I punish you, I whoop you, talk to you, keep you in the house, but none of it seems to work. So what should I do?"

He looked up at her. "I'm sorry, Mama, but I swear I ain't start it this time. The boy kept looking at me all crazy 'cause he think I jumped on his cousin at the rec center," he explained.

"Did you?" she probed.

He dropped his head. "Yes'm."

Grandma Mama just shook her head. "Boy, don't you know that these people is crazy? You can't keep goin' around jumpin' on folks. What if one of 'em got a gun, *then* what? You heard about Junior Davis? He beat up on some boy, then the boy came back and shot him dead. Ain't you scared of stuff like that?"

Daquan picked over his gizzards and mumbled, "No, ma'am."

"You ain't, huh? That's your problem. You ain't scared. Got no good sense, and I can't beat that into you. And I can't beat them streets out of you neither."

She reached in her purse and pulled out a small fold of money. Daquan recognized it immediately, because it was his.

"Now where do a twelve-year-old chile get a hundred and fifty dollars from?" she questioned.

His mind linked and unlinked until he latched onto a lie. "Me and Nut mowed . . ."

"*Hush* your mouth," Grandma Mama hissed from behind clenched teeth. "Onliest thing I can't stomach is a liar. Now you tell me the truth, or so help me God, it'll be the last lie you tell. Now, where did it come from? Did you steal it?"

"No, ma'am," he answered, shook.

"Did you rob somebody?"

"I—I . . . we—we," Daquan stuttered, ashamed to tell her the truth. "We sold some car radios."

Grandma Mama dropped her fork. "Lord have mercy, chile, you breakin' in people's cars? Don't you know them folks'll kill you?" She looked at her grandson, seeing him slipping further and further away from everything she had ever taught him. And she didn't know what to do. She had already put Jerome out for selling drugs. And she tried to get Daryl to write to Daquan, but he had his own issues that seven years in a cage had created. Grandma Mama took a deep breath, stilled her emotions, and told him, "Well, if you grown enough to take yo' life in your own hands, you old enough to be on your own. And that's exactly where you gonna be if I find any more money in my house, or if you get put out of school. Just once more, you hear me?"

"Yes'm," Daquan replied, not knowing if he should be happy he wouldn't get a whoopin' or sad because he could end up homeless.

"Now, you may as well eat yo' food 'cause you sho nuff

payin' for it," she informed him as she stuck his money back in her purse.

By the time Daquan got home, everyone was out of school and Nut was waiting for him. He and Nut had become friends over the years, especially since Pepper and Jerome hung so tight.

"Hello, Mama Watson," Nut greeted her respectfully, as Daquan helped her up the front steps.

"Mm-hmmm," she toned in a disapproving manner.

"Grandma Mama, I'll be in in a minute," Daquan informed her.

"Just remember what I said, Daquan," she reminded him, then turned and entered the house.

As soon as she was inside, Nut asked, "What's up? You on punishment or what?"

Nut knew how Grandma Mama carried it.

"Naw, man," Daquan answered. "But she found my money."

"*All* of it?!" Nut said in disbelief. "What she do, bruh?"

Daquan sat down on the steps. "She kept it."

Nut sat down next to him. "Damn, man. How you gonna buy them Jordans now?"

"Easy, get me some more. Black Jimmie said he need a kicker box and a amp," he told Nut. "Let's go to the rec."

As they walked, Daquan told Nut, "She said she'll kick me out."

"Who? Mama Watson?"

Daquan nodded.

"What you gonna do?"

Daquan looked at him. "Be more careful, ya heard me?"

Rosenwald Recreation Center on Earhart Street was the place to be for all ages of youth. The younger kids could play on the playground or draw with finger-paints, while the older kids could play basketball, cards, lift weights, or just plain hang out, like most of them did. The parking lot was always

packed—cars with booming systems, girls trying to outshine
one another, guys trying to look cool, tough, or a little of both.
Everyone from Uptown knew about Rosenwald gym in the
CP3.

As Daquan and Nut crossed the street to the rec, they
heard, "Ay, Quan, *Quan*," and out of the crowd came D.J.

D.J. was a year younger, but bigger than both of them, side
by side, in width. He came from a big-boned family, and at the
rate he was going, he'd easily be linebacker size by the time
he was eighteen, which was fine with him because he ate,
drank, and slept football.

"What's happenin'," he greeted them, shaking their hands.
"I heard you had a fight with Ray Ray today."

"I beat Ray Ray ass today, if you call that a fight," Daquan
joked as he unwrapped a grape Jolly Rancher.

"Them boys from the Parkway talkin' a lot of junk. Big
boys, too," D.J. warned him. For a big kid, D.J. didn't like to
fight. But when he did, he was like a young bull. It just took a
lot to get him started.

"Forget them fools," Nut replied. "Let 'em come 'round
here if they want to."

The three of them walked into the rec parking lot, surrounded by multiple car systems playing the Geto Boys'
"Mind Playing Tricks On Me." Daquan spotted Black Jimmie
leaning against his black Nissan Maxima, talking to two girls.
Daquan always liked Jimmie because he was smooth like Big
Daddy Kane. He was half Geechee, which gave him his dark
skin tone, and half Creole, which gave him curly hair and long
eyelashes that made the girls go crazy for him. Jimmie got his
money from fighting and raising dogs, and he loved to gamble.
He was also known for messing around with roots and potions
real heavy.

Daquan walked over to Jimmie and said, "What up, whody?
You still need that?"

Black Jimmie liked young Daquan 'cause he was 'bout his

business. He told the girls he'd see them later, then turned to Daquan. "What up, lil' daddy? What you got for me?"

"Nothin' yet. That's why I'm askin' if you still 'bout it," Daquan replied.

Jimmie smiled. "I'm 'bout it, whody. I told you I needed it, didn't I? Now how much you chargin'?"

"Two hundred. But if you give me a hundred right now, I'll only charge you fifty when I give you the stuff," Daquan proposed.

"A hundred now, huh? You tryin' to hustle Black, huh? When I'ma get the kicker?" Black Jimmie asked, folding his arms over his chest.

"Naw, I just need to handle somethin' right quick. I'll have that to you in a few days, ya heard me?"

Black Jimmie went in his pocket, peeled off a hundred dollar bill, and handed it to Daquan. "I respect yo' hustle, lil' whody. Just make sure you got the word to match. Don't let me have to send Ol' Johnny at you."

Daquan took the money, like, "I got ya, whody."

He walked away to catch up with Nut and D.J. by the ball court, but not watching where he was going, he bumped into Desiree.

"Oh, hey, Quan," the young girl flirted, as if it was an accident. Like she hadn't watched him while he was talking to Jimmie, then deliberately made sure she crossed his path.

"Oh, what's up?" he answered, backing away a step or two.

"Is that for me?" she asked, looking at the money in his hand.

He sucked his teeth and put it in his pocket. "Girl, won't you go 'head somewhere," he huffed, and brushed past her. It wasn't that Desiree was ugly. She was a cute little redbone, whose birthday was on the same day as his. Ever since they started grade school she always had a crush on Daquan, and he had always brushed her off. Back then, he wasn't into girls, and now he was into money.

Nut and D.J. watched Daquan approach, and D.J. commented, "That Desiree sho' is pretty, man. How come you don't talk to her, Quan?"

"Man, *you* talk to her," he spat. "I got more important things to worry about."

"What Jimmie say?" Nut asked, changing the subject.

"He 'bout it. I got a hundred from him now, fifty when we get the kicker. Let's go get some change."

The three of them walked around the back of the rec building where they knew there'd be a dice game going on. When they rounded the corner, the first person they saw was Jerome, serving a fiend. Jerome had gotten in the crack game and was slangin' hard, trying to come up. Gone was his boom box, only to be replaced by a Cadillac Eldorado with a banging system. His jewels and clothes let the world know he was the man to see.

"What's happenin', lil' cuz?" Jerome grinned, gold grill glistening. "What you doin' back heah?"

"I need some change," Daquan boasted, extending the hundred dollar bill to Jerome. He still looked up to Jerome, even though he didn't see him as much these days.

Jerome looked at the bill. "Y'all still breaking in folks' shit? What I tell you about that, lil' cuz? I told you, if you need money, come see me."

Daquan waved him off. "It ain't but them white boys around Saint Charles Street."

"Shit, that's the worst. Let them crackers catch you up there. Fuck around and lynch y'all lil' asses."

Jerome handed him back five twenties. "I hear about you selling some shit to these nigguhs, and I'ma beat yo' ass, ya heard me?"

Daquan pocketed the money in silence. He wanted to say something slick, but he knew better. Jerome would definitely make good on his threat, but that wasn't going to stop Daquan. The way he saw it, Jerome had his hustle, and he had his own.

*   *   *

That night, Nut and Daquan took the bus over to Algiers, the section of New Orleans where the white boys showed off their cars and cruised the strip of Manhattan, where the Palace Theater was located. Daquan thought it was funny how many white boys bumped rap music in their stereos, but didn't like blacks, a point of sociology he was too young to grasp.

They got off the bus and made their way along the street, keeping their eyes peeled for the police. This was Sheriff Harry Lee's section of New Orleans, where the whites lived and played, so being a black face after dark was a crime in and of itself. But Daquan and Nut knew the area well. It was where they got most of their merchandise from, but being young, they didn't realize that they had made the area hot.

They were moving through a small apartment complex when they spotted the lick. "Looka heah," Nut said, peering through the window of a Nissan Sentra. Large speakers were sitting up in the rear deck of the car.

"Naw," Daquan rejected. "He want a kicker box, man."

"How you know ain't no kicker in the trunk?"

Daquan didn't answer. Something about the night didn't feel right, but he tried to convince himself it was just nerves. Truth was, he was still shaken by the dream he had the night before.

He dreamed of a large church full of familiar faces, family, and friends. Even Daryl was there with Macy. Grandma Mama was the only one crying, but no one seemed to notice. They were all chatting and laughing, oblivious to the old woman's pain.

Daquan rushed over to Grandma Mama and called out, "Mama! What's wrong? Are you hurt?"

But she didn't even acknowledge his presence. "Mama! It's *me*, Daquan, Mama. What's wrong?"

Still no response.

Just then, the piano player began to play a slow, sad waltz that drew his attention to the coffin in the front of the church. He crossed the room to it, only to find the lid closed. He tried to lift it, but a small feminine hand held it closed. He looked up to see that the hand belonged to Diana.

"Don't . . . open it," she warned.

"I want to see," he whined.

"No. Don't open it," she repeated.

But his curiosity got the best of him. He opened the casket lid, admiring the thick red satin that lined the interior. His eyes traced the fabric of the suit from the pants to the small black hands folded across the body's midsection. But what he saw next made him gasp and stumble back.

The face in the coffin was his own. The hands folded in their final resting place were his hands. It was his own funeral.

"Mama! *Noooo*, I'm not dead! I'm . . ."

The words got caught in his throat because the eyes of his casketed self popped open at the sound of his own voice. The corpse sat up at the waist until they were both eye level and face-to-face.

He awoke breathless and in a cold sweat.

"Quan? Man, you hear me?" Nut whispered harshly from a few cars down. "Let's get this one."

Daquan blinked out of the zone he had fallen into, looked around, then approached Nut, standing beside a Suzuki Samurai SUV.

"Look," Nut urged.

The Suzuki was laced with a system that, even in silence, just *looked* loud. The four-speaker kicker box took up almost the whole trunk space on a slant from tweeters to twelves. The Alpine pull-out sat tantalizingly near. All they had to do was cut through the vinyl top and they were in.

"We can't carry that," Daquan surmised, referring to the

kicker. He had a smaller, two-speaker version in mind. There was no way they would be able to move that.

"Then we'll take the car," Nut smirked devilishly. "I told you I can hotwire," he reminded Daquan.

Nut had been itching to try what his cousin had taught him about stealing cars.

"Nigguh, you can't drive," Daquan accused.

"Damn lie. I can drive. Let's just get this shit and go," Nut urged him, already slicing through the top with his orange box cutter.

He crawled in through the slitted opening and Daquan crawled in behind him.

"Nigguh, you better know what you doin'," Daquan hissed.

"Just chill," Nut assured him as he reached under the dashboard, searching for the ignition wires. "Man, I can't wait till I pull up in the project wit' this," Nut remarked.

"Man, we ain't takin' this shit home! We gon' take it somewhere, get the system, and dump it," Daquan replied, killing Nut's stunt dream.

All of a sudden, the car started up, which made Daquan's heart jump for joy. But a split second later, a high-pitched wail filled the car. The alarm hadn't tripped until then because they hadn't opened any doors to get in. But now that the car was crunk, and it hadn't been disarmed, the siren screamed like a soprano being attacked by a rapist.

"What the fuck?" Daquan panicked.

Nut froze up, not knowing what to do. Daquan thought about getting out, but when he heard, "*Hey*, you!" from a man across the parking lot, he punched Nut hard in the shoulder. "Motherfucker, drive!"

The jolt of the blow brought Nut back to reality. He threw the stick shift into first gear and the Suzuki lurched forward. Although Nut wasn't experienced with a stick, he shifted into second gear at the proper time, keeping the gears in motion and avoiding the risk of getting cut off.

They raced out of the parking lot, narrowly missing an on-coming car.

"Watch out, Nut! You gonna kill us in here!" Daquan yelled angrily.

"I—I got it," Nut stammered, finally realizing that he had bitten off more than he could chew.

The way Nut swerved made a passing police car U-turn and throw on the lights and siren, which made Nut's panic even worse. He tried to make a left at the intersection, but got side-swiped, causing the Suzuki to careen and fishtail. Before they knew it, Nut rear-ended a parked car. The force of the blow, and the intensity of his anxiety, caused him to black out at the wheel.

Daquan, however, was out the door as soon as his body absorbed the impact. He was a little disoriented, but his feet were in motion to escape. The police cruiser circled around the Suzuki and pulled halfway up the curb, then an overweight white cop got out the passenger side and chased Daquan.

Daquan tried to cut through a backyard, but when he got ready to leap the fence, he was met by two red eyes and a deep-throated growl. An oversized rottweiller leaped against the fence, daring him to jump it. Daquan skidded to a stop and turned, hoping he had enough time to cut along the side of the next house, but he was met with, *"Freeze,* boy! You move and I'll shoot!" The big fat cop snarled, his police-issued .38 locked and loaded.

All Daquan could do was raise his hands in surrender.

"Ms. Watson? Is this Ms. Gladys Watson?" The authorative male voice inquired over the phone.

Grandma Mama propped herself up on her elbow and glanced at the clock by her bed. It was 11:45 P.M. Deep down in her motherly instinct, she knew the call was about Daquan, so she prayed for the best and prepared herself for the worst.

"Yes, this is Ms. Watson," she replied, now fully awake.

"This is Detective Miller of the New Orleans Police Department, and I have a . . ." she heard the sound of rustling paper, "Daquan Watson in custody. Are you his legal guardian?"

She breathed a deep, but silent, sigh of relief. "Yes . . . yes, I am."

"Well, I'm sorry to bother you this late," he said, his tone anything but remorseful, "but he was arrested in a stolen vehicle after he attempted to elude police."

No response.

"Ms. Watson?"

"I'm here," she replied.

"He's been charged with possession of a stolen vehicle, attempting to elude capture, and resisting arrest. Once his processing is completed, you can pick him up."

"And . . . if I don't?" she asked, breaking her own heart with every word.

"If you don't, then he'll remain in custody until he goes before the judge," the detective informed her. He was used to black parents refusing to take back their delinquent children. *I don't blame you*, his racism chuckled inside.

"Okay," was all she could get out before her voice cracked, and she hung up the phone.

Grandma Mama wanted with all her heart to go and get her baby, but she knew if she bailed him out this time, Daquan would feel like whatever he did, she'd come and get him out of it. But life wasn't like that. And if he was ever going to learn that lesson, now was the time.

As she rolled over to go to sleep, tears rolling down her cheek to form a salty stain on her pillow, she said a prayer for her child.

"Are you scared?"

"No."

Silence . . .

"Then why are you shaking?" Diana asked.

" 'Cause I'm cold," Daquan lied.

The truth was, he *was* scared. Not of being in a detention center, or of what the police would do to him, but scared of being alone. He shook from the coldness of solitude. He knew Grandma Mama loved him, but he wasn't surprised when the detective smugly informed Daquan that no one was coming for him. Nut had left almost immediately. His mother had come as soon as she got the call, and whooped his ass all the way out of the police station, much to the officer's amusement.

Shit, Daquan would take a whooping over this any day. The steel and hollow concreteness of his cell made him long for the familiar sting of Grandma Mama's heavy leather belt. But she had already warned him about the consequences of his actions.

If you grown enough to take yo' life in yo' own hands, you old enough to be on your own, he remembered her saying. And the memory made him curl up in a ball on his bunk, instinctually mimicking the position of a fetus in the warmth of its mother's womb. His only umbilical to life was the presence of his dead sister.

"I love you," she told him.

"I love you, too," he replied, not seeing her pigtails, but hearing her voice as if she was right in his ear.

"And I'll never leave you. I promise. Wasn't I there when you were scared of the dark?"

"Yeah."

"And when Daddy stopped writing you?"

He nodded his head.

"I'll always be here with you, Daquan . . . I promise."

The words were clear and comforting, and in his heart he could feel his hand embraced by his sister's, until he fell asleep.

5

Daquan and Nut were each sentenced to twelve months in Scotland Correctional Institute for Youth. Although they were first offenders, they were given the max because the car they stole belonged to the nephew of a wealthy Masonic businessman with friends in the court system.

Daquan leaned his head against the steel-grated window of the prison bus as it bumped along the highway, heading for Scotlandville, Louisiana. Nut sat beside him with his grill scrunched up in a screw face, trying to look tougher than the fear inside would let him be.

"I'm tellin' you, whody," Nut said to Daquan, loud enough for the other twelve juveniles on the bus to hear. "A nigguh bet' not even *look* at me wrong, 'cause I don't give a fuck about killin' me a muhfucka!"

"Yeah, I hear ya," Daquan replied in a flat monotone. He never even took his head away from the window and the sight of the passing cars.

"What's wrong with you?" Nut asked. He expected Daquan to act just as tough. "You sick or somethin'? You ain't got nothin' to worry about, nigguh—we from the CP3!"

Daquan closed his eyes. He didn't know what to expect, but he was ready for whatever. He had heard a lot about Scotland. They called it Baby Angola, a sort of stepson to the largest and most feared adult prison in Louisiana.

When they pulled up to the double barbed-wire fence of the prison, it looked like a mini penitentiary with a billboard that read: SCOTLAND.

Looking at the compound for the first time, Daquan couldn't help the eerie feeling that his life, from this day on, would never be the same. He could tell that everyone on the bus felt the same way because as the huge barbed-wire fence slid back to admit the bus, all conversation stopped. Once those gates closed they wouldn't open until each boy's sentence was over. Whatever happened while they were inside those gates, they would just have to deal with.

"Everybody out!" bellowed the potbellied redneck corrections officer, cradling a pump shotgun in his arms.

They all stood up and shuffled off the bus the best they could, making sure the heavy leg shackles they wore didn't get tangled up and trip them. One by one, they stepped out into the hot Louisiana sun, forming a single-file line. The redneck C.O. inspected the line, shoving a few guys, including Nut, over a few inches until the line was up to his standards.

"What? What did you say, boy?" the redneck hissed at Nut, because he heard Nut suck his teeth after he shoved him. "You got a problem?"

"Naw," Nut replied, fighting the urge to spit in the cracker's face.

"Then move!" The C.O. replied.

He marched them through the doors of intake into a large room. The walls were old, with peeling sky-blue paint revealing the cold gray of the reinforced steel walls. They were made to line up side by side while the C.O.s unshackled them.

A tall, burly black man walked in wearing sergeant stripes. Even though he was one of the police, he was a welcome face, especially since the other six C.O.s around them were all white. But as soon as he opened his mouth, he proved to be a true house nigguh.

"Look at you," he spat, walking along the row of boys. "Every one of you disgust me. I'm glad you're here instead of on the streets, molesting the good folk of *Looo*siana."

He stuck his chest out as if he was proud of locking up little black boys. Only two of the new inmates were white, and Daquan could see that he wasn't talking to them.

"Where you from?" the Sarge asked one of the boys.

"New Orleans, the Magnolia projects," he answered proudly.

"Yeah? You know where I'm from?" the sergeant replied, getting up in the same boy's face. The boy shook his head silently.

"A town called 'fresh off yo' ass,' and your face is making me homesick. All you gotta do is *breathe* wrong in heah, and I can make it so you don't have that luxury no more."

He stepped back to address the whole line.

"The state sent you here to be reformed. Well, I know better. I know you ain't shit and ain't gonna *be* shit, so I'm just gonna make you suffer for it. I'ma make you suffer so bad, and I *want* you to cry. I want you to call on yo' sorry-ass mammies, 'cause they can't help you. Nobody can because I run this, you heah? I run it! You will do what *I* say. When I say sit, you squat, when I say shit, you grunt, and when I say jump, if it ain't high enough, I got a whole mess of good ol' boys ta help you get airborne," he said with a chuckle, referring to the Ku Klux Klan of C.O.s behind him.

Daquan tensed up with anger, eyeing the Sarge until he recognized the look and came over to him.

"What's your name, boy?" he questioned.

"Daquan Watson."

"Daquan Watson, huh? You think you tough, DAY-QUAN?" the sergeant asked, purposely pronouncing his name wrong.

"No," Daquan replied, "and my mama ain't sorry, either."

He didn't say it in a challenging way; he simply stated his position.

"She had yo' sorry black ass, didn't she?" the Sarge taunted.

Daquan locked gazes with him, and the Sarge chuckled.

"Yeah, you think you tough. I'ma have fun makin' you cry. 'Specially when some of them monkeys on the unit have you back there runnin' around in drag." The rednecks laughed, but Daquan's mind locked on the image of the Sarge, bruised and bloody in a dark alley, begging for his life.

"Awright, strip these pieces of shit and get 'em dressed out," the Sarge ordered as he left.

They were taken further back into a damp-smelling room with a line of showerheads and a tiled floor, and told to strip off all their street clothes. Every last stitch of freedom was peeled away, layer by layer, until the boys stood bare before the eyes of the system. Their personal belongings were boxed and filed away, pending release, which some would never see, while their bodies were subjected to dehumanizing scrutiny.

"Bend over," the C.O.s yelled with glee. "Spread your cheeks . . . squat . . . cough."

Many of these young boys had been through this process before, but for those like Daquan, it was the first time, and it left a scar that cut deep through their emotions. A scar that, if left to fester, could become bitterness—and the worst kind of heart is a young, bitter one.

After the search, they were all given blue shirts and blue pants. The blue shirts indicated that they were in processing, and would be for the next four weeks. Then, they would be taken to general population and given red shirts, which to many of the hardened inmates meant fresh meat—especially the white boys.

In prison, where white inmates were the minority, racism reversed itself, and it was the whites who were at the bottom of the totem pole. They were the first victims of abuse, robbery, extortion, even rape. That became clear to Daquan once

their group was settled in the cluster of cells called the processing pod.

"Let me get that chicken," one of the black guys told a
white boy when dinner was served. He snatched the fried bird
out of his Styrofoam tray as soon as the C.O. left with the food
cart. The freckle-faced white boy didn't say a word, but his
growling stomach cried out. Although he was rather big for
thirteen, his heart wasn't as big. His friend however, a smaller
boy with shady blond hair, did protest when the same dude
took his chicken.

"Hey! Give that back!" he squealed and stood up.

The black dude wasted no time in smacking fire out of the
white boy's face, but to his credit, the smaller white boy fired
right back. His circumstance was just the opposite of his bigger friend: he was small and scrawny with a big heart. It just
wasn't big enough to keep the black dude from beating his ass
unmercifully, until they heard the keys of a C.O. coming jan-
gling down the hall.

They broke up the fight and scurried to their bunks. Daquan
just knew the white boy would tell the guard, but he didn't.
The scrawny blond had been through this before, so he knew
snitching was a no-no and a one-way ticket to the infirmary.

Daquan sat on his bunk next to Nut and watched the people around him. They ate greedily from the small trays on
their laps, eyes darting around out of fear, or like predators
looking for victims. He knew in his heart that he would never
allow himself to be a victim, but he had enough humanity left
in him to pray he never became a predator, either. He found
his thoughts drifting toward home.

Dear Grandma Mama,

*How are you doing? I am fine. Thank you for the money.
How is Aunt Melissa? Have you seen Jerome? Tell them I am in
school and doing well, especially in English class. I hate Math,
though.*

*You asked me what I've learned in here in your last letter.
I've learned a lot about myself and why I'm in here. When I get
out, I'm going to do better. I want to go to college, maybe
Grambling State, like Melissa did. I don't want to get in trouble
anymore, or go to jail. They feed you nasty food and the police
talk down on you when they tell you to do stuff. I'm not coming
back.*

*Yes, I got the letters from Daddy, and I will write him back.
I've just been busy with school and my pod duties, but I will.
Tell everyone that I love them.*

Love,
Daquan

P.S. When are you going to visit me?

Daquan put his pen down and stretched his arms over his
head. In the background, the TV echoed through the dorm,
while voices chittered and chattered at alternating decibels.

Young Daquan had seen a lot in his short time in detention.
He had only been on the yard a month, and already his mind
frame had aged and hardened. He was trapped in cages with
savages that resembled humans, but acted like beasts. On the
wall over his bed, someone had scribbled a short poem:

The Jungle Creed
Is the Strong must feed
On any Prey he can
I sat at the Feast and was branded a Beast
Before I ever became a Man

All around him, he saw the reality of those words. He had
seen cats get stabbed within an inch of their lives over card
games. He'd seen white boys molested and even raped by
older boys, some white themselves. And he had witnessed the
brutality of the racist C.O.s against all kinds of inmates. For a

twelve-year-old child to see such atrocities, there was no way he could remain a child, so Daquan grew up quickly in the short space of a month.

He even started smoking cigarettes. It wasn't because of peer pressure; it was simply a result of doing time. To do a bid, you need a vice, a hobby, or a religion. Since he was young, he chose a vice, and that vice was nicotine.

Nut, on the other hand, chose weed. He tried to get Daquan to smoke with him, but Daquan still remembered his grandma's words about the evils of drugs, and clung to them. Every day, Nut would come through, eyes bloodshot red and half closed.

"What up, whody?" he'd greet Daquan, then add, "Come on, nigguh, I got that charm."

Today was no different, except Nut wasn't high when he sat down beside Daquan.

"Whut's happenin', Quan? You goin' to chow?" Nut asked.

Daquan folded up his letter and placed it under his pillow. "Naw, I'm tired as a muhfucka, bruh. Wake me up when the movie come on."

"Fuck dat, whody, let's go out on the yard and kick it with the homies. Sleep is for lockdown," Nut replied, giving him his favorite phrase. Nut did time running. He had to have his hand in everything.

"Aiight, man, *ten* minutes, then I'm gone," Daquan stated, standing up from his bunk, and Nut followed him out the door.

Once they made it outside, it was easy to spot the inmates from New Orleans because everyone had their own corner of the yard. Smaller cities like Monroe and Alexandria had a mixture of different cats, but everyone else stuck to their set. Shreveport and New Orleans was always beefin'. Shreveport had the grassy area behind the horseshoe pit, Baton Rouge stayed near the weight pile, and the Breaux Bridge nigguhz held down the fence on the far side of the yard. New Orleans kept the basketball court because the best ballers came out of the N.O.

"Whut up, lil' whodys?" Nate, an older boy of sixteen said to Nut and Daquan, then shook their hands. Nate was in for a double homicide. He had two life sentences; he was just waiting to turn seventeen so he could be sent to Hunts Correctional Center for processing, then to Angola Penitentiary, commonly known as "The Farm." Nate was something of a legend and a good nigguh besides, so everyone looked up to him.

"Quan, you tell Jerome what I said?" Nate asked, lighting up a Kool.

"Yeah, I told him in my last letter. I wrote him through my grandma," Daquan replied, pulling out a cigarette of his own and lighting it with Nate's.

Nate nodded as he looked at the full-court game going on. A tall, lanky, brown-skin cat from the Calliope who everybody called Cee had just dunked and the CP3 was going crazy.

"Damn, Cee nice," Nate exclaimed. "Muhfucka should be in college some goddamn where, insteada wastin' his life in heah." Nate shook his head, then looked at Nut. "What up wit' you, lil' Nut? You got some of that killa?"

"Naw, Nate, I'm broke, man." Nut shrugged.

"You broke?" Nate echoed. "So how you figure on payin' D-Lo over theah? What I tell you 'bout fuckin' wit' dem' Shreveport nigguhs? They already told me you owe 'em."

Nut glanced over in Shreveport's direction and saw D-Lo eyein' him hard.

"Man, fuck D-Lo, he a buster. Why he tell you and ain't come to me?" Nut questioned.

Nate just shook his head.

"It's dumb-ass nigguhs like you get nigguhs jammed up, playboy," Nate replied. "D-Lo know if he do somethin' to you, he got problems. We Calliope. But what I'm tellin' you is, you ain't gonna be no problem for *me* if you don't cut this bullshit out, ya heard me?"

Nut was already vexed and Daquan could see it. The only reason Nut wasn't flipping on Nate was because he looked up to him, too. He was just upset that a cat he considered pussy was the reason Nate was checking him. Nate thunked his cigarette aside, then jerked his head like, *Come on wit' me.*

Nut and Daquan followed Nate down the short, grassy slope the court sat on, and waved D-Lo over. D-Lo and a fat cat called Chubbs met them halfway.

"Yo, how much Nut 'posed to owe you?" Nate asked D-Lo.

"Forty dollars," was his chin-up reply.

Nut sucked his teeth.

"I don't owe you no forty, bruh. I ain't get but three bags," Nut spat.

"The other ten, interest. Three for four back." D-Lo eyed Nut.

Nate looked at Nut and made a quick decision.

"Aiight, look, I'ma give you twenty 'cause ain't no need for this shit to escalate over no muhfuckin' get high," Nate said. He looked at D-Lo. "Take this twenty now and he'll get you the rest next week, cool?"

D-Lo looked at Nut, then at Nate. He knew Nate was a stand-up nigguh, so he figured it was best to take what he offered, since Nate was known for puttin' in work.

"For you, Nate, I'll take it," D-Lo answered.

"For Nate?!" Nut exploded. "You better be glad you gettin' that, bitch-ass nigguh!"

"Nigguh, fuck you!" Chubbs barked back. He and Nut were the same age and he didn't like Nut anyway.

Before Nate could regain order, Nut caught D-Lo with a vicious right hook that had the lanky youngster out on his feet. Daquan saw Chubbs try to charge Nut, so he threw two quick jabs, landing both square on Chubbs's jaw.

From there, it was on. Shreveport and New Orleans, lead by the Calliope, both rushed in like two armies and clashed under the hot Louisiana sun. Daquan and Nut were stomping D-Lo unconscious when Daquan felt a sharp pain in his shoulder. He looked around just in time to see some cat extracting a

homemade ice pick from his flesh, ready to sink it in him
again. He caught the boy with a right hook to the stomach that
knocked the wind out of him, causing him to double over.
Daquan pummeled his opponent's head and face until he fell
to the ground and dropped the ice pick. The burning sensation in Daquan's shoulder cried revenge. He bent over to grab
the shank. He gripped the taped handle and swung it in an
upward arc that caught the boy in the back of his thigh as he
tried to scurry away.

"*Argghh,*" he cried out, feeling the sharp steel rip through
his skin.

Daquan aimed to hit him again until he heard an ear-piercing
panic alarm go off. That meant the "riot squad" was on their
way. Everyone tried to duck and run, but suddenly the heavily
armored guards were everywhere, letting off tear gas and sub-
duing cats with their thick wooden batons. Daquan gasped for
air as the stinging gas covered the yard. In moments, he felt
his body go airborne, only to land hard on his stomach. His
arms were jerked backward so hard that blood gushed from his
shoulder wound, causing him so much pain that he passed out
to escape it.

He woke up staring at the peeling white ceiling paint of the
prison infirmary. The place smelled of stale blood and sani-
tized urine. The combination of the two aromas turned his
stomach. Daquan wanted to rub his face, but when he tried to
lift his arms, he found them both handcuffed to the iron bed
railing. The movement got the nurse's attention.

"Welcome back, Mr. Watson. How are you feeling?" the
young white lady asked, smiling.

"I'm okay," his voice cracked, still a little groggy.

"The doctor will be around to see you shortly. Meanwhile,
I'll see if I can get you something to eat," she offered.

He watched her walk away, her powder blue nurse pants
clinging to her petite hips. Hers was the first friendly face he'd

seen since he'd been locked up. On top of that, she was the first attractive woman he had seen since leaving the streets. It was his first real contact with human kindness and the feeling was awkward. It didn't last long, though, because it was replaced with the more familiar feeling of hate as the black sergeant from intake walked in, wearing a smug grin. Daquan had since learned the man's name was Tillman.

"Well, well, if it ain't the tough nigguh . . ." the Sarge quipped. "Watson, right?"

Daquan didn't respond.

"I see whoever got atcha had a bad aim," he said, referring to the shoulder injury. "Maybe you better tell me who it was, before they come back to finish the job."

Daquan had to fight the urge to tell him it was his dick-suckin' mama, but he bit down on his emotions and replied, "I don't know."

Sergeant Tillman rocked back on his heels, wearing an amused expression. "Oh really? Never seen him before?"

"Didn't see his face, Sarge."

"But he sure as hell saw *yours*," Tillman fired back. "So unless you give me a name, I'ma put you back out there so he *can* finish yo' lil' black ass off, you understand? That's what you want, tough guy?"

Daquan turned his head to one side, like, *Yeah, whatever.*

Tillman leaned in close and spoke in a clenched whisper, "You little motherfucka, don't you know where you at?! This *my* world! I run this! You think you safe 'cause you only pullin' a year? Nigguh, I can make it so you *never* see the streets again! Never . . . just try me . . . just . . . try me."

He finished up his barrage of threats just as the nurse reappeared with Daquan's tray. Tillman stood back up, smiled at the nurse while tipping an imaginary cap, and said, "Take care of him well. He's state property, remember," then walked out with Daquan's gaze burning a hole in his back.

* * *

Daquan was taken to the lockup tier and placed in a small 6-by-8 cell, just big enough for a bunk, a toilet, and a small desk in the corner. The window was barred and painted black, but over the years, inmates of the cell had scraped away, leaving names and hoods that allowed slivers of sunlight to bleed through.

"Yo, Quan! Quan, that you?" Nut's familiar voice echoed from a lower tier.

"Yeah, it's me, homey."

"You aiight, whody? They said you was bleedin' real bad! Yo, it ain't over, y'all muhfuckas know who I'm talkin' to. Quan, that shit ain't over!" Nut vowed, and a cacophony of voices shouted in reply. "Fuck y'all Calliope nigguhs!"

"Fuck Shreveport!"

"Suck my dick!"

Daquan sat down on his bunk, while the threats and abuse flew through the air, battling in his eardrums. He was ready to go to sleep, when he heard, "Yo, Quan. You okay, baby?"

Daquan recognized it as Nate's voice. He was only two cells down. Daquan walked over to the bars and replied, "I'm cool. Just wish I had a cigarette."

He heard the shuffling of shower shoes, then he heard Nate say to the guy in the cell between them, "Yo, homey, pass this to my boy in the next cell."

The guy mumbled some grudging reply, but a moment later, an ashy black hand held out three cigarettes and a book of matches to Daquan.

"Here."

Daquan took them and immediately lit one up. He allowed the nicotine to coat his nerves and bring a slight dizz to his head.

"'Preciate that, Nate."

"Yeah . . . I heard you took one fo' the team, lil' whody. You straight?" Nate asked with genuine concern in his tone.

"I'm straight, ya heard me? What about you?"

Nate chuckled.

"Shit, nigguh, I'm a soldier, so I'm always in solitary, ya dig? But ah, they talkin' 'bout leavin' me back heah till I turn seventeen, so they can send me to Angola."

Daquan blew out a stream of smoke.

"Damn, whody, I hate that it's like that. We ain't mean to get you fucked up," he apologized.

"Man, I'm a lifer. I'ma do this time wherever or till God call me home. I just ain't want none of y'all lil' nigguhs to get fucked up like me," Nate explained. He took a pull of his cigarette, then added, "Lil' whody, you coulda got killed today. You know that, right?"

Daquan looked at his shoulder and remembered the face of the boy who stuck him. A few inches more and it could've easily pierced his heart.

Nate took his silence as agreement, so he said, "Or you coulda easily kilt somebody today. That's how shit go, so you never know. Like that nigguh, Cee. He 'bout to go home, but he ride for the CP3. He coulda got fucked up, too. I'm schoolin' you, lil' whody, 'cause it's a time to go hard and a time to chill. I see you got that type of head, but Nut don't. He a soldier, but he don't think. That'll get you fucked up, ya know?"

"Yeah, but whody my boy, we grew . . ." Daquan tried to defend Nut, but Nate cut him off.

"I ain't sayin' don't fuck wit' ya peoples, naw. I'm sayin', sometimes you gotta think for you *and* him. That's all. Like I said, he a sho'nuff soldier, but plenty of them in here or six feet deep 'cause they ain't think . . . Look at me," Nate said.

Daquan nodded silently in agreement.

"So what you gonna do 'bout ol' boy that hit you up?" Nate questioned.

"I don't know, bruh. However it go."

"Then you a puppet, lil' Daddy. Real nigguhs make it go the way they want—only weak muhfuckas wait fo' shit to happen. Remember that."

6

"Watson. Mail call."

Daquan vaguely heard the voice of the C.O., but the familiar sound of paper being slid on the gravelly concrete instantly woke him up. He sat up and instinctively looked at the window and followed the slivers of light to the shadows on the floor. Being on lockdown for four months, he had learned how to tell time by the shadows. Elongated shadows meant it was close to sunset.

He got up and slid into his shower shoes to make the few steps to the cell door. He had one piece of mail, but the envelope was rather large. When he turned it over and read the name, he sucked his teeth, then tossed it on the bed while he took a piss. The letter was from Desiree. She had written him at least five times in the seven months he had been away, but he never wrote her back. To him, she was a little girl with a little girl's crush, talking 'bout a little girl's world he couldn't identify with.

"Yo, Quan!" Nut called out. "You get mail?"

The tier was usually quiet around this time, because everyone was either reading their mail, or sick because they didn't get any.

"Hold up!" Daquan shouted over the vacuum-like sound of

the toilet flushing. He waited until it stopped, then yelled, "What you say, Nut?"

"I said," Nut repeated, louder this time, "did you get any mail?"

"Yeah. You?"

"Naw, bruh. Who wrote you?"

Daquan paused before yelling back, "Desiree."

"Aw man, that lil' bitch still writin'? You ever write her back?"

"Naw."

"What the letter say?"

Daquan knew if he didn't tell him, he'd never get his push-ups done before last chow, which was his routine. He got the envelope and tore it open. Inside was a large card with a big bear on the front that read: Happy Birthday to You/*Us*.

She had crossed out the word "You" and written "Us," since they shared a birth date.

"It ain't shit but a birthday card!" Daquan yelled.

"Any money in it?" a laughing voice asked down the tier.

"Naw, whody," Daquan chuckled.

"Then what's so happy 'bout that?" The same voice laughed, and a few other cats laughed, including Daquan.

"Damn, whody, she on yo' dick fo' real."

"You might as well write back," Nut advised, wishing it was him she had written.

"The pussy must not be no good, Nut," said another voice. "Shit, I wouldn't write, neither. 'Specially since she ain't send no paper. Broke *and* her pussy ain't no good? Fuck dat."

More laughter rang out until Nut said, "Man, as good as Desiree look, I know her shit right. Tell 'em, Quan."

Daquan sucked his teeth and turned away from the door.

"Tell 'em, Quan," Nut repeated.

"Man, Nut, can't you see? He ain't fucked her yet," the laughing voice egged on.

The whole tier broke out in laughter.

"Lil' whody ain't hit it, ha? You ain't had no pussy, ha? Nigguh a virgin, ha?"

The tier was in an uproar.

"Man, fuck all y'all!" Daquan yelled through his embarrassment.

"I bet whody don't even know what the pussy look like!" Cee added, cutting on Daquan. "What it look like, Quan? And don't say a fish!"

Daquan wanted to be madder than he was, but the truth was, they were right. He hadn't had sex before. He dreamed about it, even had wet dreams, but he hadn't had the real thing. Before he could respond to the taunts of his friends, he heard the big-bellied C.O. bellowing. "Trays! Trays! Hold it down in here!" Daquan sat on his bunk and took up Desiree's card. Inside, it read:

Daquan,

I know you be gettin' my letters, boy. Why don't you write back? Keep actin' like that and I won't give you the surprise I got for you when you get out!

Tell Nut, Pam Butler said hey. I told her to write, but she ain't 'bout nothin', she just nasty. Tell Nut don't come out here and mess with her. You better not, either! You better write me, Quan, or you'll be sorry!

Your friend,
Dee Dee

Daquan sat the card down as the C.O. approached his cell. He took the Styrofoam tray and cup up to his bunk, then looked inside to find boiled eggs and mashed potatoes. He was so hungry, he forgot to curse it or bless it. In the distance he heard his man, G-Money, call out, "C.O.! Yo C.O.! I need to see you—I got hair in my tray!"

The C.O. came back to G-Money's cell like, "Where?"

G-Money held up the long strand of blond hair. "Right here."

The C.O. smugly replied, "How I know you ain't put it in there?"

G-Money looked at him, black and nappy-headed, and exclaimed, "Muhfucka, I look like I got blond hair?"

The C.O. smirked and replied, "You do now," then walked off.

"Stupid, fat bastard!" G-Money yelled after him, then added, "But I got that ass! *Believe* that!"

Everyone could hear G-Money mumbling about "gassin' him up," and they all knew what it meant. It was a mixture of piss and Magic Shave hair remover. The Magic Shave came in powder form, but once it was wet, it became like a clay putty. Used right, it removed hair, but left on, it removed skin like an acid. The piss was to make it stick in a humiliating way.

"Yo, Money, man, just chill," a sensible voice cautioned. "That shit ain't worth it."

"Naw, fuck dat, bruh—these muhfuckas keep playin' me, man! For real, I'm tired of this shit!" G-Money spat.

He was a man in a cage who had had enough. He knew the consequences of his actions. He knew what they would do to him. But the mere satisfaction of seeing that guard burnt up was enough to motivate him. Daquan called out to him, "Money! You 'bout to go, bruh! Just let dem crackers go on."

G-Money was too far gone to answer. Everyone waited with bated breath as the C.O. came back along the tier collecting empty trays. As he passed Daquan's cell, Daquan looked at him and imagined his sunburnt face peeling like a dried orange. In his heart, he knew the cracker deserved it—he just wished it wasn't G-Money who had to do it. As the C.O. reached his cell, G-Money was ready, cup in hand. The C.O. smirked at him. G-Money brought the cup through the bars and caught the man dead in the face.

"*Argggh!!*" the C.O. screamed in agony, blinded by the piss and feeling the thick putty ooze all over his grill.

"Yeah, muhfucka! Sizzle, you swine, *sizzle*!!" G-Money taunted with glee. The tier erupted in cheers and curses as the C.O. stumbled his way along the tier, nearly falling end over end off the tier.

"*Heellllp* me!" he screamed, the Magic Shave eating into his face like acid.

Another C.O. saw him stumbling down the stairs and ran to his assistance, escorting him to the nearest water supply. The dorm continued to cheer until the C.O. was gone, then the noise began to die down because they knew the victory would be short-lived. No one spoke for a few minutes, until Cee hollered, "Yo, Money, you aiight, bruh?"

"Yeah," G-Money replied, and they could tell by his tone of voice that he was moving around, preparing himself.

"You know they comin'," Cee continued. "Be strong, soldier, ya heard me?"

"Always, baby, always," G-Money confirmed.

They all saw the six officers with the extra-long batons enter, headed by Sergeant Tillman. The smirk on his face told all who could see it that this was the part of the job he loved most.

"Soldier, whody!" Cee exclaimed once more.

His voice echoed, then got trampled under the sound of twelve steel-toed boots ascending the stairs.

"You need six muhfuckas for one man, you cowards!" Nut cried out.

"Shut up or you next!" the Sergeant barked, not knowing who said it. They walked by Daquan's door without looking right or left. But he could hear them stop in front of G-Money's cell.

"Inmate Robinson, lay down on the floor and place your hands behind your head," Tillman ordered.

No one heard G-Money's reply.

"This is your final warning, inmate Robinson. Lay down on the floor."

"Hell, no!" G-Money blurted out, more out of fear than defiance. He knew it was coming either way, so he wanted to face it standing. Daquan heard the cell open, and all six officers rushed G-Money at one time. G-Money was the average size for a fifteen-year-old, so it wasn't long before they heard, "I'm down! I'm down!" But the scuffling sounds continued.

"Fuck y'all cowards! The man said he down!" Daquan hollered out, wishing he could get out of his own cell and run to G-Money's aid.

"Ow, man! I . . ." G-Money mumbled, but was cut off by a sickening wooden thud that landed on flesh. The thuds continued over and over, until they subsided and Tillman said, "Get a stretcher."

A few minutes later, a stretcher was brought up. Daquan could hear them putting G-Money on it, but he wasn't prepared for what he saw. When they carried him by Daquan's cell, he couldn't recognize his friend. His upper body was covered in blood and his head was swollen like those famous pictures of Emmett Till. All Daquan could do was lower his head. When he lifted it, Tillman was standing at his door. "*I* . . . run this," he whispered triumphantly, then he smiled and walked off.

As Daquan slept, he could feel that familiar presence that had become so much a part of his inner self. He felt like he was sitting in a squatting position, with his arms crossed over his knees and his head on his arms.

"He made you mad," she said, feeling it as much as he was.

"I wish I could kill him," he said, without lifting his head. "Fuckin' kill all these motherfuckin' crackas!"

She moved over to him and touched him lightly on the shoulder. Daquan woke up into her comforting brownness, and he could feel his frustrations melting away from the rawness of his nerves. Diana smiled at him.

"All you ever feel is hate and anger?" she asked. "Where has it gotten you?"

He thought back over the many decisions he had made in his short life, and realized that the worst ones were the ones he made out of emotion. Frustrations of not having enough made him take from others. Hate in his heart made him lash out violently against people. His anger had blinded his thinking.

"Nowhere . . . here," he mumbled before putting his head back in his lap.

"If you kill them, then where would you be? And if you keep wishing you could, but don't, it only poisons your heart."

Daquan stood up and looked at his sister. She seemed older.

"How come you don't come see me as much as when . . . I mean, when I was younger? You gonna leave me, too?" he questioned.

"I'm always with you, Daquan," she replied softly.

"But I need to *see* you. I need to talk to you, talk to somebody, 'cause I'm goin' crazy in here," he told her emphatically. "Where do you go?"

Diana walked a few feet away. The cotton of her dress, still freshly creased, made soft swooshes as she walked.

"I'm just . . . here. Sometimes, I want to see you, but I can't . . . like with Mama."

Daquan's eyes widened as he approached her.

"You visit Mama, too?"

She shook her head in despair.

"She won't let me, but I can feel her. I can always feel Mama like I'm inside of her . . . Always." Diana wrapped her arms around herself, then added, "I can feel when she's crying or mad. I can even feel when she smiles and when she laughs. But she doesn't do that much. Mostly . . . she cries," Diana explained.

Daquan was reluctant, but he asked anyway. "What about Daddy—can you feel him, too? Does he . . . cry?"

"Sometimes," she told him. Knowing what he was feeling, she added, "There's nothing wrong with crying, Daquan. I can feel when you want to cry, too." She smiled.

"Ain't no need to cry. It can't help me."

"Neither can hate, unless you let it."

"Huh?"

Diana came over to him and took his face in her hands. "You have to learn to *use* your feelings. Your tears, your anger, even your hate, instead of letting it use you."

"But how? How do I do that, Diana? Show me," he begged, but she was gone. The warmth of her palm was replaced with the cold plastic of a pay-phone receiver. He was in a phone booth outside the Calliope. The only light was the street lamp half a block away. In his ear, the dial tone buzzed loudly until the operator came on the line and said, "If you'd like to make a call . . . If you'd like to make a call . . . then *speak*!"

All of a sudden, four men with bandanas around their mouths surrounded the booth, all armed with AK-47 automatic rifles. Daquan tried to open the booth's folding door but it was jammed. The gunmen all cocked their weapons simultaneously, then one stepped up close to the glass, right up to Daquan's face, and hissed, "Game over, nigguh."

He stepped back and they all opened fire, riddling his body with hot lead. Daquan sat up on his bunk, breathless. The whole tier was quiet. He was too scared to lie down, but too tired to stay awake, and his mind wondered what it all meant.

Seventeen days later, Daquan was let out of solitary. Nut stayed longer because he kept catching infractions, which lengthened his time, but they had less than five months to go, so solitary wasn't too bad.

Daquan went back to his same pod and saw Cee, who had gotten out of the hole a few days earlier.

"What's happenin', my nigguh," Cee greeted him. "I see dem dicksuckers let you out, huh?"

"Shit, we still in heah, ya heard me? See me in five months and say that," Daquan responded.

"I heard that, lil' daddy. Look, *MTV Raps* on. Let's go check it out."

Daquan and Cee walked over to the TV area where they had *Yo! MTV Raps* blaring. The video was N.W.A's "Appetite for Destruction." Cats that knew the words were rapping as if they were Ren or Eazy; those who didn't just bopped their heads hard, feeling the nigguhs' attitude.

"That's that hard shit there, whody. Them fools is crazy," Cee commented, bopping to the music.

Daquan listened to the beat intensely. Music had always done something to him, ever since Jerome introduced him to "Planet Rock." Whenever he went out to hit a lick, he would listen to the Geto Boys, N.W.A, or Too $hort. The music always put him in the mind frame of readiness, amped him up and said what he was feeling. Without even thinking, he said, "I can do that."

Cee looked at him like, "Do what? Rap? Nigguh, you can't rap. Why I ain't never heard you wit' the rest of dem fools bangin' on tables?"

Daquan shrugged, still watching the video at the part when Dre starts blasting with that tommy-gun in the bank.

"My brother out in Cali got a record sto'," Cee told him. "That's where I'm goin' in a few weeks. He 'bout to put it down in rap fo' the N.O.," Cee announced proudly. "Lemme hear you bust a flow."

"Naw, bruh, not right now. I don't feel like it," Daquan stuttered, wondering what made him say he could do it in the first place. He had never written a rap in his life.

Cee sucked his teeth like, "Just like I said. *You can't rap.*"

Daquan looked at him directly. He hated to be told he couldn't do something, especially after being in a place like Scotland for seven and a half months, where you're told what to do constantly. The video on TV was Naughty by Nature's "Uptown Anthem." He began to bop his head to the beat, then just let it flow . . .

> *I'm the D to the Q and pack a black calico*
> *When I roll or flow, I represent the Callio'*
> *Fuck what y'all heard—I serve chumps wit' lumps*
> *If y'all stunt lil' punk—Be laid up for months*
> *Duck boy—I keeps it gutta, a Cutt Boy*
> *What up boy—Me and Nut a steal ya truck boy . . .*

While Daquan was rapping, a few other cats overheard him and came over to listen . . .

> *I'm only thirteen—But seen a whole lot, whody*
> *For all my dead nigguhz I pour out my whole forty . . .*

A few of the prison rappers came to spit a verse or two, taking turns. Daquan was a natural; the words and phrases just flowed from his lips like they had been held back for too long. When the session was over, Cee gave him dap and handed him a piece of paper. "I ain't know you rip like that, D.Q.," he joked, calling him by the name he used in his raps. "This my brother number in Cali. Call me when you get out, ya heard me?"

"Aiight," Daquan replied, putting the paper in his pocket.

For the last five months of his bid, all Daquan did was write rhymes. Everything he had been feeling for so long came out in a song. He even wrote his daddy and sent him letters in rap form.

You sat me on your lap when I was five years old
I remember that Pops, ya baby done grow'd
As I sit and reminisce all you are to me
We share the same blood. You are a part of me

Nut was just as excited about Daquan's newfound skills as he was.

"Yo, D, write me some raps too, bruh. I wanna blow up too!" Nut exclaimed, picturing them both rich and famous.

By the time Daquan and Nut jumped on the bus back home, they were ready to take on the world.

7

It felt good to be back in the 'hood. Even though the ghetto is usually considered the worst zoning in town, surrounded by waste and neglected vacancies, when it's all you know as a child, it will always be home. Vacant lots become playgrounds, milk crates turn into basketball hoops, and the projects are a world all its own.

Daquan took a deep breath, inhaling the aroma of the Calliope deep into his nostrils. The place hadn't changed—the only thing different was the "WELCOME HOME DAQUAN AND NUT" sign strung across the parking lot of his building. Everyone seemed to be there. The music was loud and the local bounce legend, Gregory D, was on the mic. All that could be heard was the boomin' bass and the latest ghetto chants:

That Calliope! Buckjump time!
That Calliope! Buckjump time!
That Third Ward! Buckjump time!

Jerome did it big for his little cousin and his homey. He had come up strong in the growing crack-and-black ice epidemic that was gripping the ghetto. The first thing Nut and Daquan saw as they stepped out of the probation officer's car was

Jerome's brand-new cocaine-white Cadillac Allante, fully laced with a booming sound system complete with AMG-style hammers. The license plate read *ROME* and was trimmed in gold plate.

The probation officer looked at the banner and shook his head.

"You two must be pretty popular," he remarked sarcastically.

"What, you ain't know?" Nut quipped, bobbing his head to the music.

He escorted the two boys to Daquan's steps, but Grandma Mama and Melissa were sitting on a bench drinking tea when they saw Daquan.

"My baby's home! Come give Mama a big hug!" she ordered lovingly.

Daquan rushed over and hugged the tears right out of Grandma Mama as she covered him with kisses.

"Mama missed you so much," she exclaimed, tears of joy rolling down her face.

"I missed you too, Mama," Daquan replied.

He kissed and hugged Melissa, who commented, "Boy, you done got so *big*. Look at them muscles. Lord, Mama, he gon' drive these young heifers crazy!"

Daquan had gotten almost a foot taller, and all those calisthenics had his young, burgeoning frame tight. Still, the comment made him blush a little.

The probation officer stepped up with Nut at his side. "Mrs. Watson?"

"Yes, that's me."

"I see that Daquan has returned to open arms, but I need to go over the terms of his probation and have you sign some papers. It won't take long."

"Okay, have a seat."

"Look at my lil' cuz, Pepper!" Jerome exclaimed.

Daquan and Nut looked around and saw Jerome and Pepper

approaching, so they ran over to them. Jerome and Pepper hugged them both, then Pepper said, "Talkin' 'bout Daquan, *shit*, look at *my* lil' brother. I bet he can still whip Quan ass!

"Bet!" Jerome joked.

Both boys enjoyed the attention, especially coming from Jerome and Pepper. Their gear and jewels said it all. The game was being very good to them. "That yo' probation officer?" Pepper asked.

"Yeah," Daquan replied.

"Mine, too," Nut chimed in.

Jerome nodded.

"Yeah, Mackey play fair. Glad you ain't get that asshole, Delaney."

Just then Mackey approached Nut. "Mario, I need to see your mother before I can officially let you out of my sight." He looked up at Pepper, taking in his whole presentation. "Hello, Novarell. How have you been?"

"Shit, I'm straight," Pepper smiled, stuntin' his twelve gold teeth with diamond cuts.

"Yes, I'm sure you are," Mackey replied, then turned to Nut, or "Mario." Mackey and Nut walked away, and Pepper went with them as well. Jerome turned to Daquan and playfully sparred with him.

"Whut up, lil' cuz? I heard aboutcha down there in Baby Angola," he told him proudly.

Daquan smiled, then replied, "I learned from the best," then he threw a quick slap-jab that Jerome just managed to dip at the last second.

"Oh, you think you ready for this?" he chuckled, then faked a left and quickly scooped Daquan and hoisted him in the air. "Maybe in a few more years and another hundred pounds."

He put Daquan down and looked at his watch. "Look, I got some shit to take care of, but I'ma come get you in the mornin'. We gon' go shoppin' and just hang, ya dig?"

"Fa sho'," Daquan said with a smile, then gave Jerome a handshake hug.

As Jerome walked away he heard, "Daquan Watson!" The voice was familiar, but when he turned around, the figure wasn't. It was Desiree, only she wasn't the skinny, chicken-legged little girl she was a year ago. She still had the same reddish-brown hair and catfish-green eyes, but Desiree had filled out in all the right places.

She looked like a grown woman, and she knew it, too, the way she sauntered over to him. She was dressed in cut-off jean shorts, jelly flip-flops, and a T-shirt, and if he hadn't grown to be five-seven, she would've been taller than him at her new height of five-five. She had Pam Butler with her as she approached him with her hands on her hips.

Daquan was utterly speechless. She definitely wasn't the Desiree that used to get on his nerves. Now, he couldn't take his eyes off her, and she knew it, too.

"*Mm*-hmm, nigguh, joke's on you, ain't it? Why you ain't never write me back?" She folded her arms over her burgeoning breasts and looked him up and down, liking what she saw as well.

"Hey, Quan," Pam spoke, giving him that eye he would've understood if he was more experienced.

"Don't speak to him," Desiree snapped, rolling her eyes, then added, "till he tell me why he play me like that... Well?"

"Man, I ain't get no letter. When you wrote me? Them people be fuckin' up the mail," he replied, saying the first thing that came to mind.

"You lyin'! That's why you make me sick! Why Tanesha's brother be gettin' her letters and I got the address from her?!"

Daquan didn't know what to say so he just sucked his teeth like, *Man, don't believe me then. What I gotta lie for?* Then he stepped off to see his grandma.

"That's alright, Daquan Watson!" Desiree yelled behind

him. "I know you want this. Walk away if you want to! Come on, Pam."

Grandma Mama looked up as Daquan approached.

"Lord, who is that chile puttin' all her business in the street like that? How old is she?"

Melissa replied, holding a half-eaten corn cob in her hand. "Essie Carol daughter. She 'bout Quan age, ain't she, Quan?" Melissa teased him.

"I don't know," he replied in a feigned aggravated tone, frontin' like he wasn't open on the new and improved Desiree.

Grandma Mama just looked at him, smiling. The prolonged gaze made him feel funny, so he finally said, "*What?*"

"Nothin'. Just seein' on how big and handsome you done got. Just like yo' daddy when he was your age. Come here, sit with Mama for a spell." Daquan sat down next to his grandmother on the bench.

"So, how do it feel to be back home? Have you ate yet? All this food, get you some of it," she told him.

She watched him load up his plate with fried chicken, crabs, jambalaya, and three cobs of corn.

"I see ain't nothin' change 'bout his appetite," Melissa quipped. "He still eatin' everything in sight."

"Ain't nothin' wrong with yours, either," Grandma Mama shot right back, chuckling. "He's a growing boy. What's yo' excuse?"

Daquan smiled as he chewed, glad to be back in his comfort zone. For the rest of the day, he enjoyed his freedom amongst friends and fun, soaking in everything. That night, he climbed into his soft bed and was happy to be off that hard bunk. As he drifted off to sleep, his thoughts turned to tomorrow, when he would see Jerome.

Daquan was up early the next morning. Being locked up for a year had conditioned his body to getting up at dawn, so instead of going back to sleep, he decided to start his day.

He instinctively picked up his pack of Camels and started

to spark one, until he remembered he was in Grandma Mama's house. She'd flip if she knew he had come home with a habit, so he dipped in the bathroom, turned the shower on hot to steam up the place, then lit his cigarette. After his shower, he tried to get dressed, but none of his old clothes fit him, so he reluctantly put back on his prison release outfit from yesterday. He couldn't wait to go shopping, because wearing the same thing two days in a row wouldn't work now that he was home. Daquan went in the kitchen, following the aroma of spicy fish and grits. When he walked in, Grandma Mama was humming one of Satchmo's melodies, fixing a plate.

"I see you already up," she commented, handing him his breakfast.

"Yes'm, I'm used to gettin' up early," he told her, sitting down and grabbing the salt without even testing to see if his food needed it. But she saw him and said, "Slow down, chile. You ain't even et none of it yet. That's why black folk pressure so high now. Too fast wit' the salt."

She sat down across from Daquan, watching him eat. "Now that you up, what you gonna do with your day?"

Daquan wiped his mouth. "Jerome 'posed to take me shoppin', then I'll probably be with him."

The smile on her face soured to an expression of disapproval.

"Daquan, do you know what Jerome do for his money?"

Daquan didn't want to look his grandmother in the face. "I guess he work."

"Look at me, Daquan," she told him. When he did, she went on, "The boy sell *drugs*. Drugs, Daquan, like the ones your mama was on and broke up yo' family."

Daquan sighed. "It ain't like he *use* 'em, do he?"

"Does it matter? He sell 'em, so *somebody* gotta be usin' 'em. Somebody's *mama*," she emphasized.

"We only goin' shoppin'," he mumbled between bites of fish.

"And Eve only bit the apple. Listen, Daquan, you don't need to get in no more trouble, ya heah? That probation man said if you get in any mo' trouble for the next three months, they gonna lock you back up. Is that what you want?"

"No, ma'am."

"Then mind what I say. I know it's summer so ain't no school to keep you busy. Why don't you try and cut some grass? Earn yo' own money," Grandma Mama suggested.

"Okay, Grandma Mama," Daquan replied, standing up and putting his plate in the sink. He kissed her on the cheek, then told her, "I'm goin' to Nut's."

"Mm-hmm," Grandma Mama responded skeptically, watching him walk through the kitchen door. "Daquan."

He turned around.

"And ain't gonna be no smokin' in this house. You wanna smoke, do it on the porch. Remember our deal we made before you left?"

Daquan nodded, wondering how she knew he'd lit one up in the house.

"I love you, but you old enough to make your own decisions, good or bad."

Daquan walked out and headed straight for Nut's, but Nut was still asleep, so he went over to Jerome's apartment on the other side of the Calliope. As he walked, he noticed that there had been a lot of changes in the little time he was away. Older people he remembered from a year ago seemed different. Like the man across the street from Nut that worked all the time and washed his beige Monte Carlo every Saturday; here it was past nine and he was walking, wearing dingy work pants and a raggedy button-up. Even some of the women he and Nut used to have a crush on seemed run down now.

He got to Jerome's spot and started to knock, but the door suddenly swung open and his Aunt Melissa was on her way out with money in her hand. Daquan's presence startled her.

"Oh, hey, Quan." She kissed him on the forehead, then

turned back to Jerome, who was standing behind her in his boxers, rubbing his eyes.

"Thank you, baby—I'll pay you back soon as I get my check."

"Yeah, Ma," Jerome answered, like he'd heard it before but had yet to see it.

Melissa left and Daquan came in, shutting the door behind him.

"What's happenin', lil' whody? What you doin' up? You still on that prison time, ha?" Jerome joked, scratching his nuts, then added, "Damn, I shoulda got Ma to go to the store. I ain't got no cigarettes."

Daquan held out his pack with a smirk.

"Damn, lil' cuz gettin' grown for real," Jerome commented as he took the pack and pulled a joe.

"When we goin' shoppin', bruh? I ain't got shit to wear," Daquan told him.

"Lemme get right, then we'll roll. You hungry? Man, who I'm talkin' to? I know Grandma Mama cooked," Jerome said as he walked down the hall. "What she cooked?"

"Cajun fish and grits," Daquan yelled to him.

He could tell Jerome missed Grandma Mama's house, but from the look of things in the apartment, he wasn't planning on coming back any time soon. The place was laced. The furniture was covered in rich brown leather, with maple wood end tables and bookcases that held a Sony stereo system. It even had a CD player that Daquan didn't understand because no one really had CDs. In those days, it was strictly cassettes. He looked around and spotted the new white Jordans by the couch, laying on their sides like Jerome had just kicked them off and discarded them. His Sega system sat surrounded by various video games, its tangled cords running from the big-screen TV on the opposite wall.

Jerome was living the life that the majority of working people couldn't afford and most of the people in the Calliope would never imagine. In a society that emphasizes hard work and education, Jerome's success didn't make sense to Daquan. He remembered Grandma Mama saying, "He sells *drugs*."

Daquan didn't like what drugs did to people, but as to what it did *for* people . . . No one could be blamed for wanting nice things.

"You ready?" Jerome asked, emerging from the back wearing blue Karl Kani shorts with a matching T-shirt and another pair of Jordans just like the ones on the floor, except these were navy blue. He grabbed his nugget watch off the table and affixed it to his wrist.

"Yeah, I'm ready."

They went out the back door to the parking lot, also known as The Cut, where Jerome's Allante was parked. He chirped the alarm, then climbed in. When he started the car, Mary J. Blige's tape was still in the deck, and "Love No Limit" popped on.

"Fuck that. Mary my girl, but I gotta ride to that Pac," Jerome explained, putting in *Tupacalypse Now* and rewinding the tape to "Soulja's Story."

They cuttin' off welfare!!
All you wanted to be, a soldier, a soldier . . .

Jerome took Daquan to the Plaza Shopping Center and let him tear the mall up. The first thing Daquan hollered was "Jordans," so Jerome copped him three pair. Daquan was a Saints fan, so Jerome copped him everything Saints, from Starter coats and fitted caps to T-shirts and windsuits. Kani, Boss, Polo, and even Used found its way into Daquan's bags. Jerome made sure he was heavy; the only stipulation was that Daquan had to carry his own bags.

"I ain't wearin' it, so I ain't carryin' it," Jerome informed him, flipping the car keys on his pinky finger.

They went to the food court and ate McDonald's.

"So," Jerome began after they sat down with their order, "you home, you geared up and shit. So now what?"

Daquan shrugged his shoulders, gobbling fries.

"What you mean, you don't know? You betta not be thinkin' you goin' back to breakin' in people shit, 'cause if you is, I'll break yo' . . ."

Daquan cut in over the threat. "Man, I ain't studdin' no shit like that."

"Bett' not," Jerome warned anyway, biting into his Big Mac. His beeper went off for the hundredth time since he'd been in the mall. He checked it, then put it back on his waist. "Gold-diggin' bitch."

Daquan had been trying to tell Jerome what he really planned to do. He wanted to rap. Maybe even go out to Cali with Cee and see what his brother was really all about.

"You know Corey Miller? He live on Erato Street in Rocheblave Courtway," Daquan asked.

"Yeah, why?" Jerome answered.

"We was locked up in Scotland, but he got out before me. He went to stay with his brother in Cali. He got a record store," Daquan told him, but Jerome just looked at him like . . . *And*?

Daquan took a deep breath. "They 'pose to be doin' this rap thing and . . . Yo, Cee said I was real good, bruh. I had the best flow in Baby 'Gola," Daquan boasted flatly, because Jerome didn't look impressed.

"So what you sayin', nigguh? You wanna rap now?" Jerome chuckled. "You wanna go to Cali and rap with dem nigguhs at a record store?"

Jerome's laughter got harder, making Daquan feel smaller and, at the same time, madder.

"What's wrong with dat? And we ain't rappin' in no store, we 'bout to have our *own* record label," Daquan fired back.

Seeing Quan was getting mad, Jerome checked his laughter. "Look, Quan, I don't know what them nigguhs doin' in Cali, but I know what's goin' on *heah*. Shit is rough and motherfuckas doin' whatever to get by. And I know you, you ain't gonna work, and if you do go to school, it won't be to learn. If I thought you would, then I wouldn't come at you like this, but since you ain't, you damn sure ain't gonna end up with the rest of these petty nigguhs breakin' in shit, robbin' liquor stores and in and out of prison. You gonna be in these streets, you might as well get something out of it," Jerome scolded him.

Daquan dropped his head, dream crushed but still alive.

Jerome leaned his elbows on the table. "Big cuz the man around heah, ya heard me? I'ma teach you how to be a man, too. I'ma school you, whody."

Daquan looked up at Jerome, hearing his grandmother's warning from so long ago. "Man, Jerome," Daquan sighed. "I don't wanna sell nobody no drugs."

"Fa sho'. I feel where you comin' from, bruh. Maybe you see it as goin' against the grain, but crack ain't what broke up yo' family. And even if it was, this shit *owe* you, Quan. It may not get yo' family back, but you can make sure you ain't gotta live like that. You wanna rap? Go 'head, rap. But get this paper so you can own yo' label, open a store, whatever. It's up to you."

"You could give me the money," Daquan accused subtly.

Jerome finished his soda as he stood up. "Ain't shit free in this world, Quan. I'll bend over backwards to help you get it, but I'd make yo' game bad if I just gave it to you. Come on, we out."

They drove back along Interstate 10 without saying a word, Tupac blaring from the speakers. Jerome kept glancing over at Daquan with an amused expression on his face. Daquan was laid back in his seat, with his head propped up on his hand, elbow on the door handle. Jerome turned down the music and asked, "What's the matter, nigguh? You poutin' on me now? Actin' like a bitch or somethin'?"

"Ain't nobody actin' like no bitch—fuck you," Daquan mumbled.

"Probably just grumpy because you ain't had no pussy since you been home. You need to use my crib so you can fuck one of dem little hookers?" Jerome offered.

Daquan sucked his teeth and leaned against the door. "Ain't nobody studdin' no bitches, man. Just take me to Nut house."

"What you mean, you ain't stud . . ." Then it hit Jerome, and he looked at Daquan wide-eyed. "Whody?! You still a virgin, ain't you?"

Jerome bust out laughing, then playfully threw a punch at Daquan that he slapped away hard. "Damn, cuz, I ain't know! Don't worry, it ain't nothin' to be ashamed of."

"Nigguh, what I got to be shamed for?! I don't give a fuck 'bout no pussy. What's so good about that shit, anyway? It ain't money!" Daquan naively spat.

"Yeah, cuz, you *definitely* ain't had none," Jerome chuckled. Then a thought hit him. He looked at his watch, then said, "Matter of fact . . ." He checked his rearview, switched to the right lane, and made a right. "I want you to meet a friend of mine."

"Who?"

"Pussy."

The moment she opened the door, Daquan caught butterflies in his loins. She stood almost as tall as Jerome's six-two height in her red stilettos. She opened the door wearing an opened robe that revealed her pink Victoria's Secret teddy that stopped just above where her panties would've been, had she been wearing any. She stood in the door provocatively, until she noticed that Jerome wasn't alone. She closed her robe and snapped, "Jerome, I thought it was just you. Who is this?"

"My little cousin, Daquan. Say hi to Mandi, D.," Jerome introduced as he and Daquan entered.

All Daquan could do was nod for staring so hard.

"He's so cute, Rome. How old are you, Daquan?" she asked, but before he could answer for himself, Jerome said, "Old enough. Look, I need to holla at you 'bout somethin'. Let me see you in the kitchen."

"Oh, okay," she complied, then asked Daquan, "You want something to drink, Daquan?"

"Naw, we just ate," Jerome told her on his way into the kitchen.

Mandi followed Jerome into the kitchen, while Daquan sat on the couch. Looking around Mandi's condo, it seemed like everybody was living the good life but him. Her living room was color-schemed in white and soft brown, set on hardwood floors.

"Jerome, is you crazy?! I ain't doin' no shit like that!" Daquan heard Mandi exclaim from the kitchen. Then he heard Jerome's voice, but he couldn't make out the words.

"This is some fucked-up shit, Jerome. I can't believe you'd come at me like this," was what Daquan heard a few moments later. But her voice wasn't as defensive as before. He knew whatever it was, it had to do with him; he just hoped it wasn't what he thought it was.

Jerome came out smiling and winked at him, then Mandi came out next with her arms folded over her breasts, an annoyed expression across her gorgeous face. She just looked at Daquan like he had done something terrible, then she spoke.

"How old are you, Daquan?"

"I told you—" Jerome started to say, but she cut him off.

"No, Jerome, let him talk for his self. If he gonna do it, he can damn sure talk," she scolded, then turned back to Daquan. "Well?"

"Thirteen."

"Thirteen," she mumbled to herself, shaking her head. "Well, *thirteen*, Jerome said you want some pussy."

Daquan looked at Jerome accusingly.

"You do, don't you?" he quipped.

"I . . . I guess." Daquan mumbled.

"You guess?" Mandi echoed. "No, you say, Mandi, I want some pussy. Go 'head."

Daquan looked at a chuckling Jerome, who urged him with his eyes. Daquan looked at Mandi standing in front of him.

"Mandi . . . I, um . . . I want some . . . pussy," Daquan finally got out.

She wasted no time grabbing his hand and pulling him from the couch. "Come on, then."

Mandi led him by the hand like she was gonna whoop him instead of fuck him. When they got into her bedroom, she sat on her waterbed and put her head in her hands, running her fingers through her hair, as the bed rocked her body up and down.

"Can't *believe* I'm doin' this," she finally said, then took off her robe, stood up, and let the teddy fall to the floor. Her cocoa brownness was flawless. Her breasts were small, but she made up for it with her hips, fat ass, and the thick thighs of a stallion. Daquan's eyes didn't blink once. She sat back down.

"What you waitin' for?" she quipped. "You don't know what to do, do you?"

Daquan shook his head. Mandi sucked her teeth and pulled him over to her by his belt. She took off his pants and stared at his limp thug muscle.

"You ain't even hard . . . *Jerome*!" she called out. "He scared to death! The boy ain't even hard!"

Jerome had his feet kicked up on the coffee table, rolling a blunt with a VIBE magazine on his lap. "Well, give him some neck!" He replied then added to himself, chuckling, "The way you blow, it'll get anybody up."

Mandi closed her eyes and took a deep breath. Then she

looked into Daquan's unsuspecting face, "You heard the man."

She slid her hand along the length of his dick, then slipped it into her expert mouth.

Daquan got hard so quick, she gagged, then relaxed her throat. She only blew him until he was right. When she took his dick out of her mouth, Daquan realized he was standing on his toes and holding his breath.

Mandi lay back and propped her legs on the bed, then pulled him down between them. She took her hand and guided him inside, and in his ears he swore he heard angels sighing. Every muscle in his body seemed to melt into her softness, except for his dick, which stayed rock-hard. It felt so good, he was frozen.

"Well?" Mandi huffed. "Hump . . . *shit*, do somethin'."

The sensual friction he felt sliding in and out was so addictive, before he knew it, he was humping like a rabbit, enjoying every thrust until he felt that sharp sensation of a building ejaculation. She felt him trembling, so she grabbed his ass and threw the pussy on him. It was more than Daquan could take. His whole body stiffened as he exploded inside a woman for the first time.

"Damn, boy! Get up!" Mandi exclaimed, wiping her face and pushing him off of her.

He wanted to tell her he loved her, but he couldn't speak.

"You drooled on me," she accused, but Daquan wasn't the least bit embarrassed.

He felt too good.

Mandi threw on her robe and went up front where Jerome was smoking a blunt.

"He *drooled* on me, Jerome."

Jerome stood up and handed her the blunt. "Take it as a compliment."

Daquan came out, pulling up his pants.

"You straight, lil' whody?" Jerome beamed proudly.

"Yeah," Daquan replied, looking at Mandi.

Jerome opened the door. "I'll be back later, lil' mama."

He and Daquan walked out.

"You better," she said to herself, hitting the blunt, a single tear tracing her cheek. "You better."

8

Jerome had created a monster. It took a few weeks of brokenness and boredom, but when Daquan finally decided to roll with Jerome, he took to the game quickly. He had convinced himself of Jerome's philosophy, that if drugs took his life, then it owed him a life. At least until he got what he wanted out of it.

Jerome showed him how to cook up powder cocaine and turn it into crack. He also showed him the more complex process of making black ice, which was to cook powdered cocaine, heroin, and PCP together, using baking soda and water as you would to make crack. The heroin converts the heated mixture to black, resulting in a shiny rock that produces a longer lasting, more euphoric high when smoked. So of course, fiends paid much more for it.

Once Daquan got the hang of it, he and Nut were constants on the spot in the Calliope everyone called The Cut, a dark, secluded area of the projects where nothing but drug transactions took place. They were in The Cut so much, their friends started calling them "The Cutt Boyz."

"The Cutt Boyz got that raw."
"See dem Cutt Boyz, they hold'n."
"Where dem Cutt Boyz, whody?"

It was all you heard. They were quickly making themselves a factor in the game. Daquan even had a friend rent out an apartment so they could handle the traffic better and give the addicts a place to get high without bringing too much heat.

But the game wasn't all sweet. Because Nut and Daquan were so young, the fiends sometimes tried to gorilla them, and some of the older boys in The Cut tried to cut their throats for sales. Being Jerome's little cousin and Pepper's little brother carried a lot of weight, but the two young hustlers still had to prove they were their own men as well.

When it came to Grandma Mama, Daquan had to stay on point so she wouldn't catch him slipping. He kept his money over at Jerome's house in his own little safe, and his extra clothes, he kept at Nut's. He would still ask her for some money, here and there, to keep the facade up, to which she would complain, "All you do is hang out with those no-good young'ns doin' God knows what. You need to get a job, boy."

Meanwhile, his name was beginning to ring bells around the project and surrounding areas as a rapper to beat. Whether it was on the block or at the Rec Center, Daquan, a.k.a. D.Q., could be heard holding a rap session with any number of other cats. It got to the point where his friends and listeners had favorites.

"Yo D, do that joint about the choppa."

"D.Q., rock that Calliope joint."

"D.Q., when you gonna put my name in yo' raps?" the girls would often flirt with him. When it came to the ladies, he had become a pussy hound, trying to stick anything willing to holler back. Because him and Nut were getting their paper up, not to mention their game tighter, they had their pick of the hoodrats around the way.

He didn't see Desiree much, and he wondered why, until one day he was going in Rose Tavern and he heard, "D.Q!" with a soft, feminine exclamation.

He turned around to find Pam Butler sashaying up in a pair of extra-tight cut-off shorts and a T-shirt that stopped above her navel. "I know you heard me callin' you, boy. I said your name three times."

Daquan put the money he was counting in his pocket and Pam's eyes followed it.

"My bad, lil' mama, but I hear you now. Whatz hap', girl?" he smiled, flashing his first two solid gold teeth on his top grill.

"You goin' to the store? You gonna buy me sumthin'?" she asked in a fake shy tone.

"Yeah, you know I got you," he replied—then they entered Mr. Dan's corner store.

She purposely got in front of him so he could watch her ass as she walked over to the cooler and got a grape soda.

"I ain't seen you wit' yo' girl lately," Daquan remarked. "Y'all don't hang no mo' or somethin'?"

"Who? Desiree?" Pam questioned, then rolled her eyes and sucked her teeth. "What you askin' 'bout her for?"

Daquan shrugged it off, while Pam grabbed two blow pops and a pack of gum. "Just makin' conversation. Lettin' you know I be watchin' you."

"Mm-hmm," she mumbled on her way to the counter. "I don't know why you studdin' her and she got a man. She went to Baton Rouge to her grandma's. He live down theah."

Daquan was on fire, but he kept his cool as he paid for her stuff and bought a pack of Camels for himself. "I ain't studdin' nobody, boo. All I'm sayin' is, how you know she got a man, if she in Baton Rouge?"

They walked out the door, then she turned to face him. "'Cause we talk all the time and she told me," Pam lied. "But if that's all you wanna know, I'll tell her you was askin' about her."

Pam turned to walk away. Something told him not to, but the sway of her hips made him say, "Yo, Pam. Hol' up, lil' mama. I'll walk you home." She stopped and put her hand on her hip until he caught up. She didn't say anything, so he quipped, "Oh, it's like that now?"

"Shoot, you da one actin' all whipped and shit," she shot back, unwrapping her lollipop and putting it in her mouth.

He watched the grape-colored orb disappear and her lips wrap around the stick and he automatically started shootin' to hit that.

"I better not walk you all the way home. Your man might see us and I'll have to whoop his ass out here," Daquan said.

"If he do, that's on him. I can walk with who I wanna walk with," Pam huffed, like her fourteen years made her grown.

"I bet that nigguh'll get mad if he saw me do this," he teased, then palmed Pam's ass and squeezed it.

Pam jumped away and giggled. "Boy, you betta stop!"

"What? You sayin' I can't do *this*," and he grabbed her ass again. This time she slapped his hand playfully.

"You betta quit, Daquan, now," she said, smiling the whole time.

"*Damn*, that thing soft, gurl," Daquan commented as they approached her house. He noticed there weren't any lights on inside. "You here by yo'self?"

"Why?" she teased, knowing damn well why. "I can't have nobody in there when my mama ain't home."

"Well, if she *ain't home*, how she gon' know?" Daquan smirked, closing the space between them.

"'Cause ain't no tellin' when she might come back," Pam replied, taking out her key and opening the door. She turned around and faced him, with the door pulled shut behind her.

Daquan walked up on her. "Then we'll hear her car. Plus, I just wanna use the bathroom."

Pam stood there eyeing him, sucking on her lollipop with a devilish grin on her grill. "You betta not get me in no trouble, boy."

She backed into the house and he followed her in, closing the door behind him.

"The bathroom down da hall."

"It's too dark. You gotta show me."

As she walked, Daquan purposely bumped into her, letting her feel his hardness.

He could tell she was getting hot because her voice was more of a whisper.

"D.Q., what is you doin'?"

He pulled her body to his and started kissing on the back of her neck. He ran his hand down in her shorts and slid two fingers inside of her, making her gasp and grab the wall.

It wasn't long before he had her shorts off and his around his ankles. They lay on the worn hallway carpet and he pushed inside. It was the warmest pussy he'd had so far. He just thought Pam had the bomb shit.

"Daquan, you gon' be my boyfriend?" Pam moaned, giving him the best her young body could give.

"Yeah, girl," he lied, caught up on how good her pussy felt. "You my girlfriend."

"For real, Daquan?" she repeated, really wanting it to be true.

"I said it, didn't I?" he replied with aggravation, because she was talking too much.

Pam got the hint, so she decided to finish the conversation in body language, rotating her hips like she learned from her mother's boyfriend, late at night, when her mother was asleep. So she used it on Daquan because she liked him, not because she was scared of him, like she was of her mother's boyfriend. Pam figured, if she had a boyfriend like Daquan, he would make the old man stop. Maybe even kill him if he loved her enough. She was determined to make Daquan love her. Before long, Daquan felt that tingling build in his stomach, urging it on until he came inside of her.

Pam kissed him like, "I love you, Daquan, I love you. You my man now, right?"

"Yeah," he huffed, heart rate just beginning to slow.

She kissed him again greedily, then told him, "You betta go before my mama come back."

Daquan got up and pulled up his shorts, while Pam sat on the floor, putting hers back on. Then she stuck her hand up for him to help her up. Daquan obliged and she led him to the door. Pam kissed him once more. "You heard what I said. right?"

"What?"

"That I love you, okay?"

Daquan's ego soared, thinking he had put that dick on her. In actuality, she was only hoping love could save her. He grabbed her ass, "I'ma see you later, aiight?" Then he walked out the door, feeling like the man.

Two days later, Daquan was on fire. When he got up to take his usual morning piss, he was half asleep until the stream of piss bust out the head of his dick and almost bent him over double. It was like he was pissing lava. He had to piss in quick spurts, in bearable increments, until he drained his bladder. That's when he noticed greenish brown pus in his boxers. Daquan looked at his dick and instinctively gave it a slight squeeze, which made the same color pus come out. He almost fainted, he was so scared.

Daquan sat on the toilet, trying to get his thoughts together. He couldn't tell Grandma Mama. He had to see Jerome. Daquan jumped up, threw on some pants and a pair of sneakers, then skidded out the front door. He ran all the way across the project and started banging on Jerome's door like a madman.

It didn't take long before Jerome snatched the door open in his boxers with a chrome nine in his left hand, screwfaced.

"What's wrong?! You alright?!" He thought some shit had jumped off from the way Daquan was banging.

Daquan pushed past him and stood in the living room. "I'm sick!" he exclaimed. All kind of thoughts went through his head until he decided it could only be one thing. AIDS.

Jerome closed the door. "Sick? Sick how?" he probed with concern.

"Man. Man. I think I got AIDS, dawg! I got AIDS!" Daquan was the closest he had been to tears in years.

Jerome ran up and grabbed him by the shoulders. "AIDS?! Naw, Dee, what the fuck? How you know?!" Jerome was just as scared as Daquan was.

"This mornin' I went to the bathroom . . . I just had to piss . . . Then, aw man, that shit started burnin' like hell! I had to piss a little at a time. Then I saw this green shit comin' out the head of my dick!" Daquan was so caught up in his explanation, he hadn't seen Jerome's expression go from worried to amusement to red from holding in his laughter. But when he did notice, he said, "What?"

That's all it took for Jerome to explode with laughter. It was more from relief than humor, because he knew Daquan and Nut were always trying to fuck something, and he didn't know if they were protecting themselves or not. But now that he knew it was only gonorrhea, he fell out on the couch in humorous tears.

"What the fuck is you laughing at?!" Daquan barked. "This shit ain't fuckin' funny!"

"No, it ain't," Jerome managed to get out between laughs. "And it ain't AIDS, neither."

Daquan felt a load leave his shoulders, but he still asked, "How you know?"

"'Cause, you stupid muhfucka, it's gonorrhea. You been burnt, that's all," Jerome explained.

"What you mean, that's all? This shit hurt."

"Believe me, I know. But it serve yo' pussy-hungry ass right. I bet you be goin' up in 'em raw, don't you? You be trickin' fiends?"

"Naw," Daquan lied.

Jerome threw a couch pillow at him. "Lyin' muhfucka," he chuckled. "But straight up, nigguh, you betta' stop fuckin' these hoes without a condom. This time it's just penicillin and shit, but next time, it could really *be* AIDS."

Daquan let his words sink in, then asked, "Where I get the shot at?"

"From Delgado Health Clinic on Claiborne Street," Jerome said, standing up. "But I'ma take you to a real doctor. A bitch see you in the clinic and she tellin' ere'body you got burnt. Lemme get dressed."

As Jerome walked in the back, he yelled, "And don't sit down. I don't want no pus all over my shit. Matter of fact, wait outside," he joked.

"Fuck you," Daquan retorted, but he had to laugh, too.

Daquan couldn't wait until he saw Pam again. After the humiliation of the doctor's visit, the uncomfortable jab of the long metal Q-tip that they ran inside his pee hole, and the needle and pills, he was *seriously* considering whooping her ass.

He got his wish a week later, while he and some of the other Cutt Boyz were playing basketball, three on three, for money. A lot of little chicks were standing around watching and flirting, but he was into the game. That is, until he saw Pam walk up. Daquan stopped dribbling and walked straight off the court, headed in her direction. Seeing him coming to her, she was grinning ear to ear until she saw the look on his grill.

"Bitch! You nasty fuckin' slut, you *burnt* me!" he accused loudly.

The whole game stopped and all eyes, oohs, and ahhs were on them. That's when he noticed Desiree walking up to find Pam.

"Wh-What?" Pam's voice quivered, more hurt by the names he called her than by the accusation. "I ain't burnin'."

Daquan fished out the blue referral paper they give you for your sex partner when you test positive for a STD. "Well, if you ain't know, you betta get yo' nasty, no-good-pussy-havin' ass checked out!"

Laughter erupted from all around, but Nut and Desiree weren't amongst those amused. Nut didn't know Daquan had fucked Pam. Even though she wasn't his girl, he had hit her before, and as he looked at the situation with Pam and Desiree, Pam was *his* piece. To hear now that Daquan was fucking her too didn't sit well with him. But he held his tongue. Desiree, on the other hand, didn't.

"Pam?! I *know* you ain't fuck Daquan behind my back!" Her high-yellow complexion was a fire red, making her freckles look like sparks.

Tears ran freely down Pam's face. She didn't pay Desiree any mind, but all she could say to Daquan was, "I'm sorry, I'm sooo sorry . . . He must've gave it to me, I didn't know." No one asked who *he* was, and from what happened next, Desiree didn't even care.

Desiree threw back and smacked fire out of the shorter Pam, but Pam didn't just fold. She turned on her like a wild alley cat. "Bitch!" Her nails clawed to get into the flesh of Desiree's face, but because she was at least six inches taller, Desiree just leaned out of the way, continuing to land blows to Pam's face and upper body.

Daquan stood there watching until an older chick named Dawn intervened. "Boy, break that shit up. They fightin' over yo' no-good ass."

Daquan sucked his teeth, like, "Shit, I ain't makin' 'em fight."

"Nigguhs ain't shit."

Someone did finally break them up, and when they did, Desiree turned on Daquan. "Oh nigguh, it ain't over! You gon' get yours, too! I *hate* you!" she exclaimed, as they pulled her away.

Get yours? he thought. *What I got to do with it?*

It wasn't like he and Desiree went together. Pam even said she had a man in Baton Rouge. He shrugged it off and nonchalantly bopped back to the court like, "Ball in."

"Lil' whody be layin' that pipe down," D-Nice, one of the older Cutt Boyz, propped him. "Got these hoes fightin' over him," he chuckled.

Daquan strutted in the lane like a peacock, passing the ball to Nut, who watched him with a touch of larceny in his heart.

After the game, their little clique went to get drunk and blazed. Daquan had vowed to himself to never touch drugs, but he did drink forties. So as they kicked it, bragging about their game highlights, Daquan knocked one off and was into his second when D-Nice commented, "Naw, I'ma tell you who put they game down. D.Q!" Everybody laughed, except Nut .

"*He* get game M.V.P."

Daquan blew out a stream of cigarette smoke, then stood up, wobbling.

"Naw, whody, the bitch tried to play me. Poppin' all that I love you shit while I was beatin' that pussy, and come to find out, the ho on fire!"

Laughter erupted.

"Shit. *I* woulda beat that bitch ass. Ask them fo' bitches that burnt me," Slim exclaimed, hitting the blunt.

"Man," Daquan slurred as he turned the forty up and guzzled it. When he took it down, he began nodding . . .

> *If a nigguh ain't shit, then a bitch is a fool*
> *I'ma hustle in da cutt, man, I'm nice with that tool*
> *They want flowers and candy, and for D to be mushy*
> *But I'm a dog in da streets, girl just give me some pussy*
> *This ain't daytime drama, lil' mama, so don't holla*

And don't follow, I crack that head with a beer bottle
Whody, pass the forty so I could . . .

"Damn, I fucked up. Hol' up."

Daquan chuckled as he lost his freestyle, fully feeling his buzz.

"Check this one, check—"

He started to rhyme again, but Nut cut him off. "Fuck all that, Quan, you ain't have to play shorty like that in front of everybody."

Daquan looked at Nut.

"Play her? Nigguh, she burnt *me*. She betta be glad I ain't beat her muhfuckin' ass like Slim said," he retorted, passing the forty to D-Nice.

"Naw, you played yourself, screamin' on her and shit. That shit wasn't cool, nigguh," Nut told him, hitting the roach.

Daquan looked at Slim. "You hear this muhfucka, Slim? Like it's a cool way to tell a bitch she burnt you, ya dig?"

Slim laughed lightly, as Daquan finished the forty, then added, "*I* know this nigguh ain't flippin' on me over no ho."

"If I am, then I'm just like yo' goddamn daddy," Nut hissed, not meaning to go there, but mad enough not to care.

Daquan didn't waste a second. He turned and fired on Nut, but Nut managed to dip most of the blows; then he lunged at Daquan's legs from his sitting position, scooped him up, and slammed him hard on his back. Daquan shot Nut a straight jab that brought blood from his nose before D-Nice and another cat, Red, pulled Nut off Daquan.

"Let that shit go, Nut. Both y'all high and drunk and liable to say anything," D-Nice told them.

"Let 'em fight, Red—shit, they aiight."

"Naw, fuck dat. You hear me, D? Nut?" D-Nice growled and flexed. He was a legend, not only in the CP3, but in every ward of N'awlins, period. He was a six-five, 235-pound stack of muscles, fresh from Angola, but he had a heart of gold. Nut and Daquan looked up to him, so there was no bucking—his word was law.

"Yeah, whody, I hear ya," Daquan replied.

"I'm straight," Nut assured him.

D-Nice let them up and said, "Now go home, y'all fucked up. And if I hear y'all fightin', I'm straight bustin' both y'all heads."

Nut and Daquan walked off silently.

The night air and his anger had sobered Daquan up. He looked up at the full moon, letting the glow distract his mind.

"Yo, D . . . I'm sorry what I said 'bout yo' daddy," Nut apologized, but Daquan retorted.

Nut put his hand on Daquan's arm to stop him.

"Say, bruh, I was just mad. I felt like you played me."

"Played you how? 'Cause I fucked Pam? Nigguh, ere'body fucked Pam," Daquan spat.

"Yeah, but you my *dawg*. We ain't 'posed to be hittin' the same ho."

"We done fucked girls together before, runnin' trains, Nut," Daquan reminded him.

"You know what I mean, D. That's different."

"Yeah," Daquan chuckled. "You was likin' Pam, that's all."

Nut smiled. "Man, fuck that shit."

They started walking again, tension lifted.

"But I am sorry 'bout what I said, for real, though. I respect what yo' daddy did."

"I don't," Daquan mumbled.

"What you say?" Nut asked, not knowing if he heard him correctly.

Daquan stopped. "I said, I don't. That shit was dumb, bruh. He ain't no soldier and I don't respect him. You think my mama give a fuck 'bout that shit? You think she go see him, or write him? Fuck no, for all he know she still gettin' high, fuckin' whoever she wanna fuck while he locked up for-fuckin'-ever. Fuck dat nigguh—I ain't got no daddy," Daquan huffed.

It had been building in him a long time, but it took someone to bring it out.

Nut didn't know what to say.

"Damn, D, I ain't know you felt like that."

"Now you do. So don't never come at me 'bout no bitch, aight? Don't *never* let nann female come between us, feel me?"

"Yeah, D. Never."

Then they dapped each other to seal the deal.

9

The late summer heat laid thicker than molasses, enveloping the Calliope in a hazy orange hue. The flies droned lazily and even the fiends awaited nightfall before they scurried about. Daquan's body was awash with sweat, and all he could think of was, *why shorty didn't have no A.C.?* He continued to pound her caramel flesh from the back, listening to their bodies smack together and her deep-throated moans. All the while, the tangy smell of sex filled the air.

"Not . . . Not so ha-hard, Quan. It's killin' me," Kimoko gasped, gripping the sheets as she bent over her half-made bed, but Daquan was trying to get it over with quickly. It was too hot to be fuckin'.

He felt a stretching effect across his dick—then it disappeared, and all of a sudden Kimoko's pussy felt wetter and sloppier, which made him pound harder.

"Ohhhh Quan! Damn, you feel good," she moaned.

The pressure in his pelvis filled his hardness as he released inside of her, pushing her body forward until she was prone on her stomach. Daquan relaxed long enough to get the strength back in his knees, then he stood up to take the rubber off. But when he looked down, it was only a band of plastic around the base of his dick.

"Shit! Muhfuckin' rubber bust, girl!" he spat, then looked at Kimoko. "You ain't got nothin', do you?"

By now she was sitting on the edge of the bed, inches from his hip. "Hell, no!" she retorted defensively. "Do you?"

"Hell, naw, and I better not now," Daquan shot right back, slipping the rubber's remains from his dick, and heading for the bathroom.

"That's fucked up, Quan. You ain't *even* had to go there!"

He heard her yell as he entered the bathroom. Daquan dropped the rubber in the toilet, then grabbed a rag and wiped himself off. He heard Kimoko approach, then she stood in the doorway with her arms folded across her naked breasts.

"I ain't no ho, Quan. I just like you. I don't be fuckin' just to be fuckin'," she informed him, rolling her eyes.

That ain't what I hear, Daquan thought to himself, but he replied, "Naw, lil' mama, it ain't like that. I was just sayin', you know, that's all. Shit, I like you, too."

Kimoko blushed away her tension. "How much?"

Daquan walked over to her. She was almost sixteen, and three inches taller than him, but height wasn't a factor, especially since everything he wanted from her was below the waist. He slid his fingers in her already dripping wetness, pulling them in and out and listening to the squishy sounds. Kimoko closed her eyes and humped his fingers, quicker and quicker until she begged, "Stop teasin' me, Quan. Put it in."

He was ready to go another round, but was interrupted by the thunderous banging that suddenly threatened to knock down the front door.

"Yo Daquan! Daquan! Open the door, bruh! It's Nut!" Nut yelled through the door. But Daquan had already slipped in balls deep. Nut banged again, this time like he was a mule kicking the door. "*Daquan!*"

Kimoko felt his attention leaving her, and her hormones purred through her throat. "Let him wait."

"Yo Quan! Them peoples got Rome and Pepper!" Nut bellowed like he was in the same room.

M.O.B . . . Daquan thought to himself. According to the old hustlers' code, there was no doubt what to do: it was always Money Over Bitches.

Daquan pulled out so fast, Kimoko almost fell to the floor. "Quan!" she whined, but he was already slipping on his clothes and walking his Jordans until they were all the way on. He unbolted the door to find Nut wide-eyed, like he had seen a haint. "Come on!" Nut barked.

They dashed across parking lots and through courtways, trying to make it to the other side of the projects. When they got there, the parking lot was full of unmarked sedans. Men in D.E.A. jackets moved back and forth, as Melissa stood near Jerome's Allante, sobbing uncontrollably into the chest of a man Daquan didn't know.

He looked around, and the sidewalks, windows, and doors were packed with people trying to see what was going on. The lights, the sounds, the very air, took Daquan's mind back to his father's arrest, and he had to blink twice when they brought Jerome out in cuffs, because the first time he thought it was his father.

Jerome saw Daquan and Nut and he tried to muster a smile, but it was so weak, he dropped his head so they wouldn't see its frailty. After him, they brought Pepper out. Daquan saw the tears welling up in Nut's eyes, but he refused to let them fall. The D.E.A. agents put Jerome and Pepper in separate cars, then pulled off, one behind the other. The other agents continued to go in and out of the house while TV cameras and reporters snapped up every detail of the event for the evening news and morning paper.

"What happened?" Daquan asked, his voice hoarse with emotion.

Nut just shook his head. "I don't know, man. I don't know.

It's fucked up, man . . . I was on my way over to the spot, and when I cut through, all I saw was cars skidding up. That's when I jetted to get you."

Daquan saw two D.E.A. agents coming out with Jerome's safe, and it was then that he realized almost every dime he had was kept in there. Everything he had hustled and saved for was being carried off right before his eyes, and there was nothing he could do about it. Daquan felt so sick, he thought he would throw up. The police had taken everything from him: his father, his cousin, and now his young life's savings. And all they had left him was the bitter, useless hatred that tasted like shit in his mouth.

"Fuck!!!" he screamed, head back, his words aimed at the sky. "Fuck!!"

Nut knew what he meant, but all he could do was drop his head. Daquan was enraged, but he tried to calm himself so he could think. Whatever he could salvage was at the spot. If they had raided that, too, he felt confident that they didn't find the dope because they had their own dope-sniffing dog to make sure it couldn't be detected.

"Let's go to the spot," Daquan told Nut.

When they got there, it was deserted. The setting sun threw elongated shadows around the perimeter as they eyed it cautiously from across the cut.

"You think it's straight?" Nut questioned.

Daquan answered with his footsteps, aimed right for the front door. He pulled out his .25 caliber chrome, a part of him hoping some police did pop out, because he felt cold enough to hold court in the streets. They entered the apartment and looked around at its trash-strewn interior. Junkies were truly junky. Even Ol' School, the cat they had holding the spot down, was nowhere to be found.

"Go check the stash," Daquan told Nut.

Daquan kicked trash around the room, looking for signs of a

recent police presence. Nut returned with four and a half ounces wrapped in plastic, then handed it to Daquan.

"This all we got? What you holdin'?" Daquan asked.

"'Bout a quarter," Nut lied.

Daquan sucked his teeth. "Damn, whody. What the fuck we gonna do now?"

No one spoke while breakfast was prepared. Daquan sat at the table with his head down on his folded arms, while Melissa sipped coffee, letting the steam soothe her red and puffy eyes. Only Grandma Mama's low hum of "Precious Lord" could be heard over the sounds of pots being scraped and plates being portioned.

"Quan, pick yo' head up. Food's ready," Grandma Mama told him, holding out a plate of eggs, toast, and hot sausage that he took and put in front of him.

"Melissa?" Grandma Mama toned, referring to the food, but Melissa just shook her head. Grandma Mama fixed her own plate, then sat down on her usual side of the table, with her back to the stove. She bowed her head in silent prayer, then began to eat.

"Has he got a bail?" Grandma Mama asked.

"A million dollars," Melissa replied flatly.

"A million—" Grandma Mama gasped. "Who they think got that kind of money 'round heah? Might as well not give him nann."

They continued to eat on in silence, until Grandma Mama looked at Melissa and remarked, "Baby, you stayin' up all these days ain't gonna make it no better. You *need* to get some rest. How you gon' make it through work?"

Melissa put down her coffee. "I'll be okay." She lit up a cigarette, something Grandma Mama wouldn't usually allow, but let pass. "Just need to see my baby, is all."

Grandma Mama nodded.

"I tol' that boy! Tol' him he need to leave that mess alone! I said—" Melissa preached to no one in particular, but Grandma Mama cut her off.

"Melissa."

"I said, these people ain't yo' friends. They'll backstab you first chance—"

"Melissa," Grandma Mama repeated, calling her daughter back from her zone. "Now, I know you love that boy. He's your only child. But whatever you told him didn't speak as loud as what you did."

Melissa looked at her with confusion. "*Did?*"

Grandma Mama put down her fork. "Melissa, you spent that child's money as much as he did. Spent it with a smile and never looked back."

Melissa's eyes narrowed. "So what you tryin' to say? I *helped* my own baby to . . ."

"You didn't help him do nothin', and you ain't the reason he there. But you sho' ain't part of the reason he *ain't* in there . . . Now, I'm sorry that you had to hear it this way, but if you want the Lord to help you through this, you got to own up to your part in it and beg His forgiveness. Go to Him with a clean heart," Grandma Mama told her, never losing eye contact.

Melissa rose slowly from her chair. "You got some nerve to look me in my face and tell me how I raised my child, when your'n sittin' his ass in the same *place*!"

"Daryl there for bein' a man, not for sellin' folks poison and takin' food outta babies' mouths," Grandma Mama retorted.

"You think it's easy out heah?" Melissa stressed. "You think 'cause folk go to church, go to work, it's food on they table? These boys out heah doin' whatever they can to get by, while you sit up in heah, stuck in a time don't exist no mo'. Ain't no rules no mo', Mama. Hard work don't get you a damn thing but pain and frustration. Look at me. A thirty-five-year-old woman wit' two jobs and I still live with my mama. Not 'cause I *want* to, because I *have* to," Melissa stated, putting her pocketbook over her shoulder. "You go right on and judge Jerome, just like them white folks do. Talkin' 'bout a clean heart," Melissa laughed mockingly, "when yours so full of self-righteousness, Jesus himself probably fall short in yo' eyes."

Grandma Mama slowly rose to her feet, bracing her weight on the table. "I'd thank you to leave now. This heah conversation is over."

She strolled out of the room, leaving Melissa to glare at her back. Melissa turned to Daquan and snapped, "You ready?"

As they drove over to the county jail, Melissa's attitude alternated between tears and curses. She smoked three cigarettes back-to-back by the time they arrived. Once inside, Daquan recognized the stench, remembering his time behind county walls. He felt like his life was just going in circles. Every turn ending right back where he had begun. The confusion of youth was becoming the hopeless frustration of dreams deferred.

"I.D.?" the redneck C.O. asked nonchalantly, as he carelessly chomped on his gum. He noticed Daquan's young eyes glued to him, and he flashed a mockingly menacing smile in return. Daquan clenched his fists in an attempt to keep his emotions from spinning out of control.

They went to the visiting booth and waited for Jerome to be brought into the room on the other side of the glass. Daquan remembered this as well; it was the last place he'd seen his father. Being here made him wonder, would this be the last time he would see his cousin, too?

They brought Jerome out in the familiar county orange. He smiled at them through the glass and they noticed a slight cut above his left eye. Melissa snatched up the phone. "Hey, baby, you okay? What happened to your eye? Did the police do it?" she rattled, firing question after question.

Jerome chuckled hard. "Slow down, Ma. I ain't got but one mouth. Naw, the police ain't do it, and I'm okay, which is more

than I can say for ol' boy who thought paper made me soft."
He smiled and threw a smooth hook at the glass, then winked
at Daquan. He smiled back.

"I know my baby can handle his own, but you still be careful, heah?" Melissa admonished in a motherly fashion.

"I will," he told her so she wouldn't worry, then added, "let
me holla at Quan fo' this time run out."

"Okay—I love you, baby."

"Love you, too. And tell Mama I love her, even though she
mad at me."

Melissa rolled her eyes. "You know how you grandma is."

She handed the phone to Daquan.

"What's happenin', whody? What's crackin'?" Jerome asked.

"Nothin' cuz. How they treatin' you?"

"Like shit, but I'ma soldier, ya heard me?" Jerome replied.

"Fo' sho," Daquan smirked.

Jerome looked over his shoulder, then gestured to the
phone and mouthed the word "tapped." Daquan nodded and
Jerome put the phone back to his ear. "Ay look, Mandi asked
about you."

"Who?"

Jerome smirked. "Come on, lil' cuz, I know you ain't forget
Mandi. The chick that broke you in."

Daquan blushed at the memory. "Naw, I ain't forget that,
just her name."

"I can dig it," Jerome chuckled, "but dig, she got somethin'
for me. Give it to—" he nodded at Melissa. "Okay?"

"Got you."

"Plus, I got some peoples I need you to see. Mandi know
who they is and I already spoke to 'em, so they waitin' on you
to come holla. It's only a few I can't reach, like that nigguh
Black.

"The Black who be fightin' dogs?" Daquan quizzed.

"Yeah, same nigguh you used to jack sounds fo'," Jerome
chuckled. "He standin' on a grip, so handle that, aiight?"

"I got you, cuz," Daquan nodded, proud that Jerome trusted him like that.

Jerome looked into his young cousin's eyes, and he felt guilty about ever getting him started in the game. He should be out playing ball, chasing bitches, Jerome thought. Instead, Jerome was sending him out to get more involved than he already was.

"You sho'?" Jerome checked.

"Yeah, I'm sho'. Ain't I 'bout it?" Daquan shot back, thinking Jerome was testing his gangsta.

Jerome smiled. "Yeah, you 'bout it. Besides, these nigguhs know, just 'cause I'm away don't mean I'm gone, ya heard? So call Mandi. Auntie got her number."

"I will, Rome."

"Cool . . . and look, I know you got hit, too. So when you get that, get you," Jerome instructed.

"Good look," Daquan replied with a sigh of relief, because he didn't know how to bring up his own financial needs. He gave the phone back to Melissa, and she talked to her son for the remaining time. Daquan just sat back, watching Jerome speak, admiring the fact that he was still Jerome. He didn't appear worried, and his composure maintained that same smoothness Daquan always tried to emulate.

Back to life, back to reality
Back to the here and now, oh yeah . . .

The sounds of Soul II Soul played softly as Daquan and Melissa rolled back home. She looked more relaxed and only smoked one cigarette. At a red light, she turned down the radio completely and looked at Daquan.

"Daquan . . . you know, Mama was right," she admitted, getting his attention before she continued. "In her own way, but she ain't say nothin' wrong. I did tell Rome that he needed to stop. But the money . . ." she shook her head, looking straight ahead. "The money just . . . make it alright. At first you're nervous, then you get used to it. You heah about people gettin' killed or goin' to prison, but you never think about it being you, until . . ."

The light turned green, and a few tears rolled down her cheek.

"I just want you to know that I know what you doin'. I know what you been doin', and . . . I want you to stop. I loved your daddy, my brother, and he gone. And Lord knows I love Jerome, now he . . ." She sniffed and wiped her eyes.

Daquan put his hand on her shoulder. "He gonna be okay, Auntie. He'll be home soon."

She smiled through her tears. "I pray so, but Daquan . . . please, baby, think about what's goin' on. Leave this mess alone, baby, please . . . before it's too late."

He nodded to reassure her, but the truth was, it was already too late.

10

"Come in. I'll be ready in a minute," Mandi told Daquan and Nut as she let them in the door. Daquan tried to smile at her, but she acted as if she'd never met him before. Nut looked around her crib, just as impressed by it as Daquan was when he came the first time.

"Damn, whody, this huh's?" he asked, amazed.

Daquan shrugged. "She opened the do', didn't she?" he quipped.

Mandi came out in a pair of painted-on jeans, a peach-colored halter top, Chanel sandals, and Chanel shades perched on top of her crinkled Shirley Temple curls. She picked up a small tote bag, hoisted it onto her shoulder, then said, "Let's go," in a tone that was strictly business.

Nut couldn't keep his eyes off of her as they climbed in her white 535i BMW. Nut was in the back, while Daquan was reclined in the front. The first stop was downtown, to drop the tote bag off to Melissa at Jerome's lawyer's office. She was already waiting in the parking lot, sitting in her late model Honda. Mandi pulled up to her car, driver's door to driver's door, and let her window down. No words were spoken as Mandi passed Melissa the tote bag. All that spoke was the sadness in

Melissa's eyes when she saw Daquan in the car, and it made him drop his head.

"How much am I supposed to give the lawyer?" Melissa asked.

"Whatever he asks," Mandi answered matter-of-factly. "That's fifty there. Whatever it is, we'll get the rest."

Melissa looked at the bag in nervous amazement. She'd never seen this much money in her whole life. "Th-Thank you," was all she could say.

"Not a problem," Mandi replied, offering Melissa a slight smile behind Chanel-shaded eyes.

Their next stop was Melphomene, a project in the uptown Sixth Ward of New Orleans. As they drove down grimy Martin Luther King Street, past a crowded Church's Chicken, Daquan and Nut knew they were out of their territory, and neither had a gun. Mandi pulled up on a group of nigguhs standing around a black Chevy Blazer, pumping "Like a Dog" by Soulja Slim. When she stopped the BM, all eyes fell on them. Daquan looked at the guys, then at Mandi, who was looking at him. "Well?" she said.

"Well what?" Daquan asked back, with raised eyebrows.

Mandi smirked. "It's apartment 109. Ask for Blue. He's supposed to have eighteen." Mandi looked back at the nigguhs again, who were now curious as to what they were there for.

"If you want, I could hold your hand," Mandi quipped, and Daquan sucked his teeth, mumbling, "Fuck you."

He reluctantly got out, followed by a more reluctant Nut. They walked past the group without a word said by either party, heads held high and hands at their sides. They climbed the steps to apartment 109 and knocked on the door.

"Who dat?" a deep growl of a male voice wanted to know.

"We here for Jerome. I'm his cousin," Daquan replied, so nervous the moment felt surreal. He heard bolt after chain-link bolt being unlocked, then the door swung open. Daquan and Nut looked up into the bloodshot red eyes of a six-foot-seven jet-black nigguh. At his leg was a red-nose pit, head lowered and silent.

"What you want?" the man asked impatiently.

Daquan looked from man to dog, wondering whose bite was probably worse. "Jerome sent me to get that."

The man glared down at him without answering, until Daquan heard another voice inside say, "Let him in, Jo-Jo."

The man slowly stepped aside and the pit sat on his hind legs beside the door. Once inside, Daquan and Nut's eyes had to adjust to the darkened setting. A young cat in a wheelchair rolled out the back, with a paper bag in his lap. "You Daquan, whody?"

Daquan felt slightly relieved to hear a word as familiar as his name being spoken. "Yeah, whody, you Blue?"

Blue nodded and held out the bag to him. "It's supposed to be eighteen, but I made it an even twenty. Jerome know what it's for."

Daquan took the bag without looking inside. "I'll make sure I tell him, ya heard?"

Blue smiled and his gold-and-diamond grill lit up the darkness. "I like you, lil' whody, you got heart. You need anything else, holla, ya dig?"

Daquan nodded, then turned for the door. He and Nut exited the apartment a lot more relaxed than when they went in. He gripped the bag tight as he headed for the car, keeping the nigguhs in his side view, but no one said a word. Most of them weren't even paying them any attention.

They got in and Daquan tried to hand Mandi the bag. "Put it under your seat," she told him, then pulled off.

The next pickup Mandi handled, but Daquan wished he had instead. They were closer to the Calliope, on Fontainebleau Street, parked outside of a brick house. What made them want to go in was the fact that there was nothing but bad-ass broads coming in and out.

"Damn! Look at that pooh shooter theah!" Nut exclaimed. "Fuck that, let's go in."

Daquan was mesmerized as well, but he kept his head. "She said wait, yo."

"Fuck takin' her so long? I gotta pee," Nut quickly conjured up, but just as he opened his door, Mandi came out carrying a leather satchel, followed by a thick redhead white girl, speaking Creole.

"*Vu tu dans deux semaines*," ("See you in two weeks.") the redhead said with a smirk.

"*Oui*," Mandi replied over her shoulder as she climbed in the car.

"Hol' up, bruh," Nut spoke, one foot out the door. "Let me go in and take a piss."

"Please," Mandi rolled her eyes, starting the engine. "Them nasty bitches want the same thing you want."

"What you mean?" Nut asked, puzzled.

"She means they want pussy too," Daquan reasoned.

"Aw man," Nut moaned, "don't tell me all them fine ladies is dykes!"

They arrived in more familiar territory, when they spotted Black's brand-new Cadillac DeVille parked at the Rosenwald Rec Center. They had checked a few other spots, but Black had a thing for young girls, so finding him there wasn't surprising. Mandi pulled up and parked facing the basketball court, and Nut saw Black with his shirt off playing a game of full court.

"We'll be right back," Daquan winked at Mandi, before bouncing from the car. Picking up all this money and riding around in a BM with a bad bitch made him bop cocky, and Nut followed suit.

They stepped around the fence, giving nods and daps to

people they knew, and approached the court. They waited a few minutes while Black's dark tone glistened in sweat, hustling up and down the court.

"Yo Black! Black! Let me holla at you for a second," Daquan requested, eyes flirting with a young broad in a pink tennis skirt.

Black heard them, but played through it, acting as if they weren't there. Daquan waited patiently another few minutes, until one of the players disputed another player's foul call.

"Foul?! Nigguh, that's bullshit! Play ball!"

"Yo Black! What up, baby, let me speak wit' you," Daquan hollered.

Black walked over with his hands on his hips, out of breath. "What up, lil' whodies?" he greeted, flashing a gold-toothed grin full of malice.

"Yo, Rome got bagged the other day, dog," Daquan told him.

Black looked around nonchalantly. "Yeah, I heard about dat. Fucked up."

"Yeah bruh, it is, and he tight right now, so he sent me to get that from you," Daquan responded, cutting to the chase. Something about Black's attitude made him feel uneasy.

Black spit a stream of saliva to his left, then looked at Daquan and Nut. "Oh, he did, huh? Look at lil' whody . . . You comin' up, ain't cha, huh? I remember when you used to steal car radios and shit." He laughed, and the people in earshot laughed along with him.

Nut was fuming. "Man, fuck that got to do with this heah?"

Black shot Nut a menacing glare. "Y'all nigguhs seen it befo'. Charge it to the game and tell Rome see me when he get out."

"What?" Daquan barked angrily.

Black uncoiled a loose, lefthanded backslap that caught Daquan in his lip and knocked him to the ground. Nut swung

on Black, but he was no match for the older, faster, and stronger
Black. He easy dipped Nut's wild overhand right and rung his
right ear with a hook that spun Nut halfway around. Black
kicked him in the ass. "Fuck y'all lil' nigguhs think y'all is,
huh?! Send a boy to do a man's job, that's what you get! Take
yo' asses back to Jerome and tell him suck my dick. My next
ride on him."

Black turned away and went back to the game. Daquan had
to restrain Nut from going back at Black. Even though they
both felt humiliated and vengeful, Daquan pushed Nut toward the car. When they reached the car, Mandi was sitting
expressionless behind the wheel, a pretty chrome nine with a
pink handle in her lap. As soon as Nut saw the gun, his eyes
filled with murder, and he lunged for it. Mandi made no attempt to stop him, but Daquan snatched his wrist back.

"Nigguh, what the fuck wrong wit' you?!" Nut huffed,
ready to fight Daquan if his response wasn't right.

"Muhfucka, calm down! We'll . . ."

"Calm *down*?! I'm 'bout to kill this fool!" Nut declared.

"Right heah? In front of ere'body?! Nigguh, *think*! These
broke muhfuckas'll break they neck to get to the phone and
get that Crime Stoppers reward off yo' black ass! Look!"
Daquan yelled and pointed at all the faces turned in their direction, including Black's. He was watching their every move,
and so was his man on the sideline, cradling a concealed gun.
Nut looked, and although he was still hot, he understood
Daquan's point.

"I'ma kill that nigguh. I *swear*, I'ma kill 'im," Nut vowed
through clenched teeth.

Daquan looked him in the eyes and vowed likewise. "*We*
gonna kill 'im, whody, ya heard me? Black's a dead man."

Mandi pulled into the parking lot of Daquan's building and
stopped the car. Nut got out without saying a word, while

Daquan gathered up both bags of money. He started to open the door.

"Quan," Mandi said.

He turned around and saw her smiling at him. "I'll see you later."

Daquan didn't know how to respond. It was the first nice thing she had said all day to him, but he was too upset to give a fuck. He got out, seeing Nut disappear around the building as he went inside.

Daquan opened the door and peeked inside, listening as to where Grandma Mama was. He didn't want her to see the bags because she would demand to know what's in them. If she saw all that money, she'd put him out on the spot, and that was the last thing he wanted. It wasn't because he didn't have anywhere to go, because he did; he simply didn't want to let her down. Daquan couldn't stand the thought of the pain he knew he would cause her.

"Daquan, that you?" she inquired softly from her bedroom.

"Yes, ma'am," he answered, high-stepping to his room before she decided to get up and come check on him. He stuffed the bags under his bed and sat down, listening for sounds of movement. When he heard none, he pulled out both bags and emptied the money on the floor behind his bed. Daquan lay on his stomach, undoing rubber band after rubber band, and counting the money until he came up with a final tally of thirty-five thousand.

Daquan knew Jerome would be disappointed, especially after Mandi told him about the two other nigguhs that owed him bad skipped town, and the way Black had played him.

Black . . .

Just thinking about the nigguh made his blood boil. He was glad he didn't have a gun right then, because Daquan knew in his heart, he would've done what Nut wanted to do as well, with no hesitation. Murder in his young mind wasn't the

heinous act most people viewed it as. To him, it was just another reaction in an arsenal of retaliation . . . Slap a nigguh,
beat a nigguh, kill a nigguh, somehow they were all the same,
just different degrees.

Being thirteen in a grown man's game had exposed him to
too much, too fast. It had desensitized his emotions to the
point that life had little value.

There was no question in his mind that Black would die,
and that thought accompanied him into the inner chambers of
his heart.

"What will you do?"

"Kill him."

"But you don't want to . . . do you?"

He looked into the darkness of the void they always met in,
and there she was. Diana's pigtails were long gone now. Her
face was a feminine reflection of his own, a fact that became
more and more apparent as the two of them aged. "Do you,
Daquan?"

". . . No," he admitted, free to be truthful with her, even if
he couldn't with his own self. "But I can't tell *them* that. I can't
even let myself feel that."

Diana came closer and took both his hands in hers. He
loved when they touched because it was a sensation of pure
understanding.

"Then why, Daquan? Why be someone you're not?" she
probed.

"I'm not, because this is who I am. It just isn't who I want to
be," Daquan explained, lowering his head. But Diana lifted
his chin and met his eyes with a smile in hers.

"Who do you want to be, Daquan?"

"Free," he replied easily. "Just . . . free. Like you."

Diana's smile disappeared. "Don't say that, Daquan. I'm
not free."

Daquan looked off into the impenetrable darkness and said, "I just don't wanna feel no more, Diana. It's like, it keeps building inside of me and I don't know the answers. Every emotion is a question, you know? And I don't know how to get it out."

She caressed his cheek. "Then cry."

"I can't."

"You won't . . . but you can. Release it, Daquan. before it takes you under . . . release it, let it out. Murder isn't the answer," Diana explained.

"It's the only one I got, Diana. So if I cry, I'll let his blood be my tears."

The next day, Daquan awoke with a throbbing headache, and he couldn't unknot his stomach. Even the smell of Grandma Mama's gumbo didn't give him an appetite for anything other than blood.

He showered and dressed quickly, then tiptoed out the door, because he didn't want to see Grandma Mama's face, knowing what he had in his heart. Daquan went straight over to Nut's and found him sitting on the front stoop, smoking a cigarette. They nodded a silent greeting, then Daquan picked up Nut's Camels and lit one up.

"How we gonna do this?" Nut asked solemnly, like there was no question it was getting done.

Daquan blew a stream of smoke out, and replied, "Get us a fiend's car, you know, grab them thangs and lay on the nigguh till we can creep 'im."

Nut looked over at him. "You know where he stay?"

Daquan shook his head, "But we know where he be. Trust me, he won't be too hard to find."

Nut nodded in agreement, then thunked his cigarette to the pavement. He got up and went in the crib, then returned a few minutes later, shirt bulging with the print of two gats, a nine and a .38. He handed Daquan the nine, and he tucked it in his jean shorts. "Let's go see if we can get Ol' School car," Daquan suggested.

It didn't take much convincing to get the old, rusty Oldsmobile from the dope fiend called Ol' School, especially after Nut offered him a hundred dollars for the whole day. Ol' School had heard about what Black did, and by the look on their faces and the bulge in their waists, he knew what they intended to do. He hated to see boys so young get caught up in the game that had drug him down, but he knew he was powerless to stop them, so he just told them, "Ya'll watch yo'-self, ya heah?"

Daquan got behind the wheel and started the fifteen-year-old engine, then slammed the rusty door with a loud squeak.

For the rest of the day, they stalked Black from spot to spot. They first spotted him getting lunch from Mama's Kitchen. They kept their distance, but never lost sight of him. The later it grew, the more anxious they became, and all Daquan could think of was what he had told Diana: *If I cry, his blood will be my tears*. He was living for the moment those words came true.

Black moved through his day, totally oblivious to what or who was in his midst. He knew Jerome was heavy, but Black felt safe because Jerome and the go-hard nigguhs that rode with him were behind bars. In his mind, if Jerome had to send little nigguhs to get his paper, then he definitely didn't have anything to worry about.

He didn't know how wrong he was. As the evening moved on, Daquan and Nut had followed Black to liquor stores, to gambling spots, to the Magnolia, and back to Black's dope spot; but each time, there was always a gang of people around. They finally got a break when Black pulled up on Apple Street and blew the horn. It was dark by now, but Daquan could see the person coming out was a female. She sauntered over to Black's Caddy, got in, then they pulled off. Nut cocked his gun and hissed, "I don't give a fuck where he goin', this time I'm smokin' him."

"I'm wit' you, whody," Daquan assured him.

They followed Black to the Rosham Red Motel and allowed him to get a room and go inside. Once he was in, they pulled around to the rear and got out, looking around.

"So what, we just knock on the do'?" Nut asked, puffing on a cigarette. "What if she answer?"

"Naw, Nut, we gonna make the nigguh come out to us to get it," Daquan smirked.

"How?"

Daquan looked around the parking lot until he saw a nice, softball-sized piece of concrete, then went and retrieved it.

"With this."

Nut looked at him with confusion.

"One of us gotta be in the car, while the other one bust his car window, then slide up under it. As soon as he come out, pull off so he'll think the nigguhs got scared or somethin'. Then blast his ass, ya hear me?" Daquan explained, already knowing he'd be the one under the car.

"You drive," Nut replied, gripping the gat like the grudge that was in his heart.

"Muhfucka, you drive better than me," Daquan lied. He wanted to pull the trigger as bad as Nut. "And if shit get hot, I'ma need you behind the wheel."

Nut thought about it momentarily, but shook it off. "Man, fuck that. *I* wanna burn his ass!"

Daquan sighed hard. "Nut, just drive the fuckin' car, aiight? I got this. I'ma handle it for both of us. Plus, you fatter than me—you might can't even fit under theah."

"Man, I—"

Daquan cut him off firmly. "Nut, we wastin' time. Damn, nigguh gonna be done finished," he huffed and walked away.

Nut paused for a moment, then went and got the car. Daquan crept up behind the Caddy and pulled out his nine. When Nut backed up behind him, he cocked it back, took a deep breath, and smashed the driver's-side window completely with the concrete chunk, making Black's alarm go crazy. He quickly dropped and rolled under the car, feeling the heat of the transmission on his face.

"What the fuck?! Hey!" Black came out, shouting, as Nut skidded off around the building. Black was clad only in boxers, hard dick poking a tent in the material.

The sound of his own breathing was heavy in Daquan's ears, and it felt like his heartbeat was pounding in the finger that he had poised on the trigger.

"Punk muhfuckas!"

"Baby, what happened??"

"Take yo' ass inside!" Black demanded.

Daquan could hear Black's bare feet hitting the pavement, coming closer and closer, until his toes were directly beside Daquan's shoulder. Daquan closed his eyes for a second, then reopened them as he slid his torso from under the car, raised the gun, and fired twice into Black's stomach while he leaned in the window to see if anything had been taken.

The girl, wrapped in a dingy white sheet, was only a few feet from Black when the shots cracked the silence. Seeing Black stagger back, she let out a piercing scream. Daquan came out from under the car and fired again, hitting Black in the chest, when he noticed Black had a revolver in his hand, one he never got to use.

As Black fell back on the concrete, Daquan stood over him and hissed, "Charge *this* to the game, nigguh," then fired twice into Black's skull, opening it up like a cracked egg.

The girl was frozen in horror, but her scream had brought a

few people to the windows of rooms. Daquan didn't think twice, but he regretted all three shots he pumped into her head, from almost point-blank range. By the time her body hit the ground, he had dashed into the safety of the darkness and jumped into the car with Nut.

11

Jerome looked into his cousin's eyes and knew everything he had heard was true. There was no mistaking the eyes of a killer, no matter how young or old, male or female. He sat on the other side of the Plexiglas, looking at Mandi and Daquan, and he realized they were all he had to count on.

"Man, I ain't even gonna ask 'bout that shit right, 'cause I already know. But . . ." his voice trailed off, so Daquan picked up the slack.

"I understand what you feelin', cuz, but what can I do? The muhfucka chose for me, you know?" Daquan explained, his mannerisms more fluid, more relaxed than the week before. Murder had made him a man.

Jerome nodded knowingly. "So what now? It ain't like before, Quan. You can't just walk away—you know that, right?"

"I ain't tryin' to, Rome. I'ma ride wit' you, dog," he announced proudly.

Jerome looked at Mandi, who gave him an inquisitive look in return. Jerome rubbed his face and sighed. "Cool. Them nigguhs who skipped town really put me in a bind. Them peoples ain't find nothin', but my lawyer said one of us talkin'. I don't know who yet 'cause we all separated. I got word to

Pepper and he on it, too. 'Tween the both of us, we'll find out."

Daquan nodded and Jerome continued.

"Anyway, the lawyer sayin' he need at least another fifty, maybe seventy-five, and I ain't got it. That what you got is all I got in this world, but . . . I got a way to get it."

Daquan's eyes took on a dedicated gaze. "What you need me to do?"

Jerome looked at Mandi, and she subtly nodded her head, so he continued. "Mandi gonna school you, cuz. Just holla at her. She good peoples, Quan, and she like you. Listen to her," he explained.

"I got ya, cuz, ya heard me?" Daquan assured him.

"I know, baby boy, I know," Jerome replied with a tinge of regret in his tone.

"Put Mandi on."

Daquan gave Mandi the phone, and she took off her earring, put it to her ear, and said, "Hey, baby, how you doing?"

"I'm good, baby girl." He gestured to Daquan, "Take care of him for me, okay?"

"Have I ever let you down?" she smirked. "You just hold your head and think about what island you takin' me to after all this is said and done."

Jerome chuckled. "Shit, we can hit all of 'em. After being in heah, Gilligan's Island'll be a paradise."

Mandi laughed, then blew him a kiss. "I love you, baby."

"Yeah, I know."

Mandi's attitude had totally changed toward Daquan. She was less guarded in his presence and she smiled more easily. Daquan liked the way she carried herself, and he felt better about himself because a woman like her had taken him in. She even took him to Canal Street to shop, using her own platinum cards to foot the bill. She bought him clothes by designers he couldn't even pronounce, in styles he'd only seen grown men sport on runways and in magazines. Daquan was tall for his age, so when he dressed in a suit, he looked well beyond his quickly approaching fourteenth year.

She bought him ostrich-skin shoes with a belt to match, and she insisted he wear the outfit out of the store. "You're not going to be lookin' like a little hoodlum with me, Quan," she said, smiling.

They went to Cafe Du Monde for lunch, and Daquan found that Mandi spoke French fluently.

"*Quel est le plat du jour?*" ("What is the special of the day?") she asked the waitress, as they sat along the railing bordering the sidewalk.

The white, stringy-haired waitress was startled by her fluency, but replied. "*Plat du jour est* shrimp po' boy."

"*D'accord*," ("Okay") Mandi replied. "*Je voudrais deux*," ("I would like two") she said, holding up two fingers, and the waitress walked away.

"You French or something?" he asked.

Mandi giggled. "No, baby, I just know how to talk to people."

Daquan looked around the restaurant at all the tourists taking pictures and discussing sights to see. He chuckled to himself, wondering how many of them wanted to see the real N'awlins.

"So why you buy me all these clothes?" he asked as the waitress returned with their po' boys.

"Because, the people I'm taking you to meet believe in first impressions. So if you dress like a common thug, they'll treat you like one," Mandi explained. "If I don't love anything else about New Orleans, I definitely love the food."

"Where you from?" Daquan probed, enjoying the smell of their sandwiches himself.

"Here, there," she expressed vaguely, "but mostly there." She smiled, then dug into her meal.

"These people . . . where they at?" he asked, mouth full of shrimp.

"Houston."

"They Jerome connect or something?"

"No . . . mine," she answered, wiping her mouth. "As soon as Jerome's connect heard what happened, they cut all ties."

Daquan sucked his teeth. "That's fucked up."

"No, that's business," she shot right back.

He looked her in the eyes. "But you do business wit' him, right?"

"Yes."

"Why you ain't cut all ties?"

Mandi's cheeks dimpled as she replied, "That's personal, but it's because of that, that I'm dealing with you. Don't misunderstand—this is for *Jerome*, not you. But you stand to make a lot of money in the process . . . if you can cut it." She broke it down, then leaned back in her chair to see how he was taking it.

"I can cut it," he stated from his gut.

"We'll see," she replied, signaling for the waitress. "I have to go take care of a few things."

The waitress came over and Mandi said, in English, "Check, please."

He changed back into his old clothes at Mandi's, then she drove him back to the Calliope. Daquan saw Kimoko with her arms folded and her lip poked out, waiting on him to show up.

"Damn." Daquan swore in an exasperated tone that made Mandi snicker.

"Looks like somebody's in trouble."

As soon as they pulled up and parked, Kimoko was all up on him before he could even close the door.

"Nigguh, you got some nerve pullin' up wit' anudda bitch in my face, like we ain't kickin' it!" Kimoko spat, head rolling like a bobble head.

Mandi ignored the comment, telling Daquan, "Close my door, and be ready by eight."

Kimoko bent down and hissed, "'And who the fuck is you 'posed to be?"'! You got somethin' on ya' rabbit-ass mind?"

Mandi slid the Chanels down onto her face and drove off, blowing a kiss at Daquan.

"She *better* be gone, 'fore she get that Beema fucked up! And where *you* going?!" Kimoko yelled, when she saw Daquan walking off.

"In the house, girl. I'm tired," he replied lazily.

"You ain't shit, Daquan Watson! You . . . ain't . . . *shit*!" Kimoko hollered as he shut the door in her tear-stained face.

Grandma Mama had seen the whole thing, so when he came in, he heard her call his name, "Daquan."

"Ma'am," he answered, with a slightly irritated strain in his voice.

"Don't sass me, child—come heah," she called from the kitchen. He came in reluctantly, and Grandma Mama asked, "Why is that child out there hollerin' at you like a white-mouth mule?"

"Man, I don't know," he shrugged, ready to go lie down. He had a lot on his mind, and he just wanted to be alone until he could sort it all out.

"And who was that lady in that fancy car? Daquan, what are you doin' in them streets?" she demanded to know.

"Nothin', Ma. She just tryin' to help me wit' my rappin'," Daquan lied.

Grandma Mama shook her head with a curious smirk on her face.

"What?" he toned, wondering why she was looking at him like that.

"You too grown for me to look at now?" Grandma Mama chuckled softly. "You lookin' more and more like yo' daddy every day. Act like him, too, wit' all them gals chasin' after you. Don't you bring no babies home you cain't raise, ya heah?"

"Yes'm . . . I'm goin' to my room," he told her, trying to keep the conversation short.

"You hungry? I got wings in heah."

"I already et," Daquan said before closing the door.

He felt drained—not physically, but mentally. He expected the murder to have more of an effect on him, but the fact was, he felt nothing. But the drain came from all that Mandi had told him, and the way he knew Jerome was counting on him to come through. Daquan had no doubt whether he could handle whatever Jerome asked, but the thought of so many possibilities excited and exhausted him at the same time. He lay across the bed, fully dressed, only to fall asleep moments later.

They say everything is bigger in Texas. Daquan was hoping the same held true in the dope game. Mandi rented a burgundy Grand Prix for the six-hour drive to Houston. Daquan had never been out of New Orleans, so the sights along the way were all new to him. Each passing city brought memories of the inmates at Scotland and their senseless turf wars: HAMMOND, LAPLACE, GONZALES, BATON ROUGE, LAFAYETTE, LAKE CHARLES, BEAUMONT, HOUSTON.

"Was that your girlfriend yesterday?" Mandi asked as they drove along Interstate 10 West.

"What? Kimoko? Hell, no, she ain't my girlfrend," Daquan replied, screwing up his grill.

Mandi snickered. "She seems to think so."

"Well, she ain't," he said, still trying to get used to wearing gators. They weren't anywhere near as comfortable as sneakers, but they did make his feet feel pampered.

"Are you fucking her?" Mandi quizzed, never taking her eyes off the road.

Daquan didn't know what to say, not knowing if the wrong answer would fuck up any chances of Mandi letting him get another shot, but his silence gave him away.

"Yeah, you fucking her . . . but if you plan to keep doing so, make sure she knows that's what it is. If you keep lying to these little girls, having them think they're someone they're not, it could blow up in your face," Mandi schooled him. "A lot of guys in prison right now because their girl got mad and dropped a dime, you follow me?"

"Yeah."

Then, as an afterthought, Mandi added, "She's cute, though."

And Daquan shot right back, "Not as cute as you."

She looked at him with a curious smile. "Yeah, you're definitely Jerome's blood type."

Daquan nodded in and out for the rest of the trip, until he felt Mandi nudge him and say, "Wake up. We're almost there."

Daquan slowly sat up in his seat, stretching his arms out in front of him. They were already in Houston, driving along Old Spanish Trail. Daquan had always thought of cowboys and horses when he thought of Texas, but Houston was a mega-sized city.

Soon, they drove past the metropolitan section of the city and entered the *real* city inside the city—the part of Houston known as the Fifth Ward. Daquan felt like they were right at home. He saw the same squalid conditions, the same vacant lots, and the same stoic expression filling the faces that he passed. It was then that he realized the 'hood was everywhere.

"The guy's name is Jorge. He's a Mexican. When we get there, let me do all the talking, okay?" Mandi instructed him, in a calm but authoritative tone.

"Fo' sho'," he agreed. He wasn't too keen on Mexicans no way. The ones he ran across in New Orleans never spoke English and acted as if they didn't like strangers around.

Mandi pulled up to a medium-sized brick building on the corner of Alvacade Street and drove into the parking lot. She got out her lipstick, applied a fresh coat, checked it in the mirror with a kiss, then opened the door, like, *Let's go*.

Daquan got out, and the grainy surface of the pavement grated under his hard-bottom gators. He brushed his slacks off, adjusting his crotch in the thin material, then followed Mandi's short-skirted thighs around the building. Above the door was a sign that read LA BONITA, with the silhouette of a naked woman bent over, so he knew they were at a strip club. Inside, the midday crowd was scanty, but a few topless females danced from table to table, or carried drinks to the horny patrons.

Mandi went up to the bar and signaled for the bartender, a pock-faced Mexican with ex-con written all over his mannerisms and bulging biceps.

"*Yo estoy aqui para ver a Jorge*," ("I am here to see Jorge") Mandi articulated fluently to the bartender.

"*Jorge debe de ser un chico con suerte. ¿Te esta esparando?*" ("Jorge must be a lucky guy. Is he expecting you?")

"*Esta puerta siempre esta abierta pa Mandi*," ("His door is always open for Mandi") she replied, dimpling her cheeks seductively.

While the bartender grabbed the phone, Daquan looked around the bar. A red-haired Latin chick was working the pole, completely naked. She writhed her way down, ending with her legs spread-eagled, exposing her red pubic hairs and beckoning to Daquan with a wiggle of her index finger. His dick stood up in his pants, eager to comply, but the bartender said, "*Vete para dentro*," ("come inside") which Daquan took as their green light, because Mandi gestured for him to follow her into a side door, just off the bar. The bartender hit a switch, and the heavy steel door popped open. They entered onto a short staircase that ended at the threshold of another door, which Mandi knocked on twice.

"*Bienvenido!*" ("Welcome!") Daquan heard a male voice say from the other side. Mandi turned the knob and they walked into Jorge's office. The blood-red carpet was so thick, the door would only open halfway. Jorge was standing in front of his desk, talking on the phone. Mandi walked over and gave him a hug and a kiss on the cheek.

"*Te ves muy bien. ¿Como estas?*" ("You look good. How are you?") Jorge asked, eyeing her whole package. He finished his phone call, hung up, and gave Mandi his full attention.

"*Estoy bien. Quiero que conozcas a alguien. Este es Daquan,*" ("I'm fine. I want you to meet someone. This is Daquan.") Mandi introduced, gesturing to Daquan.

Jorge held out his hand, with his huge diamond pinkie finger cocked to the side. "*Gusto en conocerte,*" ("Good to meet you") he said, and Daquan shook his hand, but didn't reply. He looked at Mandi.

"He doesn't speak Spanish," Mandi informed him.

"Oh," Jorge chuckled. "*Lo siento!* ("I get it!") I thought he was the silent, tough-guy type. "How are you, Daquan?"

"I'm good," Daquan replied, happy to be able to understand what was being said.

Jorge looked at his Rolex and said, "I was on my way out, but for you I have, ah . . . ten minutes."

Mandi answered, "And I have—" she ended her sentence by holding up three fingers, then reversing her palm and holding up five fingers.

Jorge mimicked her hand gestures questioningly. "That's all? What, business a little slow?"

"It's for my friend. He's in a bind, and if you could help him out, it could be very prosperous for us all in the long run," Mandi proposed.

Jorge chuckled, "Not everyone gets to enjoy a long run," he philosophized, then looked at Daquan. "*El muchacho . . .* How old are you, Daquan?"

"Fifteen," he lied smoothly.

"And you want to, ah, do business with me?" Jorge inquired.

"Mandi said you a good guy to know, so yeah, I'm 'bout it," Daquan responded.

Jorge laughed hard. "'Bout it? I like that. 'Bout it. Okay, Mandi, I'm 'bout it," he told her, getting off his desk and looking at his watch. He kissed her on the cheek and informed her, "By the time you get back, they'll be expecting you, okay? I gotta run, but I'll be free in an hour. You gonna wait?"

"No, but be sure to call me when you've got more time to spend," she answered with a subtle hint in her request.

Jorge smiled, holding the door for them.

Daquan was nervous all the way out of the club. He couldn't wait until Jorge got in his Benz 300CE, so he could tell Mandi, "I ain't bring the money."

He expected her to be upset, after driving all the way to Houston and telling Jorge what they had, and he left it at home. But the remark didn't even break her stride as they approached. "I know, because I didn't tell you to."

"So why we come all the way to Houston fo' five minutes?" he asked, sounding confused and slightly agitated.

She stopped and turned to Daquan, "Because Jorge had to meet you to deal with you. Now it's a go. He has a spot in Slidell. We take the money there and pick up the weight. The people I deal with don't stand on corners, Quan, or run dope houses, so you can't just pull up, cop, and blow. They sell heroin by appointment only. This was your appointment. You're in, so relax," she explained, then started to open her door.

Daquan echoed, "*Heroin*? I thought we was coppin' yay."

She turned to him, puzzled. "Didn't Jerome tell you?"

"Naw, he ain't tell me shit," Daquan answered, upset.

"Is there a problem?" Mandi wanted to know.

Daquan looked off toward the street, watching the moving traffic. Heroin . . . Jerome knew how he felt about heroin, and he was vexed that he hadn't told him. But he felt committed because Jerome needed the money, and he wanted some money too. He remembered Jerome telling him, "Dope owes you a life, whody."

He turned to Mandi and said, "Naw . . . naw, ain't no problem."

He got in the car silently, and Mandi watched him, wondering what was wrong.

12

By the time school rolled back around, Daquan had both feet planted firmly in the game. He and Mandi had a system that operated like clockwork. They'd pick up the weight from Jorge's spot in Slidell, then Mandi would hit Blue and the dykes off, while Daquan, Nut, and Big Ace went hand to hand in the CP3 and surrounding areas. Nut wasn't feeling the fact that Daquan wouldn't take him along when he re-upped, but it wasn't Daquan's decision. It was Mandi's.

"He's too young-minded, too wild, and he doesn't think, Daquan," she had told him when he brought it up. "He's a block nigguh, so let him play his position—no more, no less."

But Nut had the feeling that Daquan didn't trust him. It wasn't only the connect, but he saw Daquan changing. He still stayed G'd-up in the hood gear, but he would often put it down casual, especially when he went with Mandi, leaving Nut to wonder where they were and what they were doing. But they had the block so hot, and the money was so sweet, Nut never dwelled on it long.

While Nut splurged on chicks, clothes, jewelry, and blunts, Daquan stacked his paper, enabling him to cop a black '88 Cadillac Eldorado for his fourteenth birthday, which he kept parked several lots away from Grandma Mama's watchful eyes.

The only thing in his life that didn't elevate with his game was his dreams. They had continually gotten worse, until he was sometimes literally scared to go to sleep. He'd purposely hustle hard, staying up until he would just fall into a coma-like state, praying he wouldn't dream.

But it didn't work.

He dreamed of his death often, always calling out for Diana, but she wouldn't come. One night, he dreamed he was back in the Magnolia. It was the day his father killed Teddy, but he wasn't five years old any more. His mother was naked and on her knees in the bed with a belt tied tight around her upper arm.

"Come on, baby," she purred to him. "Come give Mama what she *neeeeed*," she begged.

All he could do was stare until his father busted in and pinned him against the far wall. "What the fuck you doin' in heah!? I'ma kill you!!" he threatened, wrapping his big, vise-like hands around Daquan's throat.

"Daddy, it's me! It's . . . *me*!" he wheezed, feeling his knees get weak. "It's your . . . son."

"My son?!" His father laughed wickedly, not loosening his grip. "You ain't none of my goddamn son! I'ma kill you!"

His father shoved him hard against the wall and headed for the closet. Daquan tried to run, but a hand grabbed his ankle so tight that he yelled out in agony. He looked down and saw that the hand restraining him was Teddy, with half his body blown away.

"Naw baby boy, don't you run. I got mine, now you gonna get yours!"

Daquan finally shook loose, but by the time he did, he was looking down the barrel of his daddy's gun.

"Die, nigguh, die!" His daddy screamed, unloading shot after shot into Daquan's head and body until he closed his eyes and all he saw was light. He opened them to find Diana sobbing over their mother's body. Daquan ran over and hugged her to him, begging her, "Don't cry, Diana, please don't cry."

"But . . . Daquan . . . why?" Diana sobbed. "Why? You killed Mama."

"No! I didn't—" he started to deny, but Diana and her mother's body began to fade away. "No, come back, I didn't kill Mama! I didn't kill her!"

He woke up in a cold sweat, still saying, "I didn't kill her!" He looked around and he was home, in his bed.

Moments later, Grandma Mama knocked softly, then entered with concern in her eyes. "Baby? You okay?" she asked, sitting on the side of his bed.

"I'm—I'm okay. Just had a bad dream," he told her, thanking God that it was a dream.

Grandma Mama wiped the sweat from his forehead, then she spotted the tattoo on his stomach that read "Cutt Boyz."

"Daquan, what is that? You done went and got yourself marked??"

Daquan quickly got out of bed and threw on his T-shirt. "I ain't *marked*. It's a tattoo," he replied, trying to get his stuff to take a shower and avoid her questions.

"I know what it is—what is it for? You 'posed to be in a gang now?" she asked, watching his every move.

He stopped and looked at her. "It ain't no gang. It's just a tattoo, no big deal. I gotta get ready for school."

Daquan tried to leave, but Grandma Mama called him back. "Daquan." Her tone of voice made him stop and look at her. "I don't know what you doin' out here, but *you* know, and it ain't right with your *soul*. Dreams is from the soul, boy, and if they tryin' to tell you something, you better listen."

Daquan fiddled with his towel, saw she was finished, then left without saying another word.

The first day of school in the ghetto is always a fashion show, and Daquan planned on winning first prize. While the chicks sported the latest flava of tight jeans and booty shorts, and the dudes were draped in the freshest hood apparel, Daquan took it to the grown and sexy. He was only fourteen, coming to school in his own Cadillac, pumping Pimp Daddy and dressed in gators and slacks. His three-and-one-half-inch-wide herringbone accentuated his royal blue silk shirt and matching Kangol, which he wore to the back.

Nut was killing it, too, rocking a green Adidas velour sweatsuit with money-green Forums. As they parked, slamming Cadillac doors, Daquan could smell the wetness of the young pussy trying to get their attention.

"Hey, D.Q.!"

"Come here, Nut!"

"You gonna take me home?"

They were turning heads of students and teachers alike. The teachers just looked on in awe and dismay, not only at Daquan and Nut, but at the many children adorned in the finery that street life had brought to their young lives. But Daquan was the only kid pushing a Caddy to Fortier High, so they were the real ghetto stars admired by everyone, except the few who hated from the sidelines.

Daquan and Nut definitely had their share of haters, but nigguhs knew that the Cutt Boyz went hard, so if you were gon' bring it, you had to be ready to go just as hard. Most weren't, so the hate only took the form of hard stares and mumbled curses.

Daquan and Nut were in separate homerooms, so they navigated the crowded hallways in opposite directions, mingling and flirting well into the late bell. By the time Daquan got to homeroom, most of the class was already seated, and the skinny, middle-aged white teacher was taking her roll.

"Mr. . ." she peered over her glasses at the attendance sheet, "Watson. So glad that you could finally join us. Please, find a seat."

Daquan ignored her sarcasm, scanning the room for a vacant

spot he preferred. The girls who had corny dudes next to them rolled their eyes, wishing that the seat was vacant. Daquan finally spotted a seat next to a kid he knew named Leon, and sat down.

"What up, whody?" Daquan greeted, shaking his hand and settling back.

"What up, D.Q? Yo, I'm glad you heah, 'cause I needed to holler at you," Leon answered.

Daquan looked at him. "What's happenin'?"

"*Mister* Watson," the teacher scolded from the front of the class. "I said find a seat, not disrupt the class in doing so," she huffed.

Daquan sucked his teeth as she continued.

"Good morning class, my name is Mrs. Widmir and I will be your homeroom teacher. Many of you, I already know from last year, but there are a few new faces. When I call you, please stand up and introduce yourself to the class."

While they did that, Leon turned and whispered to Daquan, "Say whody, what a nigguh gotta do to roll wit' the Cutt Boyz? I'm tired of eatin' beans and rice ere' night, ya heard me?"

Daquan chuckled. "I dig, whody. But them Cutt Boyz ain't doin' nothin' the next man ain't doin'."

"*Shiiit*," Leon slurred, "them boyz stuntin' 'cause yo' shine blindin' me right now."

They both laughed a little too loud.

"Mr. Watson! This is the second time I've had to call your name. If there is a third time, you can spend your first day of school with the principal. Is that clear?" Mrs. Widmir warned.

"Yeah," Daquan mumbled, like, *Whatever*.

"Now, stand up and introduce yourself to the class."

Daquan reluctantly stood to his feet, but when he saw all eyes on him, he smiled and greeted the class, "What's up, whodies?!"

The class started laughing, but Mrs. Widmir calmed them quickly.

"And what school did you attend last year?" she asked.

"The one in Baby Angola. I was locked up," he informed her proudly, his attitude saying, *But look at me now.*

"Sit down, Mr. Watson," she responded solemnly, her attitude saying, *It figures.* For the rest of the class period, her voice became a drone, the words blurring together meaninglessly, and he decided right then that school wasn't the place for him, except for two periods. He told Leon they were, "The one befo' school to pick a bitch up, and the one after, to drop her ass off!"

Leon chuckled. "I dig it, whody, just make sho' you holla at me."

"Fo' sho'!"

The bell rang and the halls recongested with the energy of young black bodies posturing, pimping, and punch-lining their way from class to class. Daquan had decided to stay this first day, but after that, he planned on attending just enough to keep truancy—and therefore, Grandma Mama—off his back.

Around lunchtime, he spotted a thick little redbone chick in a purple tennis skirt sashaying her way to the lunchroom, when he flashed her a smile. Once she returned it, he slid up on her like, "Say, lil' mama, you ain't gotta eat that bullshit if you don't want to. Let me take you somewhere and feed you." He grinned, making her giggle.

"What you got in mind, D.Q.?" she inquired, using his name to let him know she already knew who he was.

"Shit, it's whateva wit' me—you know I'm 'bout it. But it ain't no fun if my homey can't have none," he ran it.

"What?!" she snapped, ready to flip.

"Naw, I mean, I know you got a friend fo' my man, lil' Nut?" he asked.

"Oh," she replied, her nerves relaxing. "Where we gonna go?"

He held out his keys to her and told her, "Let me worry

about that. You just go on and get her, then go to the car, ya heard me? I'ma go get Nut and then you'll see."

She took the keys with a seductive smile, just happy to have them. "Y'all gonna get some beer?"

"Whatever you want, lil' mama. I just hope you gonna do me the same way," he gamed.

"Hm-mmm," she hummed, like she heard that before but wasn't past hearing it again. She strutted off, and the sway in her hips made Daquan shake his head like, *Fuck school*. Then he went off to find Nut.

It didn't take long to locate Nut. He was in the bathroom, rolling dice. The game was 7-11, and he was winning and talkin' shit because of it.

"You fuckin' wit' a Cutt Boy, whody. I'ma break y'all broke muhfuckas!" Nut boasted, shaking the dice, click-clack, in his hand. He released them, letting them tumble and skip until they careened off the wall to three and five.

"Point eight," Nut bellowed, putting down two fifty-dollar bills. "Who want it?"

He grabbed the dice as money hit the floor to fade or bet him. Daquan came in and said, "Yo, Nut. We gotta bounce, baby."

"Hol' up, Quan," Nut said over his shoulder, then kissed the dice. "Box cars!" he called out, but rolled a six. He scooped the dice up, as more bills hit the floor in several different piles. "Oh, y'all nigguhs nonbelievers, huh? Okay . . . *Jump* Katy!" He rolled again, but this time he rolled four.

"Nigguh, bring yo' ass on," Daquan repeated, "while all the teachers at lunch, yo!"

Nut rubbed the dice on Daquan's shirt.

"Since you in a hurry, hurry up and gimme eight," he exclaimed, then released the dice with a flick of his wrist. The dice bounced and softly grazed someone's foot, then spun and hit two fours.

"Eight! Gimme my muhfuckin' money!" Nut chuckled, but a slim, light-skin nigguh named Eddie stopped him.

"Fuck that, it hit his shoe! Roll over!" Eddie demanded, mad that he just lost a buck-fifty.

"Roll over?!" Nut laughed. "Ain't nobody stop dice! Fuck that shit you talkin'." Nut bent down to pick up the rest of his money.

"Nigguh, you think Black whooped yo' ass, touch my—" Eddie began, but never finished, because Nut caught him with a left so pretty, it broke his jaw on impact, sounding like a firecracker exploding.

Eddie staggered and dropped, while Nut stomped him over and over. "You see what we did to Black, don't you?! Huh? Fuck around and be next!" he screamed, stomping Eddie unconscious. He then bent down and took the rest of Eddie's money out of his pocket.

"Damn, Nut, you ain't gotta do whody like that," a chubby, dark-skin nigguh from Eddie's set passively protested.

Nut spun around and pulled a .38 from his waist. "Nigguh, what you say?! You got a problem?! Muhfucka, you empty your pockets too then!"

Daquan stood there, making sure no one tried to move on Nut, but at the same time fuming over his audacity.

"Matter of fact, all y'all nigguhs empty yo' shit! Now!" Nut barked, then smacked the chubby nigguh because he was moving too slow.

Nut and Daquan picked up all the money, then left the bathroom. Nut tucked the gun and they began to run down the vacant corridor to the parking lot. The girls were already in the car, sitting low in the front seat. Then they jumped in and pulled off.

Daquan was fuming, but Nut was laughing and the girls sensed the tension. "Y'all still gonna get some beer?" Redbone asked from the backseat, but Daquan shot her a look through the rearview that made her forget about an answer.

"Man, Nut, you's a *stupid*-ass nigguh, whody," Daquan spat angrily, and Nut's laughing was making him angrier.

"Fuck dem nigguhs, Dee. Pussy-built nigguhs ain't ready fo' no soldier!" Nut growled, still amped with adrenaline.

"I'm talkin' 'bout that shit you said! You think them nigguhs ain't hear you?! You think they won't run to them peoples behind that shit?!" Daquan blazed him, making a right turn.

Nut knew he was wrong for speaking about what they did to Black, but he was offended by the way Daquan was coming at him. "Them bitches ain't gonna do shit or say shit! And if they do, they can feel it the same muhfuckin' way!" Nut exclaimed, feeling invincible in his pride.

Daquan sucked his teeth and mumbled, "Mandi right—you don't think."

"Mandi?!" Nut said. "You lettin' that bitch think for you now, whody!? Fuck her and fuck you, too!"

The girls in the back were ready to go back until Daquan pulled into the liquor store parking lot. He turned to Nut, like, "Lemme holla at you."

They both got out and Daquan went up to a shabbily dressed man hanging outside the store, asking him to go in for them. Daquan gave him the money and when he walked away, Daquan turned to Nut.

"Nut, we got a sweet thing going, so we can't fuck it up by carryin' it any ol' kind of way, ya dig?" Daquan told him, speaking calmly but firmly. "We in this together."

Nut fidgeted around, looking every which way but at Daquan. "Yeah, man, whatever. But I know I'm tired of hearin' about that Mandi bitch, whody. She don't even fuck wit' me, so how we in this together?"

"She fuck wit' me, and that's all that count. I make sure you straight, don't I?" Daquan quizzed.

Nut sucked his teeth, so Daquan added, "What you want us to do? It's her connect, so it's her rules. When we connect, then fuck her—until then we gonna ride this shit out. You wit' me?" Daquan extended his hand and Nut shook it.

"I'm just sayin', Dee," Nut began, "we the ones out heah slingin' this shit, so she need to respect that, too. Shit, all that time you be wit' her, you ain't check her yet? I bet you ain't even fuck her. Well? Did you?"

Before he could answer, the man came back with two bags and gave them to Daquan, then asked, "You want y'all windows shined? Got my stuff right over theah."

Daquan gave him a five-dollar bill and answered, "'Preciate that, whody, but we in a hurry."

The man looked at the two doe-eyed girls in the backseat and whistled. "I can see why."

Nut and Daquan walked back to the car.

"Well?" Nut reiterated.

"Well what?"

"Nigguh, you know what. Did you fuck her?" Nut's lust wanted to know.

"Yeah."

"Lyin' muhfucka."

"You anudda one. I did . . . once," Daquan admitted, as they reached the car.

Nut laughed at him like, "Once? You must ain't hit it right!"

Once they got to Nut's, they broke open the Boone's Farm wine. It didn't take long before the pound of the music, the blunts, and the strawberry spirits had the girls horny, with Nut and Daquan eager to please.

Nut's chick was a little plain to look at, big-boned with a flat ass. But when she came out of her shirt, and her big, firm cocoa-brown breasts fell out, Nut began to suck on them like a newborn baby. He worked her out of her jean shorts and a slight fish odor filled the room.

Daquan grabbed Redbone's hand and led her into Nut's room. He ran his hands up her skirt, palming her petite ass and sliding a finger inside of her, making her grunt feverishly. He could tell she was tight, and he could just imagine how it would feel, but he wanted more than pussy. Daquan pulled down his pants and sat on the edge of the bed, but when shorty took off her clothes and tried to get on top, he put his hand on her shoulder to stop her advance, with her chin inches away from his erect manhood.

"Come on, lil' mama, you know what I want?" he crooned smoothly.

"*Uh-uh*, D.Q., I don't do that," she resisted, just ready to ride his dick.

"That's 'cause you never did it wit' me," he replied, trying to stand his dick up in her face, but she moved her head. "Plus, how you gonna be my girl, and we can't even do that?"

"I ain't your girl."

"But I want you to be, lil' mama. You think I'da gave any ol' body my keys? *Hell* naw, but if you don't feel the same way . . ." He turned his face like he was hurt, pouring his young game on her naive ears, strong.

"But I never did it before," she whined.

He had to fight back the cheese-eating grin he felt behind his lips. "Act like it's a lollipop, and hold your teeth back," he explained, gently guiding her head to his.

She was reluctant, but the sounds of her friend getting fucked made her hornier, and Daquan's hollow promises made her willing to try. She opened her red-lipstick-coated lips and took his hardness in her mouth, bobbing gently. It was a sensation she'd never felt before, but she could see the effect it was having on Daquan, and that heightened her own. She remembered what he said about a lollipop, so she began to lick around his head sloppily and suck greedily. Forgetting to always keep her teeth back, she scraped him a few times.

"Damn, lil' mama," Daquan winced, "watch yo' teeth."

Daquan could tell she was new at this, and he felt proud in his game to be her first. Just the thought of it almost made him bust in her mouth. She was no way like he remembered Mandi. She wasn't even as good as some of the fiends with vacuum mouths and deep throats that he occasionally tricked with, but he felt he could school her in time.

Daquan pulled her up on top of him, and she tried to kiss him, but he turned away.

"Oh, you can't kiss me now? It's yours."

"Yeah, but I don't wanna suck it," he retorted, slipping his dick in her now sloppy wetness. Daquan couldn't believe how tight her muscles held him, and for whatever she lacked in her head game, she knew how to work her hips.

She cocked one of her legs up into a squatting position and leaned back, giving Daquan a full view of himself long-dicking her dizzy. She gyrated her hips to the rhythm of his motion, moaning his name over and over. Daquan flipped her over on her back, pinning her legs on his shoulders, and began to pound until he came deep inside of her. Daquan tried to pull out, but she wrapped her legs around his waist.

"You better not tell nobody what I did, D.Q., and you better meant what you said, too," she insisted.

He was a little irritated by her feminine demands. "What I'ma tell fo'?" he lied, ready to brag to Nut. "It ain't nobody business but ours."

His beeper went off, so he got up and pulled up his pants to retrieve it. He saw it was Mandi's number, so he grabbed Nut's cordless phone and went to the bathroom to piss and clean himself off.

He dialed as he peed, ready to go finish shorty off again, when Mandi answered the phone. "Where you at?" she asked in an urgent tone that let him know there was a problem.

He flushed the toilet, replying, "At Nut's."

"I'll call you right back," she said, then hung up.

Something was definitely wrong. He got out a clean rag and wet it with soap and water, but when the phone rang he caught it mid-ring. "What's up?"

"Quan." It was Jerome on three-way from jail. "You there?"

"Yeah, Big Cuz, what up? The lawyer get the rest of the money?" he asked, because he could hear the stress in Jerome's tone.

"Yeah, yeah, he straight. But yo . . . *Fuck*," Jerome cursed, temperature boiling.

Now Daquan was mad, too, knowing something had happened.

"Yo, listen. Remember I told you a niz-ziger was ta-zall-kin'?" Jerome slurred, using the street code of concealed speech.

"Yeah."

Jerome got quiet, then said, "It's Pi-zeppa-iz-eppa."

Whatever hardness Daquan had left in his dick went straight to his heart.

"*What*?!"

"Man, it's them peoples! I siz-zeen the sta-zate-mezent my siz-zelf," Jerome informed him.

Daquan rushed out the bathroom to make sure Nut hadn't picked up the phone, but he found him fucking the big-boned chick from the back. He returned to the bathroom to find Redbone taking a piss, so he went in the bedroom.

"You still there?" Jerome asked.

"Yeah . . . yeah, whody, I'm heah," he answered, meaning it in more ways than one.

I need you to go see lil' mama *now*, ya heard me?" Jerome ordered, referring to Mandi.

Redbone walked back in the room, still naked, and hugged him from the back, sliding her hand in his boxers, but he moved her away.

"Yeah, I can do that, whody. Fo' sho'. I'm on my way." He clicked off and closed his eyes, trying to clear his head of the drunkenness and confusion. *Pepper, a snitch?* he thought, then turned back to the chick and told her tersely, "Get dressed, we gotta go."

* * *

Daquan left Nut and his chick at Nut's house, then dropped Redbone back at school. He knew he had no business driving, because he was definitely drunk, but he fought it off well enough to push the Caddy to Mandi's.

As he drove, he tried to make sense of it all. How could Pepper flip like that? He and Jerome had grown up together since youngens. They were always best friends—if you saw one, you saw the other. They probably fought each other more than anyone, but they'd be even tighter five minutes later. Now this?

Their friendship made Daquan think of his and Nut's. They were close the very same way. Nut was his man and he loved him like the brother he never had. But he couldn't help but wonder if they would ever grow apart. Or even, if push came to shove, would Nut do him the same way? He tried to shake the thought, but it followed him all the way to Mandi's.

When he got there, she was waiting for him. As soon as his Caddy door closed, her front door opened. She emerged wearing a pink house robe that stopped about thigh-high.

"Hey, Quan," she greeted, closing the door behind him. "You want something to drink?"

Daquan pulled on the cigarette he was smoking once more, then crushed it in the ashtray as he sat on the couch. "I'm good."

Mandi sat next to him. He rubbed his hands on his face, oblivious to the fact that she was watching him. Then she finally said, "So what do you think?"

He removed his hands, saying, "I think it's fucked up! Rome put that nigguh on when he ain't have nothin'! He always broke bread with that nigguh, *always*!" Daquan barked.

Mandi nodded solemnly. "This is true, but sometimes, the more you give a person, the more they want."

Daquan couldn't help but think about his earlier argument with Nut. Mandi continued, "Very rarely is there honor among thieves, which means, if someone is a thief, then he'll steal from anyone. It's hard to trust people, Daquan, even if you want to. Women know this—it's why we don't usually trust other women, although we will usually trust the wrong man . . ." Mandi added with a smirk. "So what do you think we should do?"

Daquan looked at her. "Do?"

"The feds are going to let Pepper out, in order to go after Jerome's connect. No one knows about this except Jerome, because of an inside source of ours. If Pepper comes home and finds the connect, Jerome'll never see the streets again," Mandi explained, then stopped to let her words sink in.

Daquan shook his head with bewilderment and hatred coursing like twins through his blood stream. "Muhfuckas talk that loyalty shit, bustin' guns and shit. But when it comes down to it, it don't mean shit," he hissed.

"But that isn't all," Mandi continued. "If Pepper is released, *and he will be*, the first place he's going is to Nut. Nut will tell him what he is doing, which leads to you. Do you understand?" she probed.

"Yeah."

"So . . . what do we do?" she asked again, this time with the whole picture painted in vivid colors with hints of bloody red.

Daquan looked at her, then looked away, because he knew she was asking him to kill Pepper. She slid up closer to him, crossing her legs and exposing her smooth thigh all the way to the panty line.

"I know this is hard for you, Daquan, but Jerome told you, there's no turning back. Once the game begins, no one controls it, because it's cause and effect," she explained, gently taking his hand. He took it away and looked her dead in her eyes.

"Don't ever try and play me, Mandi," he told her in an icy tone, referring to her subtle advances. "I know what's up, and if I'ma do it, I'ma do it, but don't think you can rock me into it."

Mandi smiled approvingly. "Okay, Daquan, I respect that,

and . . . I respect you. It's good to know you do catch on fast," she complimented him, then gave him a sincere peck on the cheek.

"When he getting out?"

"Any time soon. Just be ready when he does."

I can't kill Pepper . . .
But he snitched . . .
Jerome may never see the light of day . . .
Pepper gotta go.

Daquan's thoughts fought his inebriated emotions as he drove down Broad Street heading back to the Calliope. The sounds of MC Eiht's "One Time Gaffled 'Em Up" filled the Cadillac with the killa Cali sound, putting Daquan in a killer's state of mind. He tried to keep from swerving, looking at the road through half-closed eyes and smoking a Newport in the New Orleans twilight, trying to comprehend the nature of the game he had chosen to play. It all came down to every man for himself. Shit was all good as long as money was rolling and everybody played their position. But when greed set in, or fear, even jealousy, it became a game of cutthroat, and only the strong survived.

Daquan pulled into Nut's parking lot and got out, chirping the alarm behind him. He stumbled as he approached the steps, mumbling a return greeting to a passing man. When Nut opened the door, he had to look away, avoiding eye contact by rubbing his eyes and shuffling past him.

"What up, whody? Where you been?" Nut asked nonchalantly, his mother's voice cursing from the kitchen over coming home to a house smelling like funky pussy.

"Wit' lil' mama," Daquan lied. All he wanted to do was change clothes and get away from Nut. But Nut followed him into the bedroom, bragging about his early episode.

"I'm tellin' you whody, shorty a muhfuckin' freak! She might not look all that, but she sucked my dick and ere'thang. You okay?" Nut inquired when he saw that Daquan wasn't reacting to his words.

"Headache, dog," Daquan mumbled, putting on a pair of bargain-basement jeans and an Oakland Raiders T-shirt, clothes Grandma Mama had bought him.

"Nigguh can't hold his liquor," Nut chuckled, and Daquan's mind instantly answered back, *Neither can your brother*, but he choked off the thought.

"I'm gone, bruh," Daquan mumbled, putting his jewelry in his pocket and walking into the living room with Nut right behind him.

"Aiight, Dee, we'll get up," Nut replied, closing the door behind him. He sensed something in Daquan's demeanor, but shrugged it off and went to eat dinner.

Daquan walked home with his head down and his hands stuffed in his pockets. All he wanted to do was go to bed, but when he opened the door, the first sound his ears picked up was a woman's sobs. He looked straight into Kimoko's tear-stained face, then his grandmother's stern expression. Grandma Mama was trying to console Kimoko.

"Well, I can see *some* of the things you out there doin', boy," Grandma Mama quipped. "You know this child is pregnant?"

Kimoko looked straight into his eyes, trying to hold back the tears. The word "pregnant" momentarily threw Daquan, but it wasn't hard enough to make it through everything else in his mind and reach all the way to his heart.

"It ain't mine," he retorted, closing the door behind him.

"I told you, Mama Watson," Kimoko sobbed, putting her face into Grandma Mama's shoulder. "I knew he'd say that!"

"Daquan Watson! Have you laid wit' this chile?" Grandma Mama demanded to know, but Daquan just sucked his teeth and looked away. "Daquan," she repeated.

"Yeah, Ma," he answered reluctantly.

"So how you gonna fix yo' mouth to say it ain't yourn?" Grandma Mama asked with righteous indignation.

"I'm goin' to bed," he mumbled, starting for his room, making Kimoko cry harder.

"Boy, don't you walk away from me," Grandma Mama warned him, struggling up off the couch. She approached Daquan and said, "This gal ain't got no reason to lie and pin a child on you."

Daquan softly chuckled, because she didn't know the other half of his double life. Kimoko had every reason to pin a child on him, as heavy as he was in the street. But Grandma Mama took his smirk to be insolence, and she slapped him in the head. "You think this is funny? What's wrong wit' you, Daquan? This child is finna have a baby. Say it's yours—you gonna let it grow up without a daddy?"

"*I* did," was his icy cold but simple reply. It was so cold, it even froze Grandma Mama's tirade, making her remember that she wasn't talking to a young man, but a fatherless child.

Their eye contact lingered a few moments longer, then he walked into his room and shut the door behind him firmly.

13

The cafeteria of Alcee Fortier echoed with screams and pandemonium, while Nut lay bleeding on the floor, holding his left side. Daquan looked from Nut to the pretty caramel girl laying on the other side of the lunch table, teachers hollering everywhere.

The gunshot still echoed in Daquan's mind as he scanned the many scared and confused faces. Just moments earlier it was lunchtime. Laughter and loud talk filled the cafeteria. The sun shone brightly through the elevated windows, while the kids filed through the line to receive a lunch of pizza and cookies.

Nut and Daquan came in, just to be seen, not having been in school all day. The caramel girl, whose name was Vanessa, liked Daquan and had asked him to sit with her at lunch. "Why sit in heah, when McDonald's right down the street?" he offered, but Vanessa shook her head.

"'Cause I ain't leavin' school, that's why," she replied firmly, but followed it with a smile.

It was her smile that intrigued Daquan and kept him at her. He went through the line with Vanessa, while Nut slap-boxed with another Calliope homey. Neither one of them saw Eddie come in, spot them, then hurry out. Nobody did, except a teacher, who thought nothing of it.

As Daquan and Vanessa got their trays, Eddie came back in with a green bandana tied around his face, but Nut had his back to the door. Eddie pulled the chrome .38 from his bag, and hollered, "*Yeah*, muhfucka, you thought it was over?!"

No one knew who he was talking to, because his wasn't the only voice yelling. But the glint of the chrome caught Daquan's eye and he turned to see the first flash of fire jumping from the barrel.

"Nut!" he hollered, but it was too late.

The bullet hit Nut in his side, spinning him around and then dropping him to the floor in agony. Eddie wasted no time in aiming the gun in Daquan's direction, but Daquan already had his .38 in hand. He didn't get a shot off because people were running everywhere. But that didn't stop Eddie. He fired six more times in Daquan's direction. Five slugs struck brick or glass, but one found the soft flesh of Vanessa's upper chest.

Everything had happened so fast that Daquan could only react, but he couldn't protect. The shot that narrowly missed him lifted Vanessa off her feet, knocking her back across the table.

Eddie dashed out, leaving the scene. Daquan kneeled next to Nut's body, taking the gun from his waist. He started to dip, but Nut grabbed his elbow.

"Don't leave me, whody," he begged. "I'm dyin'."

"You ain't dyin', Nut. Just hold on till them peoples get heah," Daquan told him.

"Stay wit' me, Dee," he asked, his voice getting weak.

It was killing Daquan, but he had to get out of there with those guns. "Nut, I ain't leavin' you, dog. But I gotta get these gats outta heah fo' them peoples come, aiight? I'll be to the hospital, I promise. You ain't gonna die, you ain't," he told Nut.

"Okay, bruh," Nut gasped.

Daquan took one more look around, his eyes stopping on Vanessa's body, the sounds of sirens in his ears. Two people had gotten shot, but over a hundred would carry the scars. It was like death was all around him. He knew that it could easily be him on the floor instead of Vanessa. He dipped out right before the paramedics and police arrived.

Daquan went and changed his clothes, leaving his jewelry and Caddy in the Calliope, then taking a cab to Charity Hospital on Tulane Avenue. He didn't bother to ask any of the nurses for any information as he made his way along the emergency corridor. He went from room to room until he found Nut laid up in a hospital bed with an I.V. in his arm, asleep. He walked over to the bed and gently tapped Nut's other arm. His eyes fluttered open, and he smiled when he recognized who it was.

"My nigguh, what's up?" Nut slurred, the medication making him too drowsy to keep his eyes open for long. Daquan looked at Nut's shirtless body, his eyes stopping at the gauze on his side.

"How you doin', baby?"

Nut kept his eyes closed. "It went right through, whody, but it burned like hell. Now, I'm so high I can't feel shit."

Daquan smirked, relieved to see Nut's situation wasn't too serious.

"They say somebody else got hit real bad, though," Nut told him. "Some girl—she might die."

Daquan dropped his head because he knew Nut was talking about Vanessa. "Don't worry 'bout that, bruh, you just lay up and get right, ya heard me?"

Nut opened his eyes and looked into Daquan's. "That nigguh tried to *kill* me, Dee. Bitch-ass nigguh tried to kill me. I'ma make 'im suffer bad. Eddie 'bout to see what it mean to be 'bout it, 'bout it," Nut promised.

Daquan nodded in agreement, when a nurse walked in.

"Who are you? You aren't supposed to be back here," she informed him, acting like she was ready to call security.

"I was just leavin', miss, just leavin'. We'll holla, Nut," Daquan said, shaking Nut's hand.

"Fo' sho'."

Daquan dipped out of emergency and entered the waiting room. He saw a large group of black people, mostly women, and he knew exactly who they were. As he walked, he looked into the face of a woman who had to be Vanessa's mother. She had the same caramel complexion, full lips, and the same soft-brown, chinky eyes, except hers were puffy and red from crying. Vanessa's father was holding her hand, while several other family members surrounded them, sitting and standing. They all looked up when he approached.

"I-I'm a friend of Vanessa's," Daquan said softly.

Just the name made her mother cry harder, but her father nodded him a manly appreciation.

"How is she doing?" Daquan asked, scared of the answer he might receive.

Her father took a deep breath and answered, "It's in the Lord's hands now—them doctors is only His instrument through which His mercy will flow." His voice had the quality of a preacher's and the faith of a man, which made Daquan feel good just hearing it.

He looked down at the shabby sneakers that he had thrown on just in case the police were there. "Well ... um ...." He looked at her father, and said, "Whatever, like, the bill is ... I wanna help pay for it, if you'll let me."

The whole family, even her mother, looked at him. They looked at his wardrobe, and saw a little boy who barely had clothes on his own back.

Daquan added, "Whatever I have to do, mow grass, wash cars, I'll do. I know Vanessa would do it for me."

Her mother stood slowly and opened her arms. "Come here, baby." She smiled through her tears.

Daquan timidly approached until he felt the warmth of her embrace and the coolness of her tears on his face. "God loves you, child," she sobbed. "God loves you."

God loves you.

God loves you.

God loves you . . . Those words echoed through his day and followed him into his dreams, filling the vision with creamy whiteness and golden rain. The rain tasted like honey on his tongue, and felt like silk on his skin.

Daquan didn't notice Diana appear until she inquired, "How long will you live like this?"

He redirected his attention from the falling rain to his sister. Her dress was white, but the golden rain left no trace as it fell upon her.

"Until I find a better way," he replied.

"Where have you looked?" Diana wanted to know. "Besides the life that's tearing us apart inside."

There was no way he could lie to Diana, because she knew him as he knew himself. Here, there were no illusions.

"What else is there, Diana? Work like Daddy, and all those other people, barely staying afloat? So sooner or later I gotta find somewhere to hide, like in a bottle or a pipe, or a needle like Mama? I'd rather be dead," he admitted in an exasperated whisper.

"God loves you, Daquan," Diana smiled. "Remember? Never forget that. Never. If you do, then you're truly lost."

"I feel lost now," he mumbled.

"You have a good heart, Daquan. All you need to do is follow it. Don't let the world make it bitter," she explained.

"It just ain't that easy, Diana, to follow your heart. What if it's wrong?" he questioned.

Diana smiled angelically. "You can never go wrong if you

truly believe," she told him, then disappeared, leaving him to the golden rain.

That night, he slept more peacefully than he could remember. A restful sleep, free of the demons that he felt were becoming more and more his motivation. A deep, dreamless sleep that lasted throughout the night and into the next morning.

When he awoke, he found Grandma Mama sitting on the edge of his bed, watching him sleep. It felt strange to find her there, expressionless, but all he could say was, "Good mornin', Mama."

"Mornin', Daquan," she responded, still with no trace of emotion.

Daquan sat up in his bed and asked "Is everything okay?"

"How's Anthony?" was her response.

He knew she had heard—hell, she had to. It was all over the news and all over the Calliope by the time the police got to school.

"He's okay," Daquan assured her.

Grandma Mama nodded.

"Somebody must've been prayin' for that boy."

"Yes'm."

"Daquan, I told you a long time ago that I know it's hard for you to have to live like this. We always been poor as long as I can remember. But I've tried to do what I can for you, to raise you right," Grandma Mama said, and Daquan's gut felt like it knew where she was going.

"I knew you'd get in some devilishment out theah, but . . ." She opened her hand and dumped six .22 caliber shells onto the bedspread tented over his lap.

He cursed in his mind.

"Then I found these," Grandma Mama finished, looking at him with the same pained expression she once gave Jerome.

Daquan was mad at himself, because the bullets went to a

gun he didn't even have anymore. He'd forgotten that he had stashed the bullets in his drawer. He was a little bit upset with Grandma Mama too because he felt like she had violated his privacy.

"So you searchin' my room now, Mama?" he asked.

"You bringing guns in my house, Daquan?" she shot right back. "Is this what happened at school, and almost got Anthony killed?"

Daquan got out of bed, knowing in his heart it would probably be the last time. The thought made him sick because he could see the disappointment in her face starting to show.

"Grandma, I ain't doin' nothin', I swear. Them just some bullets. It ain't no gun," Daquan tried to reason, but she wasn't hearing it.

"Daquan," she articulated slowly, closing her eyes, because every syllable was more and more painful. "If you old enough to have a gun . . ."

Daquan hurried over to her, dropped to his knees, and wrapped his arms around his grandmother's waist. "I'm sorry, Grandma Mama, I'm sorry," he blurted out. He wanted to cry for the pain he was causing her, but he couldn't. He wasn't apologizing in an attempt to stay, but she thought he was, so she steeled her emotions against giving in to the pleas of her grandchild.

". . . Then you're old enough," the tears welled up in her eyes, "to be . . . on your . . . own." She finally managed to get it out.

"I'm sorry," he whispered.

Grandma Mama started to hug him back, but she knew if she did, she wouldn't let him go, so her arms hovered above his body until she fought them down. She prayed that he'd see the error of his ways and come back, but she had to let him go. To allow him to stay would be to shelter him against consequences she felt were inevitable. She said a silent prayer that he'd come to his senses before Daquan ended up like Jerome or worse. She had no idea how deep Daquan already was.

"I've . . . I've got breakfast ready, and you can eat if you'd like. After that . . . I want you out of my house with nothin' but the clothes on your back," she instructed him, then slowly rose, breaking Daquan's embrace and leaving him sitting on the floor, looking after her.

"I'ma do right, Grandma. I promise," Daquan vowed, knowing he had to go but promising himself and her that it wouldn't be for nothing.

Grandma Mama paused in the doorway, but she didn't speak or look back. Her shoulders raised and lowered as she took a deep breath, then left the room.

Moments later, Daquan had himself ready to go. He didn't want to, but he knew her mind was made up, so there was no use dragging it out. He could hear her slowly stirring a pot. The occasional scraping of metal against metal was the only sound. He stepped out into the morning sun and headed for Nut's house. Daquan knew he could stay with Nut if he wanted, but knowing what was to come, there was no way he would stay there. He didn't want to get his own crib either, so that left only one other place: Mandi's.

He'd stay with Mandi until he figured out his next move.

Daquan knocked on Nut's door, then waited until his mother came to the door and let him in. Nut's mother took the half-smoked cigarette from her lips, and said, "Hey, Quan, how you doin'?"

"I'm okay. How's Nut?" he asked.

She waved him off like it was nothing. "That boy is fine. They say the bullet went right through. I told him 'bout that foolishness. I hear tell of y'all. Y'all better be careful," she rattled off, pausing only to hit her Salem Light.

"How's Jerome?" she inquired.

Daquan didn't even want to talk about that situation knowing what her son had to do with it. He almost said, *Ask your snitchin'-ass son*, but instead he shrugged and mumbled, "He don't call much. I just came over to get my clothes."

"What's wrong?" she probed, because she knew why he kept them there.

Going in Nut's room, he yelled over his shoulder, "Got kicked out."

"Kicked out?" he heard her echo, while he grabbed his clothes and sneakers, stuffing them in black trash bags. He heard her slippers stop in front of the door. "Mama Watson put you out? What you do?" she wanted to know.

Daquan didn't want to talk, so he packed quickly, yelling to her, "I don't know, man."

"What you mean, you don't know? Where you gonna go? You need to stay heah?" she offered.

He grabbed all three trash bags by their necks and replied, "Naw, I talked to my cousin. He said I could come over theah," he lied, heading for the front door.

"You sure?"

"Yes, ma'am. Tell Nut I'll be to the hospital tomorrow," he told her, opening the door.

"He'll be home today, but Quan," she called as he turned to go, "you got a couple of dollars? I'm outta cigarettes."

Daquan dug in his pockets, pulled out a ten, and handed it to her, thinking there was no way he'd ever stay there.

"Thank you, baby," she replied, stuffing the bill in her ample bosom.

He carried the bags to the car, threw them in the backseat, then pulled off.

14

*If I die, let me die, just bury me high
Hurry up and get it over, 'cause I'm dyin' inside.
A young nigguh with big bank and big nuts to match
Started off in The Cut, Cutt Boyz dressed in black
Picture me having visions, nightmares of my death
On da sidewalk bleedin', I breathe my last breath
Call me crazy, society made me, it's cool
D.Q., only stay true to the tool.
Hustle or die, whody, I could never be broke
Full of blunt smoke, the Calliope is Cutt Throat.*

"Whody, I'm telling you, you need to be *nation*, my nig-guh," his friend Rosco exclaimed, bigging him up to the fullest.

He and Daquan were standing outside the spot, waiting for Nut to arrive. Daquan had been staying with Mandi for a couple of weeks now, but he still kept it hot in the CP3. The money was flowing like water, and Jorge was getting more and more comfortable with him. However much weight Daquan bought, Jorge gave him an equal amount on consignment. The Cutt Boyz were heavy in the game, and they wore the medallions to prove it. Taking a page from Death Row, they all got gold-and-diamond medallions that said "Cutt Boyz" with their name at the bottom.

"I hear you, whody, I hear you," Daquan replied, pulling on his Camel. "I wish it was that simple."

"It *is*," Rosco assured him. "Nigguh, we got this paper now. We can go hard and get you some shit out for real."

Daquan paused thoughtfully but he was interrupted by the sounds of Nut pulling up in his '89 Monte Carlo, bumping Scarface. Nut hopped out, medallion swinging, and ran up, wide-eyed.

"Yo!" Nut exclaimed.

Daquan looked at him and laughed.

"Nigguh, you look like you been smoking that shit."

"Nigguh, fuck you," Nut retorted, still excited. "Pepper beat that shit!"

Rosco got amped, but Daquan remained stoic.

Nut continued, "Whody just called and said his lawyer said them peoples gotta drop the charges, bruh! I knew he was comin' home!" Nut was ecstatic.

Daquan's blood boiled. He had been preparing himself for this moment, but deep down, he had also been hoping that somehow it wouldn't be true, that Pepper would change his mind and hold it down. But to hear he was actually on his way made it official, and virtually signed his death certificate.

Nut noticed the expression on his face and said, "Yo, I asked about Jerome for you, too."

"What he say?"

"He said, since they on the same charge, ain't no reason why he ain't gonna get his dropped, too," Nut told him. "Don't worry, Dee. Rome gonna beat that shit," he expressed, trying to comfort his friend.

"I know," Daquan replied firmly, the true meaning of his words known only to him. "I know."

"We gotta throw whody a party, ya heard me?" Rosco proposed. "Bring big bruh home in style."

"You ain't know?" Nut agreed, shaking Rosco's hand.

"Yeah, yo, in style," Daquan smirked and shook Nut's hand, too. "But dog, I gotta go. I'm 'posed to see Vanessa in the hospital," Daquan informed them, relieved to have an excuse to leave. Her mother had beeped him the day before to let him know she was feeling much better and was strong enough to talk.

"Yeah? How lil' mama doin'?" Nut asked sincerely.

"She talkin' now, bruh," Daquan answered.

Nut nodded with a screwface forming on his grill. "Yo, that bitch-ass Eddie fuckin' lucky them peoples found him 'fore I did. Soon as he get out, that fool gonna die," Nut vowed, remembering the burn of the bullet.

"Fo' sho', whody, ere' dog has his day," Daquan quipped. "I'm Audi."

He dapped up Rosco and Nut, then strolled though the courtway. Rosco turned his attention to an upcoming sell, but Nut continued to watch Daquan until he disappeared. Something was wrong with him, Nut knew, but he wasn't speaking on it. They had been down too long for Nut not to notice, but he let it go, only to file it away in his mind for another time.

Daquan got to the hospital around two P.M. and found Vanessa asleep. The sun's rays shone through the window blinds and cut across the white hospital sheet and the brownness of her exposed arm, into which an I.V. tube ran. Daquan looked at her peacefully sleeping, looking like a young caramel angel. The guilt he felt for her condition welled up in his chest.

Vanessa's eyes fluttered open, and she smiled when she saw him standing in the doorway. "Hey, Daquan," she greeted in a whispery voice, hoarse from lack of use.

Daquan entered the room and stood at her bedside. "What's happenin' lil' mama? How you?"

"Better," she said with a tight-lipped grin of resolve. "What time is it?"

"Around two."

"What day is it?"

"Wednesday."

"Then why you ain't in school?" she chuckled, making him grin.

"I left early to come see you," he lied.

"Liar," she giggled. "You ain't even been, have you?" Vanessa probed, looking at him with concerned eyes that reminded him of Diana's.

He shrugged.

"You know how I do, Ma. School just ain't for me."

Vanessa turned her head on the pillow, closing her eyes. "I was *sooo* scared I was going to die, Daquan," she admitted, and Daquan had to look away from the tears running onto her pillow. She looked at him and said, "Are you scared, Daquan? I mean, to die?"

Death seemed to be his constant companion, so fear had never been a factor. "Naw, Nessa . . . I ain't scared to die. But if I get killed, I want revenge."

She reached over and took his hand. "That boy who shot me wanted to kill you, Daquan. I don't know why, all I know is I could see it in his eyes. Maybe that's why I didn't die, because it wasn't meant for me. But, I'm scared for you, Quan, because if you ain't scared to die, then what is your life worth?" she asked sincerely.

Daquan couldn't answer directly because he had never thought of the question before. What *was* his life worth? He had the car, the clothes, and the jewels that turned people's heads whenever he passed. Yet the only eyes that mattered to him were Grandma Mama's, and he had etched disappointment into them. He had the money and the product, but he also had murder in his heart for a man that had been like an older brother to him. And he had come out unscathed in a shooting, yet he stood over the bed of a child who literally paid his debt, and he wondered, was his life worth *that*?

"I just wanna live, lil' mama. Whatever that's worth, then it'll be the price I pay," he replied solemnly.

She gripped his hand tighter.

"And I'm not mad at you, Daquan. I'm not even mad at the boy who shot me. I wanna live, too, Daquan, but my life is worth more than letting someone make it bitter." Vanessa spoke from an old soul.

Daquan leaned over to kiss her on the forehead. "I dig you, lil' mama. Maybe when you get outta heah, we can hang out . . . finally go to McDonald's," he chuckled.

Vanessa smiled.

"It's a date," she said, "and I'ma hold you to that."

Daquan nodded.

"You ain't gotta do that. I'll be the one to pick you up," he winked. "I'll be waitin' on you."

He kissed her hand before letting go of it, then turned for the door.

"Daquan," she called.

Without turning around, he replied, "I will," then looked back, wearing a smirk.

"Be careful," she said anyway, even though he had anticipated her remark.

The steam from the shower put a thin layer of sweat on his forehead as he sat on the toilet smoking and talking to Mandi, who was taking a shower. "Yeah, Rome already told me," Mandi replied to his earlier question about Pepper's release.

He eyed the shadow of her naked silhouette behind the light yellow shower curtain. Daquan watched her wash her breasts, moving in circular motions toward her stomach. He had seen this sight many times since he had moved in—even seen her naked—but her body still intrigued him. Especially since she wouldn't give in to his subtle flirtations.

"Muhfucka talkin' 'bout throwin' his snitchin' ass a party," he huffed, blowing out a stream of smoke. "I'ma throw him a party, aiight. A second line." In the old New Orleans tradition of the jazz funeral, the second line was the group of mourners who follow behind the coffin just for the music, dancing all the way to the cemetery.

Mandi laughed as she turned off the shower. She peeped around the curtain and said, "Could you hand me a towel?"

He admired the soft bend of her shoulder, following it to the forearm and slight hint of her right breast, concealed decorously behind the shower curtain. Mandi noticed him looking at her and smirked, "Mannish ass."

"Mannish?" he echoed, going in the bathroom closet to bring her a large peach-colored towel. "I'm a man."

"Oh yeah?" he heard her quip, drying off in the shower. He walked into the bedroom as she asked, "What makes you a man?'

Daquan didn't bother to answer. He grabbed the remote and flipped the channel to BET. It was close to eleven P.M., so all that was on was BET News. He sucked his teeth and turned to HBO.

Mandi came out of the bathroom with the towel wrapped around her, her wet hair pulled back in a ponytail. "Well?"

"Well what?" he questioned back, putting out his cigarette in the ashtray and kicking his Jordans up on the bed, only to have Mandi slap them down.

She grabbed the lotion, then sat at the end of the bed with her back to him. "What makes you a man, as you say?" she asked in an amused tone. Before he could answer, she let the towel fall to the bed, exposing her back down to the tip of her crack. The blood in his dick rushed to the head. He could see the sides of her breasts jiggle as she moved, making the waterbed rock.

"'Cause I am," he finally replied, not knowing what else to say.

She looked over her shoulder, like, "'Cause I am? Is that your definition of a man, Quan?"

She continued to rub lotion on her legs and thighs, distracting him momentarily.

"A man handles his business—you know, gets the job done. And that's what I do," he bragged, thinking about how her titties would taste in his mouth. She passed him the lotion, saying, "Here, do my back." He leaned over and took the bottle, squirting some in his hand.

"A man," she began, "knows his limitations. He doesn't have anything to prove, because he knows who he is. If someone tests that, then he *responds*, he doesn't just react."

Daquan heard most of what she was saying, but his mind was focused on how smooth her skin was as he ran his hands all over it.

Mandi glanced over her shoulder and checked, "Did you hear me?"

"Huh? Yeah."

"What did I say?"

He sucked his teeth. "I said I heard you."

"Boy, gimme my lotion," Mandi chuckled softly, taking the bottle from him and putting it on the floor. She picked up the oversized Dallas Cowboys T-shirt off the bed and slipped it over her head. When she stood up, Daquan caught a glimpse of her firm, round ass before the T-shirt dropped the curtain on the show.

"I ain't got nothin' to prove," Daquan stated, letting Mandi know he did hear her, "not to you or Jerome. So it ain't like he pushin' me into anything. I grew up in these streets, so I know the rules. Muhfucka violate, he dealt wit', regardless of who he is."

Mandi took her hair out of the ponytail, letting it fall down past her shoulders. Even though it was a weave, it looked like it belonged to her from birth. She smiled at his understanding, but frowned when she saw him kick off his shoes and start taking off his pants. "What do you think you're doing?"

"I'm sleepin' in heah," he informed her.

"Oh, you are, huh?"

"I'm tired of sleepin' in the guest room, 'cause I ain't no guest," Daquan responded, slipping under the covers and grabbing the remote.

Mandi crawled up on the waterbed and got in next to him. "Then that's what you do. Sleep."

"That's what I said, ain't it? Sleep. But yo . . . you know, it's always whatever wit' me," he added with a smirk.

Mandi got comfortable with her back to him. "Good night, Quan."

Distant voice . . .
Calling his name . . .
Dial tone . . .
Ringing . . .
Ringing . . .
Ringing in his ear . . .
Broken glass, then . . .
The heat . . . The light . . . bright, bright light, and the sounds of gun-fire, jerking and twisting him around and down, down and around.

"Game over, nigguh," *the deep voice gloated over his twisted body.*

The dream was vivid, almost too vivid. But for the first time, Daquan didn't wake up in a cold sweat. He didn't wake up at all, just kept sleeping as a curious expression spread across his face.

It was a smile.

Jerome had picked up some weight during his stint in the county jail. Daquan could tell from the chubbiness apparent in his cheeks and around his midsection. He had also let his beard grow out into a trim five o'clock shadow that framed his face. Daquan came alone to see him, and it was a surprise to Jerome, who hadn't expected any visitors today.

"What up, lil' cuz? You miss ol' Rome or somethin'?" Jerome joked, playfully punching the glass.

"Somethin' like that, fat boy," Daquan sniped, then added, "You be in there any longer, you'll be big as a house, whody."

Jerome laughed at that. "Just eatin' good, baby, and layin' up. Shit, from what I heah, you gettin' fat in them streets. Cutt Boyz keep it hot, ya heard me?"

"Fo' sho', Rome, just holdin' fort till you touch. You know I got you." Daquan winked. "What your lawyer talkin' 'bout?"

Jerome shrugged, "We just waitin' on ere'thing, you know?" he replied vaguely, but Daquan knew exactly what he was talking about.

"Then, you ain't got nothin' to worry about," Daquan assured him with strong resolve.

Jerome rubbed his face. "You still rappin', lil' cuz?"

"Fo' sho'."

"Stick wit' that. I be hearin' them nigguhs on the radio, and they ain't half as good as you. Do somethin' wit' that. That theah is your real meal ticket, 'cause you can't do this forever, you know?" Jerome schooled him. "I been readin' the Bible and shit, bruh."

"You ain't gonna come home no preacher is you, whody?" Daquan quipped, only half jokingly. He'd seen a lot of cats catch cases and get prison religious.

Jerome laughed lightly. "Naw, whody, just trying to make some sense of this thang called life. Grandma Mama wrote me."

Daquan just looked at him. The mere mention of her name made him feel ashamed. "She love us, D.Q., and she gettin' old. We need to get her outta them projects, man."

"I know, Rome, I wanna get her a house. But you know she won't accept money from me," Daquan admitted.

Jerome nodded. "Just . . . when we get this situation straight and I get out, we'll put our heads together, ya dig?"

"Okay."

"You alright?"

"Yeah . . . I'm straight," Daquan replied.

"You fuck Mandi again yet?" Jerome grinned mischievously.

Daquan smirked. "Naw, man, she won't gimme no play."

"What you mean, no play? Nigguh, I taught you betta than that," Jerome smirked.

The guard appeared behind Jerome, announcing the end of the visit by his presence. Daquan eyed the officer hard, but he avoided eye contact. Jerome saw it in Daquan's eyes and tried to lighten the mood. "It's almost over, lil' whody, ya heard me? Then we can let these muhfuckas have this bullshit."

"I got you, whody."

Jerome stood, saying, "And do me this. Read Psalms 35 in the Bible, aiight?"

Daquan stood, too. "I will," he said.

"Fo' sho'. We all need answers, baby," Jerome jeweled him, then made his way back to his cell.

15

Pepper came home a few days later, and Nut did it big for his return. He had Pepper picked up from the county jail in a cocaine-white stretch Benz limousine, the back of which Jerome was able to see from his cell as it pulled off. He took it as a final slap in the face, and more confirmation of his decision to make him bleed.

Inside the limousine were two bad-ass bisexual Creole chicks that wasted no time in welcoming Pepper back to the free world. Nut stayed back in the Calliope, but he went to meet Pepper at the suite he rented for him. He went alone, telling Rosco, Daquan, and the other Cutt Boyz that he didn't want nobody to see his brother until he was G'd up and at his best. That was just fine for Daquan, who didn't want to see the rat-ass nigguh anyway, at least not until it was time.

"Damn, lil' daddy hookin' Pepper up," Rosco exclaimed. He loved to see people coming home get their proper due after being drug through the white man's system.

"What you expect, whody?" one of the other Cutt Boyz replied. "That nigguh Pepper be a real G."

"Hell, yeah, you can't keep a good nigguh down," Red added.

Knowing what he knew, Daquan couldn't stomach any more talk of Pepper's G-status, so he quietly excused himself and went to his Caddy. He was riding around, checking his other spots, picking up money and re'ing nigguhs up, when he received a beep. It was from Vanessa's house, so he wasted no time stopping at the next available phone booth.

"I thought you said you'd be waitin' for me?" Vanessa teased over the phone.

"Your mama said you wasn't due home for a few mo' days," he replied in his defense.

Vanessa giggled, like, "I know, I'm just messin'. But, I'm home now," she signified.

"I'm on my way, lil' mama."

It took some convincing to get Vanessa's parents to let Daquan take her out for some ice cream, especially since she had just come home. Then, on top of that, he was driving what he claimed was "his cousin's car." But he had footed the whole hospital bill, something her parents would've taken years of debt to pay off, and he promised he'd have her home in an hour.

He took Vanessa to Baskin-Robbins on upscale Saint Charles Street, and they talked and laughed over banana splits. After that he took her to Audubon Park, where they walked and talked some more, until they got tired and rested on a grassy hill.

"What you thinkin' about?" she asked.

"Nothin', shorty."

They were both just laying on their backs, watching the clouds parade across the sun-hazy sky.

"The clouds look like they're moving so slow," Vanessa mused, "but when you look at their shadows on the ground, you see they're really movin' fast."

"Yeah . . . Like life, huh?" he responded.

"I guess so."

They lay quiet a few more minutes—then Vanessa turned to look at him and asked, "How's your friend? The other boy that got shot."

He continued looking at the clouds. "I ain't got no friends, lil' mama."

Daquan was thinking about what lay ahead. He had murder in his heart, but his eyes were watching God. Vanessa raised up on one elbow, propping it under her head, with her body facing him. "But I thought y'all were friends? What's his name, Nut? Don't y'all hang together?"

Daquan sat up, wrapping his arms around his knees. "You could hang wit' a muhfucka ere' day and still not know what he might do when the sun go down," he reasoned, pulling up blades of grass and tearing them into little pieces that he tossed into the wind.

Vanessa sat up next to him, leaning on her palm. "Did he do somethin' to you?"

"Naw."

"Well, what happened?" she persisted.

Daquan took a deep breath and sighed, because he liked Vanessa too much to get irritated by her. "I just . . . don't let nobody get too close to me, Nessa, that all," he said with a shrug.

"Well, what do you do when you wanna talk to somebody? Don't you ever feel like that?" she questioned, because her world was one of inclusiveness. Her family unit had beat the ghetto odds and stayed bonded. They even ate together on Sundays, from distant cousins to her mama's mama, so she didn't understand being alone.

Daquan looked at her and replied, "I got someone to talk to."

"Who?"

He paused, studying her expression. "You sure you wanna know?"

"I asked, didn't I?" she quipped in a playfully sassy manner.

"Come on, I'll show you."

DIANA WATSON.

Vanessa read the headstone, then looked at Daquan.

"My sister," he explained. "She died at birth before I was born." Daquan gazed upon the headstone as well. The flowers he had left there a few days earlier were still fresh.

"When I got somethin' on my mind, I just come sit out heah, and say what's on my mind," he told her, fiddling with his fingers and nugget ring. "Or like sometimes . . . I see her in my dreams."

"What does she look like?"

Daquan studied her to make sure there was no trace of mockery or ridicule in her question. Satisfied, he answered, "Like Mama-Daddy gumbo," he chuckled, and she did also. "Different features from both . . . like me, I guess. She look like me."

"Then she must be beautiful," Vanessa complimented with a soft smile.

"Yeah, I guess she is. Whenever I see her she be like the age she 'posed to be. Like twenty-two, if she was livin'," he ended sadly, and Vanessa took his hand.

"She *is* livin', Daquan. As long as *you* remember her, she'll always be livin' in your heart," Vanessa said, then looked at the tombstone. "When my grandmother died, I saw her in my dreams. She said, 'Vanessa, remember that I love you. But I have to go away now. Be good, and if you need me, I'll be there.' I woke up and my mama got a call later that day that she had passed. I was real young, like five, and I never told nobody," she confided, "until now."

Daquan's insides smiled with his lips. "So you don't think I'm corny or nothin'?" he asked. He had never told anyone about Diana, except Grandma Mama, because he thought people would think he was crazy.

Vanessa giggled.

"No, I don't think you're crazy . . . not for that, anyway," she laughed. "But if you ever need someone else to talk to, I'll be theah."

Their eyes lingered on one another for a moment, then

Daquan looked at his watch, saying, "Yo daddy gonna kill me, lil' mama. Let me take you home."

He walked her up on her porch, just as the Louisiana twilight spread across the sky. Inside, they could hear the TV and the sounds of family and laughter.

"You wanna come in?" Vanessa invited.

"Naw, Nessa, I gotta go to this party in a minute," he replied.

She nodded. "When you gonna call me?"

"In the mornin'."

"Promise?"

"Promise," he winked.

The moment was awkward for Daquan, not because he didn't know what to do, but he didn't know if he should. Vanessa saw it, so she leaned over and took the initiative. She kissed him, allowing his tongue to taste hers. For Daquan, it was like his first kiss, the kiss of innocence. He had kissed to convince, kissed to fuck, or kissed to be kissing, but never kissed someone because of what he felt inside.

They broke the kiss and Vanessa looked up at him through hooded eyes. "Good night, Daquan."

"Good night, lil' mama."

"I'll see you in school," she said with a smirk.

"Fo' sho'," he replied as he bopped back to the Caddy. "Fo' sho'."

Nut rented one of the biggest halls for Pepper's homecoming party—The Riverboat Hallelujah in the Seventeenth Ward, and everyone was there to celebrate. The Cutt Boyz outta the Calliope were doing it, so the streets came through to see how. Nut had DJ Gregory D to provide the bounce, and the party was crunk before Nut and Pepper even arrived. They were still in the stretch Benz, pulling up at the front door. Pepper got out, stunting in a cocaine-white tuxedo with tails, cane, and white derby. Around his neck was a bejeweled

Cutt Boyz medallion, and a Creole bisexual on each arm. Nut hopped out, still keeping it gully, dressed in a fatigue outfit with jewels everywhere and a big-butt chocolate bunny under his wing.

Inside, Mandi and Daquan played a booth, facing the front door, so they saw Pepper and Nut as soon as they came in. Everybody was showing Pepper love, and chicks was on his dick like he was a star for real.

Daquan pulled on his Camel, exhaling the smoke through his nose like a dragon. "Look at this muhfucka heah. Ain't no shame in his game, huh? Do his own man dirty, and still show his face," Daquan fumed.

Mandi followed every move Pepper made. "That's why you always keep your grass cut," she said, "so you can see the snakes."

Daquan knew sooner or later Pepper would want to see him, and he dreaded the moment. He managed to put it off for twenty minutes, mingling with chicks.

"Yo Dee! Nigguh, *there* you go!"

Daquan heard Pepper's voice call out to him. He turned around and saw Pepper approaching by himself. He made his way through the thick maze of people, then came right up and embraced Daquan with both arms. Daquan could imagine Pepper with a knife, stabbing him in the back, but he could also imagine the look of surprise on Pepper's face when Daquan's knife sank into his back first.

Pepper stepped back and admired Daquan. "Damn, you gettin' big as shit, whody. You damn near tall as me!" Pepper exclaimed, getting a kick outta his own comment.

Daquan fought his own rage down and proceeded to put on an Oscar-winning acting job. "How you, whody? Damn, it's good to see you!" Daquan cheesed. "You beat them peoples, huh?"

Pepper's eyes slightly flickered, something Daquan would

have never noticed had he not been expecting it. "Yeah, lil' Daddy, they fuckin' wit' a Choppa City Soldier, ya heard me?"

Daquan could taste the spit he wanted to release in the man's face. Pepper went on. "And believe me, whody, Jerome gonna beat it, too. Ain't shit they can do to him." Pepper squeezed his shoulder, looking at Daquan proudly. "Man, them Cutt Boyz is keepin' it hot, ya heard me? I'm proud of y'all nigguhs."

It was then that Daquan noticed the Cutt Boyz medallion around his neck. It was identical to his own and it made him sick to his stomach to see Pepper with it on. Pepper saw his staring and gloated.

"Nut had it waitin' when I got out—you know I'ma rep it fo' sho', 'cause I heard y'all doin' big things."

Daquan could almost hear the snake-like hiss in the S's of Pepper's words. He changed his expression, looked around like he was about to confide something, then leaned over. "Yeah, I needed to talk to you abut that. My connect got hit by them peoples, so we fucked up right now . . . But ahhh, I got somethin' we can do to get right."

Pepper looked at him greedily. "You know I got you, lil' Daddy."

"Okay, well, look . . . don't tell *nobody*, not even Nut. Not now. He too fuckin' hotheaded, and I need a soldier that can think, ya dig? So look," Daquan glanced at his watch, "be ready to bounce when I give you the signal. Me and you gon' take care of this heah, then slide back 'fore the party even over."

"I got you, whody," Pepper replied, shaking Daquan's hand. "Just gimme the word."

As the night went on, Daquan's heart rate increased in anticipation of what was going down. He wanted to make sure they could exit undetected, and hopefully Nut would be gone or too drunk to notice. Nut was almost there already, staggering around, wilding for the night. He smacked some N.O. East nigguh just because he could. Daquan even noticed Kimoko up in his face once or twice, Nut's hands all over her juicy ass. Her pregnancy was showing slightly, but her titties had swollen up and she was definitely looking good.

Daquan kept checking his watch—then, around 1:45, he felt the time was right. He slid up on Pepper with a car key in his palm then shook Pepper's hand, embracing him with the other arm. "It's the black Buick Regal out back. Check under the seat—it's a nina. I figure you ain't got no gun on you, do you?" Daquan whispered.

"Naw."

"You might need one, so I brought it for you," Daquan replied. He didn't want Pepper to be nervous or catch on because of how Daquan was going about things. If he gave him a gun, he figured he'd feel safe, even though Daquan was toting his own murder weapon.

Daquan watched Pepper make his way out of the hall, and he wasn't far behind. Once he got outside, he lit a Camel and surveyed the scenery. The spot was still packed. The few people outside were either on their way in, or coupling up and on their way out. Daquan stepped around the building, quickening his pace until he reached the Regal, and found Pepper in the passenger seat. He flicked his cigarette away as he got in, cranked the engine, then backed out.

"You got that?" Daquan quizzed.

Pepper held the black steel. "Right heah, whody. Where we goin'?"

Daquan checked the rearview. "Nigguh say he got four of them thangs fo' fifteen apiece, but he a buster, so we just gonna take 'em off his hands fo' sho'. Only thing is, ain't no need to kill 'im—that's why I ain't bring Nut. He don't understand shit like that."

Pepper nodded. "Who the nigguh is?"

"Nigguh from out Gentilly. Sleepy," Daquan lied, but used a real name.

"Punk-ass Sleepy? He come up like that theah?" Pepper asked in amazement. Daquan looked at him hard.

"You'd be surprised what muhfuckas out heah doin'."

They went to the Fourth Ward of N'awlins, the Warehouse and Factory District that was almost abandoned, and definitely deserted at two o'clock in the morning. Daquan killed the lights as he pulled between two buildings. Up ahead in the distance, they could see a car parked.

Daquan squinted through his cigarette smoke, the orange light of the tip illuminating the silhouette of his face. "You see anybody in that car?" Daquan questioned suspiciously.

Pepper leaned forward, the only sound being the movement of his body against the material of the seat. "I can't tell. Just pull up there."

Daquan squinted again. "Sleepy a scary muhfucka. Lemme see the gat."

Pepper handed him the nine. Daquan cocked it back—the sound of its interlocking chamber twanged metallically in the silence. "Come on. If shit ain't right, we Audi."

Both of them got out of the car and closed the doors quietly. Daquan took one more hit, thunked the cigarette to the pavement, and hissed, "Pepper, not only is you a fuckin' snitch, but you a dumb muhfucka."

Pepper froze in his tracks, then spun to face Daquan a few feet away.

"A *what*?!" Pepper's voice boomed.

Daquan raised the gun, holding it sideways, grinning. "Fuck, you think we wouldn't find out? Huh? You think you gonna rat on my family, then ride wit' me on a lick, nigguh? You must really take us for lames."

Pepper's heart pumped pure fear, realizing there was no way he could lie, so he begged. "Quan, please—"

The first shot cut his sentence short and blew a chunk of bone and flesh out of his kneecap. Pepper hollered, then fell to the ground in agony.

"Don't cry now, whody—let yo' mama do it for you when they find your bitch ass wit' yo' dick stuck in your mouth," Daquan growled, walking up to stand over him.

"Them . . . them people, man," Pepper groaned. "It wasn't my fault, I told Rome not to fuck wit' that nigguh, and he turned out to be a fed. Man, they was talkin' 'bout life, whody. What could I do?! They ain't give me no choice," Pepper tried to reason.

"Me neither," Daquan replied coldly, pumping two shots into his chest and three more in his face. The involuntary nerve reflexes were the only thing that kept Pepper's lifeless body jerking and twitching. Daquan bent down and snatched the Cutt Boyz chain off his neck then stuffed it in his pocket. He quickly went to the trunk and got out a canister of gasoline. After wiping down the door handles and steering wheel, Daquan doused the inside of the car, then the outsides, and laid a trail to Pepper's body, where he emptied the rest. He pulled out a book of matches, using one to light the book, then tossed it in the car's interior. It didn't take long before the car filled with flames that snaked their way along the concrete to Pepper's body, turning him into a human pyre.

He jogged over to the car in the distance—a whoo-ride Chevy Corsica—jumped in, and left Pepper's body to cremate in the fiery darkness.

Daquan walked into the bedroom to find Mandi sitting up in bed, reading *Dutch*.

She looked into his face as he walked over, taking Pepper's chain out of his pocket, then dropped it in her lap. No words were spoken as he lay down fully clothed, one arm over his eyes. Mandi put down the book, kissed him on the cheek, then snuggled under him with her head on his chest.

* * *

Sunny days, bright clothes, and big brass playing the melody of "This is for My Homies"—the second-line in Pepper's honor was even bigger than his coming home party. In the tradition of New Orleans funerals, the whole block was jampacked with family, friends, and foes alike, umbrellas and handkerchiefs swaying and skipping to tunes as the hearse carrying Pepper's body led the celebration.

Everywhere you looked, people wore "Pepper R.I.P." shirts with a picture of Pepper's face heat-pressed across everyone's chest, even children and toddlers. Daquan wasn't into the second line, but he participated anyway. It wasn't because of any anger he felt over what Pepper had done. That was gone, replaced by a feeling of shame. Especially after hugging Pepper's mama and seeing the pain in her eyes.

Nut's mind wasn't there, either. He moved mechanically with the procession, numb to his surroundings. When Daquan saw him, it was like a hard blow to the chest to see his friend's condition, a condition he had caused. He started to go over to him, but Kimoko was right there, wrapped around him, and she snuggled closer when she saw Daquan looking in their direction. Daquan moved on with the crowd, hoping it would all be over soon.

Moments later, Nut approached, a blank expression on his face. Daquan hugged him, but it seemed like he had a knife in Nut's back, and part of him wished Nut had plunged one in his. His guilt created an emotional distance that Nut could sense. Nut started to say something, when he noticed Mandi off in the crowd. He pulled back from Daquan with fire in his eyes. "Fuck that bitch doin' here? Fuck you bring her for?"

"Yo Nut," Daquan began slowly. "I know how you feel about ol' girl, but she just came to pay her respects, too," Daquan explained.

Nut fired right back, "Fuck her respect! That bitch don't

fuck wit' me, so get her the fuck away from me," Nut demanded.

"Aiight, whody, just chill. I'll do that," Daquan conceded.

"Yeah, you do that," Nut spat, still confused about the strangeness in their embrace. Daquan's guilty mind made him wonder if Nut's tone meant that he suspected something, even though it had nothing to do with accusations.

Daquan walked away, approaching Mandi, and told her, "We Audi. Nut don't want you here." He looked over at Nut, who was staring in their direction.

Mandi turned her face, putting on her shades, like, "That makes two of us. We need to handle something, anyway."

The two of them made their way to Mandi's BMW when Kimoko saw Daquan and yelled, "Daquan! Daquan, you hear me!"

He started to keep walking, but then he and Mandi stopped. Kimoko came up, belly protruding in front of her. "I don't give a fuck about that silly bitch, but you still the daddy of my baby and you better start actin' like it," she huffed. Her voice was raised enough to turn a few heads, so Daquan tried to bounce before it got ugly.

"Go 'head wit' that bullshit, Kimoko. Ain't nobody tryin' to heah no baby shit," he replied.

"Oh, you gonna heah it, nigguh, believe me—payback is a bitch," she promised.

Daquan couldn't take no female threatening him, so he lost his head and discreetly spat dead in her face. Kimoko was so shocked and felt so humiliated, all she could do was cry.

"Dig, bitch," Daquan sneered. "I don't give a fuck about you or that bastard in your belly. But keep runnin' yo' mouth and I *promise* you, the next line'll be for you!" He didn't speak loudly, but with cold calmness.

Daquan and Mandi got into her BMW and pulled off, leaving Kimoko wiping tears from her eyes and saliva from her face. Mandi glanced over at Daquan, sunk low with his seat back and eyes closed.

"Is it yours?"

"I don't know," Daquan admitted.

Mandi sighed hard. "Didn't I tell you to quit fu—"

Daquan opened his eyes and glared at Mandi, cutting her off. "You don't tell me shit, ya heard me? 'Cause that ain't none of your goddamn business," he hissed.

"What the hell you mean, it ain't my business?! You *make* it my business when you don't *handle your* business!" Mandi accused.

"I'll handle it," Daquan fumed. "I'll murder that stupid bitch and her goddamn baby."

As soon as he said it, he regretted it, just thinking about Diana. Mandi glanced over at him, then spoke calmly. "Look, Quan, I'm not trying to run your life. I'm just trying to keep you on point. A woman scorned is the most vindictive creature on earth. Just throw her a couple of dollars, make nice with her, and when the baby's born, you can see for sure," she suggested.

Daquan rubbed his hand over his face. "I hear you—yo, I'll take care of it."

"Okay . . . yo," Mandi giggled, mocking his speech pattern, trying to lighten the mood.

Daquan smiled, then quipped, "Besides, I'm sayin' . . . I gotta fuck somebody."

Mandi knew what he was getting at, so she replied, "Please, boy, all those little girls I see you with, blowing up your beeper. Like, what's her name? Oh yeah, *Vanessa*," she sang, making Daquan blush.

"Yeah, that's her name, but we just friends."

"Mm-hmm," Mandi hummed skeptically. "Tell me anything."

Daquan snickered, looking out the window. He noticed

they were in the Sixth Ward, near Canal Street. "Where we goin'?"

"Jorge's in town. He wants to see you," Mandi answered.

Daquan hadn't seen Jorge since those first five minutes in Houston. Jorge had started fronting him weight on consignment, but he just sent word to his distributor in Slidell to do so—he never came himself.

"What he wanna see me fo'?" Daquan wondered.

"That's what we goin' to find out."

Jorge was staying at the high-rise Hilton hotel overlooking the Mississippi and Riverwalk. His suite was almost on the top floor. Mandi and Daquan stepped off the elevator and approached his door. She knocked three times lightly in smooth succession, then moments later the door opened and a linebacker-sized Mexican with a ponytail filled it almost completely. He smiled politely, then stepped aside to allow them in.

Inside, the spacious suite spread out, with a bar in one direction and in the other a curved leather couch and ceiling-to-floor windows. On the couch was a gorgeous blond Mexican in a jean miniskirt that was too mini to be a skirt, and stiletto-heeled, snakeskin cowgirl boots. Her luscious thighs were crossed so high, Daquan figured there was no way she had panties on.

Jorge came out of the bedroom, dressed casually in a silk shirt and slacks, carrying two cigars. "*Hola*, Mandi, Daquan, *como estas*?" ("Hello Mandi, Daquan, how are you?")

"*Bien*," ("Good") Daquan replied proudly, because Mandi had been teaching him Spanish.

Jorge smiled. "I see Mandi's been working with you." He turned to Mandi and kissed her hand. "I wish I had a teacher so beautiful to teach me a few things, eh?"

Mandi blushed as Jorge added, "Have a seat."

When Daquan and Mandi sat, Jorge sat next to the blond chick, extending a cigar to Daquan, but he declined. Jorge looked at Pepper's picture on Daquan's T-shirt and chuckled. "He looks like somebody we know, no?"

Daquan glanced down at his shirt. "Yeah, I guess he does."

Jorge lit his cigar, then nonchalantly pulled the blond woman's crossed legs onto his lap and started caressing her boot. "In my country, snakeskin boots are very expensive. Very. But... these were cheap—do you know why?" he questioned, looking at Daquan.

"Why?"

"Because," he grinned, "I caught the snakes myself. Every ... last ... one of them. Then I skinned them." He chuckled as he puffed. "But I'm no, how you say, shoemaker. So I paid for that, but I supplied the material. I hate snakes, Daquan, like a mongoose. And you, my young friend, have proved that you feel the same way."

Daquan nodded.

Jorge looked at the big Mexican and instructed, "Pedro. *El foto.*" ("The photograph.")

Pedro walked over, pulling a picture out of his pocket, then handed it to Daquan. It was a picture of some black cat coming out of a barbershop.

"His name is Trell. He's from Baton Rouge. I've dealt with him several times, directly and indirectly, and everything has gone well... up until now," Jorge explained, smoking his cigar, pinky extended, studying Daquan's reactions.

Daquan gave the picture to Mandi, and looked at Jorge. "Okay." he said, but his tone asked, *What's that got to do with me?*

"I like you, Daquan. I think you can go far in this business if you choose. So... I'm giving you a choice," Jorge stated simply.

"To do what?"

"Solve a problem for me and expand yourself. Trell has become very disrespectful. He doesn't want to pay me, and when he does, it's always short. I've given him several chances, but . . ." Jorge shrugged. "You see, Daquan, I am a business-man, not a gangster, eh? This situation, I need a gangster, someone who understands this kind of situation, you follow?"

Daquan took the picture from Mandi and looked at it with a curious grin. "Yeah, I follow. This some kind of reward for killin' my man's brother, huh? If I woulda killed his mama, what would you give me then, a fuckin' gold watch?" Daquan quipped sarcastically.

Mandi moved to placate Daquan, but Jorge liked his blunt-ness, so he replied, "If his mother was a snake, then she would deserve the same fate. This is a business, amigo—there are no friends, no family, just business. That—" Jorge pointed to the picture of Pepper on his shirt, "is the price of doing business, and that—" he pointed to the picture of Trell, "is a business opportunity. Reward, yes, gift, no—but ultimately, the choice is yours."

Jorge sat back, puffing on his Cuban, and eyed Daquan cu-riously. Daquan handed the picture to Mandi, then replied, "I'll take care of it."

Jorge's face spread into a smile as he, Daquan, and Mandi stood up. "I knew you would, amigo, I knew you would. And when you do, we'll make it snow in Baton Rouge!" Jorge laughed, but Daquan only smirked.

"I know you did—that's why you called me."

With that, Daquan and Mandi exited the suite.

16

That next Sunday, Daquan found himself in church. Vanessa had invited him to spend the day with her and her family, and he gladly accepted. Daquan needed a break from the grind of the game, the treachery of the streets, and the burden on his shoulders. He needed peace, and he was determined to achieve it, if only for a day.

The reverend spoke about Psalm 35, and it was like an omen for Daquan, because that was the same chapter Jerome had told him to read—although he never got around to it.

"Plead my cause, O Lord, with them that strive with me, fight against them that fight against me . . ." the reverend's voice boomed, speaking of the enemies, but it made Daquan wonder, what if you're your own worst enemy? Because that's how he felt. Listening to the sermon made him think of Jerome, awaiting trial for being his own worst enemy. He thought of Nut, bereaved over the loss of his brother, lashing out and wilding every chance he got. Daquan looked around at all the people in church, listening, nodding in agreement, and he wondered how many of them faced death and destruction every day, because those were the ones who really needed salvation, but he saw none of *those* faces in attendance.

After the service, they went to Vanessa's house to have Sunday dinner and he met her whole family. Even though she was an only child, her family was close, so cousins were almost brothers and sisters. It was like a family reunion, with all the laughter and food.

After they ate, he and Vanessa went outside to sit on the porch swing and enjoy the evening breeze. Daquan was as full as a tick, and he had to fight his after-dinner cigarette jones because too many people were coming in and out.

"Y'all eat like that ere' Sunday?" Daquan inquired.

"Almost every Sunday. Sometimes we all go out," she replied. "What does your family do?"

"Do?"

Mo' money, mo' murder, he thought guiltily, but he answered, "My Grandma Mama cook all the time, but never on Sunday."

"Oh," was all Vanessa said, and they both got quiet.

"I like your family, though. They cool," Daquan complimented.

Vanessa nodded, but he could tell she had something on her mind.

"You okay?" he probed.

Vanessa looked at him a moment before she replied, "I—heard about your friend's brother. They were talking about it in school, and some kids even had T-shirts. They said it happened after that party you told me about . . ." Her voice trailed off, like she was reluctant, but finally she asked, "Is everything okay?"

He glanced at her, "Like what?"

"I mean," she sighed, "Daquan, everybody in school be talkin' about the Cutt Boyz and how 'bout it they are, and I know you're one of 'em. So if somebody killed your friend . . ."

Daquan gave her a confident smile. "What, you think we're a gang or somethin'? It ain't like that, lil' mama. Whatever happened to Pepper, we don't know, so we can't do nothin' if we don't know who did it," he lied.

"I know what you do, Daquan. I may not be from the Calliope, but I can see. Maybe even stuff you don't. And I just want you to be safe, because I really like you," she expressed, telling him what had been on her heart for so long.

Daquan leaned over and kissed her gently. "I 'preciate that, Nessa. 'Cause you . . . I kinda dig you, too."

"Just kinda?" she teased.

Daquan snickered. "Naw boo, I dig you. I dig you a lot."

"And I dig you, too," she replied, mocking his Calliope twang.

Just then Mandi pulled up in the BMW and blew the horn. Daquan and Vanessa stood reluctantly and descended the steps holding hands. "I'ma call you later, okay?" Daquan checked.

"Alright," she said, then gave him a quick peck on the lips, glancing over her shoulder to make sure nobody saw them.

Daquan strolled to the car, loosening his tie and already going in his pocket for a cigarette. It was lit by the time he closed the door.

"Ain't that cute. *Quan got a kiss*," Mandi sang sarcastically.

Daquan blew out the smoke and lowered the window as she pulled off. "You jealous?"

Mandi didn't reply, but got right down to business: "The chick I sent up to Baton Rouge gave me the info on Trell. He doesn't trick or hang out anywhere in particular, but he is married with a little boy, and his wife loves to spend his money."

Daquan smoked as he listened.

"He's got a solid team, so it'll be hard to go at him. I figure the best way to handle it is snatch up his wife and son, because that's his only weakness," Mandi explained.

Daquan was looking out the window and didn't respond. Mandi glanced over at him and quizzed, "Are you listening, or is your mind elsewhere?"

Daquan looked over at Mandi with an annoyed look on his face. "Man, I'm thinking, aiight? Can't I think without talkin' or somethin'?"

"Well, say something. I'm talking about some serious shit and—"

"And I heard you, yo. Fuck is you trippin' fo'?"

"No, *you* trippin'," she retorted.

His beeper signaled the end of round one. He looked at the display and saw it was Rosco's code. "Swing by the CP3. That's Rosco."

Mandi didn't say anything, she just made the necessary turns to head in that direction. When they got to the spot, Rosco and the rest of the Cutt Boyz were standing around Rosco's Blazer. Daquan got out and greeted everybody, then turned to Rosco and said, "What up, big homey?"

"Man, it's Nut. Whody on some shit, fo' real," Rosco said, exasperated. "You gotta talk to him."

"Where he at?"

"Inside."

When Daquan went in, the place was empty, which was unusual for their dope spot. It was a mess, as always, but when he saw Nut, he was in worse shape than the apartment. The front of his pants and shirt were covered in blood, and he was pacing back and forth, smoking a cigarette. When he saw Daquan, he stopped.

"What up, whody? How you?"

Daquan looked from Rosco to Nut, like, "What the fuck happened to you?"

"How you know? Rosco called you? Them nigguhs trippin'," Nut replied, chuckling. "Everything aiight now."

Daquan saw he wasn't getting any answers from Nut, so he turned to Rosco. "What happened, Rosco?"

"This muhfucka kilt Ol' School!" Rosco exclaimed, still in a state of shock himself.

"*What*?!" Daquan barked, snapping his head around to look at Nut.

"Naw, tell him everythin' if you gonna tell the shit!" Nut demanded.

Daquan couldn't believe his ears. Ol' School was an old coon in the Calliope, born and raised. He used to be a major player in the '70s and early '80s, but he got that monkey and started shootin' "That Shit" in his bloodstream. Still, everybody loved Ol' School because he was always willing to help out. The hustlers respected him because he knew how to get money, which was why Daquan had him running the spot.

Now he was dead, bludgeoned to death with a lead pipe over a hundred dollars.

"Nigguh *been* owing me, whody," Nut huffed. "Then he had the nerve to pop shit! To *me*," Nut emphasized, hitting his blood-covered chest. "Fuck that. Nigguhs fuck up, they gonna feel it. Whoever want it can get it!" Nut fumed, pacing again.

"Where the body?" Daquan asked Rosco.

"We got rid of it," Rosco replied.

Daquan nodded, then stated, "Shut it down for a coupla days."

Rosco understood, but Nut growled, "Fuck, you mean, shut it down? I said shit is straight."

Daquan approached him. "Ain't shit straight, Nut. This place gonna be hot behind this shit, so we shuttin' down," he repeated. "Besides, me and you gotta handle somethin' in Baton Rouge."

"Yeah, like what?"

"I'ma holla," Daquan let him know, heading for the door. "Until then, shut it down, ya heard me?"

Nut sucked his teeth and left the room, while Rosco just shook his head at the whole thing.

Mandi and Daquan didn't speak all the way home, and once they got there, she went straight to the shower, while Daquan jumped on the phone. He laid back on the bed in his Sunday suit, listening to the phone ring, until he heard Vanessa's sweet voice on the other end, like a breath of fresh air.

"Hello? . . . Can I speak to you?" he charmed. "Was you sleep? . . . Naw, I just got in," he told her.

Daquan reached for the remote and clicked on the TV. He flipped through a few channels, then stopped on BET's *Video Vibrations*. En Vogue was singing about "Giving Him Something He Can Feel."

"Yeah, yo, it was fun . . . next Sunday? Let me . . . of course I wanna come, but you know how it is, lil' mama."

Mandi came out of the bathroom wearing a purple terry cloth robe. Daquan didn't notice her rolling her eyes when he said, "Yeah, I was thinkin' 'bout you, too."

"Daquan, I need to use the phone," Mandi finally said.

"In a minute," he said without even looking at her.

Mandi turned her back, going in her drawer and pulling out a pair of yellow panties. She took off her robe and tossed it on the chair, going about the room totally naked. Daquan's eyes widened, seeing her apple-shaped ass jiggling as she went over to the dresser and grabbed the lotion.

"Huh? Say that again, Nes . . ." He had to ask, because Mandi's luscious shape had him distracted.

Mandi stood in front of the mirror, applying lotion to her arms and face, then her neck and shoulders. Her hands massaged her firm breasts, and Daquan got as hard as a rock just watching her lotion herself all over. Hard enough to yawn and say, "Damn, lil' mama, I done laid heah and got sleepy as hell. Yeah, I'll be—" His sentence was cut short as Mandi bent all the way over to put lotion on her calves and feet.

"Huh? Yeah, school. Fo' sho' . . . okay . . . you, too." He hung up just as Mandi slid on her panties and put a camisole over her bare breasts. Daquan wanted to make his move, because he knew her body was calling, but when she turned around and he saw the ice grill she wore, the mixed message bewildered his young hormones. Mandi slipped into bed with her back to him and got comfortable.

"I thought you had to use the phone," he questioned.

"You took too long," she replied flatly.

Daquan started to say something, but decided against it and went to get something to eat.

Blackness . . .

He was familiar with the darkness, but this time it was different. It felt strange to him, because she was usually waiting for him, and her light brightened the void. Now there was no light, only cold darkness. He couldn't even feel her presence, so he called out, "Diana! Diana, where are you?"

But there was no answer.

"Diana!" he repeated.

Daquan moved around, but everything was so black it was like his eyes were closed, even though he could feel them wide open. "Why won't you answer me, Diana? I know you can hear me." He tried to feel her presence, but it wasn't there.

"Are you mad at me? Did I do something wrong? *Speak to me*!" he cried out, desperate to be heard.

"What do you want me to do, huh? What? What can I do, Diana, because I can't go back! Black . . . Pepper . . . Ol' School . . . Vanessa . . . Didn't you tell me you'd never leave me?" His guilty conscience turned to anger.

"You *promised* me, now you actin' like everybody else. You gonna just turn your back on me? Okay . . . *Leave*, then, go away. Go back to wherever, and stay wherever the heck you are! I don't need you, you hear me, Diana? I don't need you, yo . . . I don't need nobody . . . no fuckin' body," he was mumbling now, sliding to the hard surface and putting his head on his arms.

"I don't need nobody."

Baton Rouge, Louisiana, is basically a college town about forty-five minutes from New Orleans. The state capital is

proud home of timber forests, ocean fronts, swamplands for al-
ligators, the LSU Tigers, and the Southern University Jaguars.

But Daquan wasn't there to see the sights; he was there to
put in work. He and Nut rode into town in a gray work van
and went straight to the Days Inn motel, where Mandi's chick
Donna was staying. Daquan pulled up and blew the horn, and
a few minutes later, Donna came out. Daquan recognized her
as the redheaded white girl from the dyke spot he supplied
through Mandi.

Donna walked around to the passenger side and opened the
door, while Nut climbed in back to the empty cargo space of
the van.

"What's up, Daquan?" Donna greeted, then looked over
her shoulder at Nut. "And friend."

"That's my man, Nut. Nut, this Donna."

Nut nodded, sitting on the floor as Daquan left the motel.

"Did Mandi tell you what's up?" Donna inquired.

"She left that for you," Daquan lied, wanting to hear what
Donna had to say, just to make sure everything checked out.

"Okay, well, Trell's wife doesn't work, she just spends his
money. They have a three-year-old son, who she usually takes
everywhere she goes." Donna checked her watch. "Her favorite spot is the mall. The whole time I watched her, she hit
the mall at least three times a week. Of all the spots, the mall
is the best place to snatch her up."

"The *mall*?" Nut echoed from the back. "Wit' all them people around? Why can't we just snatch her from the crib?"

"They live in a gated community. Getting in and out is like
Fort Knox," Donna explained, then added, "Everywhere else,
her face is familiar. The gym, the grocery store, the jeweler. At
the mall, she is just another face in the crowd. I figure we flatten her tire, and wait till she comes out. With the van parked
behind her, and her car in front of her, the few seconds it'll

take to get her in the van won't be a problem," she surmised, pulling out a Newport and flicking her lighter to the tip.

Daquan glanced over at her with a smirk. "You sound like you done did this befo'?"

Donna winked at him with a smile.

"It's only 11:30. She doesn't leave the house until one, usually. You guys hungry? I am. Let's go get something to eat."

Daquan and Nut had already eaten, but they went to Burger King to kill time. While Donna ate, Daquan's beeper went off. He saw it was Vanessa's code, so he went to the phone booth and called her.

"What's up, lil' mama?" he said when she answered.

"School," Vanessa remarked, talking from the school pay phone. "And why ain't you here?"

Daquan dug the way Vanessa tried to keep him in line—it showed she cared. But at the moment he was into something much deeper than science class.

"I had to take care of something, Nessa. I might be gone a few days. I'll call you when I get back, okay?"

He didn't hear anything.

"Vanessa."

"Just . . . be careful, okay?" she asked, with sincere concern in her voice.

"I will. See you later," he replied, then hung up and got back in the van.

"It's about twenty minutes to his crib. Down the road is a convenience store. We'll wait there because she has to pass that way to come to town. You ready?" Donna inquired.

Daquan started the engine, still thinking about Vanessa's words.

They drove out into the more rural section of Baton Rouge, where the money lived. They passed golf courses and expensive car dealerships as they drove to the convenience store and parked, facing the street.

Most of the faces that drove past were white, so Daquan was glad to have a white face in the van too. He slouched slightly to make himself less conspicuous. Looking at Donna, he thought of Mandi and smiled to himself. She knew how to handle her business down to the smallest detail. He could see why Jerome had her on the team. His mind went back to a few nights before, and the way she had acted. Getting naked in front of him, getting an attitude when he was on the phone with Vanessa. He knew Mandi was catching feelings, but the way she kept him off balance with her hot and cold spells threw him off. He felt like . . .

"Here she comes."

His thoughts were cut short by Donna's words. Daquan sat up quickly, like, "Where?"

Donna pointed with a hint of urgency in her tone.

"Candy-apple red Benz coupe."

She had just passed the store, but Daquan had time because her car got held up at the light. Daquan eased the van into traffic a good three cars back. He could see her head slightly above the headrest.

"Damn, you go, girl," Donna remarked, adding, "That's a new car, too. That's why she caught me off guard."

"Yeah? Well that nigguh betta still have the receipt fo' that shit, 'cause I want the Benz money too," Nut said in a menacing tone.

The light greened, and traffic pulled off. Daquan kept a safe distance in following her. Her first stop was McDonald's, where she got a Happy Meal for her son. Next, she went to someone's house and stayed inside almost a whole hour.

"What? She fuckin' on the nigguh or sumthin'?" Nut asked, getting impatient.

"Naw, this her mama's house."

When she came out, Daquan noticed that she was white. He hadn't seen her clearly up until then. The most he had

seen was her arm at the drive-through window, so he just figured she was high yellow. But now he could clearly see her
features. She had a dark, tanned complexion, almost olive-
toned, with chestnut brown hair. She was wearing a loose-
fitting jogging suit, so he couldn't see her proportions, but he
could tell she was short.

"That nigguh married to a white bitch?" Nut asked, surprised.

"What's wrong with that?" Donna wanted to know, although her tone didn't sound offended.

"Man, all these bad-ass black chicks out heah—*hell*, no.
Man, get this nigguh!" Nut demanded, irked by the fact that
Trell's wife was white.

They made several more stops, two of which gave them a
chance to grab her had they been in a better position. Then
she finally went to the mall. By now, the mall was sufficiently
crowded that she had to park near the back of the enormous
lot. She got out, holding her son's hand, but he was walking
too slow, so she scooped him up in her arms. Donna reclined
her seat, making Daquan look at her. She saw the question
mark in his eyes, so she answered. "Might as well relax. She
gonna be a while."

Nut sucked his teeth, pulling out his gun. "Fuck that, Dee.
Pull up beside her and I'ma snatch her ass in heah."

Daquan was ready to do it, but she was already too close to
the mall entrance. "Donna, go flatten her tire."

She nodded and got out. Daquan checked his watch and
saw that it was nearly four o'clock. They had been waiting all
day, and he was getting restless like Nut. He lit a cigarette to
calm his nerves while he watched Donna walk up on the
Benz, crouch down beside it momentarily, only to reappear
folding a switchblade and sticking it in the back pocket of her
shorts. Daquan saw right then how simple it was to get got.
Trell's wife was walking around the mall, not a care in the
world, unaware of what was about to happen to her. It made

him think about his own life, and how this could be Vanessa if she became a part of his world. Daquan promised himself that he'd protect her, but deep down he knew he couldn't. No one was safe, because death was always right around the corner. Shit like this was the price for loving a nigguh in the game.

The price of doing business, he remembered Jorge telling him.

Forty minutes later, Donna spotted her coming out of the mall. "Damn, I guess she done already bought one of every-thing in there."

Daquan took a deep breath and glanced over his shoulder at Nut. "You ready?"

"Muhfucka, I *been* ready," Nut retorted, opening the sliding door, then holding it shut by the lever.

Daquan pulled the van out of the parking space and went around one row of cars to reach the one Trell's wife was parked on. She was already looking at the tire, holding her son. As they pulled up, she kicked it in frustration. Daquan pulled up beside her, startling her slightly, but when Donna leaned her smiling white face out the window, she smiled back weakly. "Are you okay? I see you have a flat."

Trell's wife pushed a lock of hair out of her face and replied, "Fuckin' tire. I just *bought* the fuckin' car, too!"

Donna got out, closing the door. "I know how it is. A lot of times, when cars sit in the lot for a while, the tires deflate. Do you have a spare?"

Trell's wife glanced in Daquan's young face. "I would really appreciate it."

"Pop the trunk."

Trell's wife chirped the alarm, then went around the trunk, setting her bags by the driver's door. She carried her son around to the rear of the car, then put him down. Her back was inches from the van's door, so Nut wasted no time in sliding it open. The sound behind her made Trell's wife quickly look around, but she was powerless to stop Nut. He yoked her up with his forearm around her throat, choking off her scream.

Her son yelled, but Donna snatched him up by his arm and quickly hopped in the back of the van, sliding the door shut behind her.

"Go," Donna huffed to Daquan.

He looked around, nervously trying to see if any attention was on them while he pulled off calmly. The whole ordeal seemed to him to take longer than actually it did, but as he left the mall parking lot, he saw no one looking in their direction.

"What's your name?" Donna asked her intently.

Trell's wife's eyes were wide with fear. "Pa-Pamela, Pamela Brooks. Please don't kill me. Please. I'll . . ."

Donna shushed her, caressing her face. "Okay Pam, listen real good. You stay calm . . . cool. We're going somewhere. When we get there, and we get you out, you be just that—cool, ya hear? Act up and we'll kill you and your son, understand?"

Pam nodded briskly, cradling her sobbing child.

Donna directed Daquan to a modest apartment complex, where they drove around the rear to one of the last apartments. Daquan made sure the coast was clear. He tucked the .38 in his waist, while Donna slid the door back, reminding Pam, "Remember, nice . . . and easy, and you'll live."

"O-Ok-Okay," Pam stuttered.

Nut got out with his arm around Pam's neck like they were a couple, but his pistol in her ribs like the hostage she was. Donna carried the boy and Daquan brought up the rear, looking from apartment window to apartment window. Donna opened the door, to everyone's relief, and they all went in.

Inside, the apartment was totally empty. The only thing in the room was a phone sitting in the middle of the floor. Donna went in the hall closet and pulled out a duffel bag, then threw it to Daquan.

"There's duct tape, handcuffs, and a few other things in there. And I made sure you had something to eat in the kitchen, okay? You straight?" Donna asked.

Daquan looked at Pam and her son sitting on the floor, while Nut stood over them with his gun pointed at them.

"Yeah, we got it."

"I'll tell Mandi," Donna replied, then left without another word. Daquan looked out the window and saw Donna get in an old Chevy Nova and pull off. He turned back to Nut and said, "Cuff 'em."

Nut dug in the duffel, extracting a pair of handcuffs and the duct tape. "Put your hands behind your back," Nut ordered Pam, and she quickly complied. Daquan squatted down to be at her eye level and spoke calmly but firmly. "Dig, lil' mama, this heah ain't about you, it's about Trell, so don't make you and your baby theah no problem for us, ya dig?"

"I-I understand," Pam replied nervously, but slightly relieved to at least know what this was all about.

"Now we gonna call yo' man and you gonna introduce the situation. Make him understand this heah ain't no game, and we'll handle the rest, ya got me?" Daquan asked, reaching for the phone.

"Yes, yes. I'll cooperate," she spoke quickly. "We won't be a problem."

"Okay, what's the number to where he at?"

She gave Daquan the number. He let it ring five times before the answering machine came on. He snickered, "You wanna leave a message? He ain't home."

"His car phone, call his car phone," Pam suggested.

She gave him that number, too, scared just thinking what would happen to her if they couldn't reach him. Trell answered on the second ring.

"Yeah."

Daquan held the phone in front of her face, and Pam cried, "Trell, please! If you don't do what they say they're going to *kill* me and Mikey!"

Daquan put the phone to his ear in time to hear Trell respond. "Pam! *Pam*! What's happenin'?! Do what *who* say?!"

"Me, nigguh, do what *I* say," Daquan growled into the phone.

"Who dis? Muhfucka, do you know who I am?! I'll . . ." Trell began to threaten, but Daquan cut him off, and said, "I know exactly who you is, nigguh. A muhfucka wit' a problem. Listen."

Without warning, Daquan smacked the shit out of Pam and let Trell hear her painful cries. "You hear that, huh? You still wanna talk or is you listenin'?"

Trell's heart was twisted with agony. "I'm listenin', I'm listenin'," he replied, humility filling his voice.

"Aiight, that's better. You know the drill, lil' Daddy—you got what we want, we got what you need, so it's on you if we reach some type of understanding, heard me?" Daquan stood up and stretched his legs.

"What . . . what you want?"

"Ten of them thangs and a hundred large, and don't say you ain't got it, 'cause if you do . . ." He nodded to Nut, and he smacked little Mikey to make him holler, "Daddy, Daddy, they're hurting me!"

Trell's eyes were so filled with tears he had to pull his Jag over to the side of the street. "Please, man, don't hurt my family. I'll give you that, I will. I got it and I can put my hands on it right away. Just tell me what to do."

Daquan smiled because this was easier than he thought it would be.

"Put yo' hands on it, lil' daddy, and I'll call you back in fifteen minutes," Daquan instructed him, then hung up and looked at Pam. "My bad, but your husband wanted to play tough, so I had to break his bitch ass down."

Fifteen minutes later, Daquan called back and quipped, "You ain't at the police station, is you, nigguh? You ain't like that, is you?"

"Naw, man, no police. Just tell me what to do with this,"

Trell begged, and the strain in his voice let Daquan know he was serious.

"You ever been to the N.O.?"

"Yeah."

"Then go. I'll give you time to get theah," Daquan replied, then hung up again.

Nut was sitting on the floor staring at Pam.

"Trell must really love you, shorty, 'cause he carryin' it real good so far," he told her, and she breathed in relief, praying it would all be over soon. Daquan checked his watch, then looked at Nut. "Watch them, whody, I gotta piss."

Daquan walked down the hall until he found the bathroom, then took him a piss. He washed his hands, splashing some water in his face. Ten kilos of heroin and a hundred thousand dollars, Daquan thought to himself. The job was too easy. He thought about all the hustlers and ballers with wives and kids, even mamas and grandmas, he could easily get at, and he thought about saying fuck the dope game and just snatching muhfuckas up for a living. He wouldn't have to worry about feds and fiends. Just take the dope and distribute it. Jorge had turned him onto a new hustle, without his even knowing it.

Daquan went back up front and his eyes widened to find Pam on her knees furiously sucking Nut's dick with the gun to her head.

"Nigguh, what the fuck is you doin'?" Daquan snapped.

Nut just laughed. "Shit, she said she'll do *anything*, whody. Fuck it, we got time to kill." Nut put his other hand on her head and pumped her bob harder, making Pam gag on his dick. Daquan snatched up little Mikey off the floor and carried him in the back. Nut was starting to get on some real bullshit, but Daquan felt like he could only blame himself, because he had started him on this path in the first place. He sat Mikey down on the floor, then ran his hands over his face in an attempt to clear his head. When he took them down, he was a little surprised to see Mikey staring at him through narrowed eyes, his little fists clenched.

"I'm not scared of you," Mikey stated with childlike firmness. "Why are you doing this to us?"

Daquan looked into his little eyes and recognized that look of hate, just like he had when he was a little boy. "It's your daddy, lil' man, not you."

"My Daddy's gonna kill you," Mikey replied. He obviously loved his father very much and believed that he could do anything.

Daquan sat on the floor. "Yeah, I'm sure he would if he could."

In the background, Daquan could hear the sounds of Pam's moans and Nut's grunts. From the sound of things, he couldn't tell it was being done at gunpoint.

"When I get big, I'ma kill you," Mikey vowed.

Daquan smiled. "Yeah, maybe you will, lil' Mikey—ere'body gotta die sometime."

Lil' Mikey stood trembling, unable to hold back the tears any longer. "I *hate* you! Why don't you leave us alone?" he sobbed, wiping his eyes with the back of his little fist.

Daquan wanted to hug the little dude, but he knew it would do no good. All he could say was, "I'm sure you do, Mikey. I'm sure you do."

When the moaning and heavy breathing stopped, Daquan led Mikey back to the living room. Pam was sitting Indian-style with just her shirt on, while Nut pulled up his pants. Mikey ran over to his mommy and hugged her neck. She lifted her cuffed hands to his head, her teary face streaked with mascara.

"Your turn, whody," Nut smirked.

"Naw, whody, I'm only here for one thing, yo," Daquan responded, picking up the phone and checking his watch. The phone didn't even ring one full time before Trell answered. "I'm in New Orleans."

"Good. Now, go to the Third Ward, out in the Magnolia. Got me?" Daquan checked.

"Okay . . . let me speak to my wife," Trell requested.

"When you get to the 'Nolia," Daquan told him, then hung up.

"Can—Can I go to the bathroom?" Pam asked timidly.

"I'll take you," Nut told her, putting his hand under her armpit and jerking her up. Mikey tried to follow, but Daquan stopped him.

The sun had set when Daquan talked to Trell again. "You in the 'Nolia? Okay, drive all the way to the back. You'll see a dumpster. Put the package in there—once we make sure it's what it's supposed to be, I'll tell you where to go to get yo' peoples."

"You said I could speak to Pam," Trell reminded him.

"Talk fast," Daquan warned him, then held the phone to her ear. Whatever he said made her cry and reply, "Okay . . . okay . . . I love you, too."

Daquan hung the phone up. He knew if everything went as planned, that would be the last time she ever spoke to Trell again. Ten minutes later, his beeper went off. It was Rosco's code, the signal that everything was everything. Daquan showed Nut the code, and they both smiled. He turned to Pam and assured her, "It's all gravy now lil' mama. Yo' man came through on his end—now it's time to come with ours."

Her face brightened slightly and she hugged Mikey tightly. She thought he meant he was letting her go, but that would only be after he led Trell into the death trap that was waiting for him. Daquan picked up the phone again and dialed Trell one last time.

"Okay, Trell, you did your part. Now I'ma do mine. Go to the other end of the 'Nolia. Look for a blue van, and we done."

Trell breathed with relief, thinking his wife and child would be inside. Once they were safe at home, he planned on bringing it to them 'Nolia nigguhs like they had never seen before.

But he wouldn't get that chance.

Rosco and the rest of the Cutt Boyz were waiting in the blue van at the other end, equipped with Choppas, AKs, and Tec Nines. Once Trell stopped, he would never start again. Fifteen minutes later, when Rosco beeped him with nine zeroes, Daquan knew it was over. He showed it to Nut, who smiled and looked at Pam.

Daquan started to tell her she was free, that he was letting her and the boy go. He opened his mouth to say it was over, but Nut didn't give him a chance. He swiftly raised the gun and let off three shots in rapid succession, two in Pam's head and one in Mikey's chest, blowing his little body halfway across the room.

Daquan was speechless and enraged. He shoved Nut hard enough to knock him on his ass. "It was *over*! It was over! We was 'posed to let her go, you stupid muhfucka!"

"She saw our faces," Nut spat like a maniacal Tupac in *Juice*.

Daquan paced with his hands over his eyes, shaking his head. "What the fuck is wrong wit' you, nigguh? Huh?"

His attention was distracted by a small, weak voice, a voice that belonged to Mikey. "Mommy . . . Mommy, he-help me," he begged, a gaping hole in the right side of his chest.

Both Nut and Daquan looked at the boy, amazed that he was still alive.

"Mm—Mommy—"

There was no way Daquan was taking him to the hospital, even if he knew where it was at. And he couldn't leave him there to suffer for God knows how long. There was only one thing to do. Nut looked at him dead in the eyes. "Now what, whody?"

Daquan looked at his crazed partner and saw the same answer in his eyes. Daquan turned his back and walked down the hall to wipe the prints off anything he had touched. The echo of the single shot removed any desire to do this for a living. He promised himself that there was no way he was ever going to do this again.

17

Daquan sent Rosco and the rest of the Cutt Boyz down to Baton Rouge to set up shop. They brought the heat to the nigguhs who caught feelings over Trell's murder, and spread love to the nigguhs that just wanted to get money. Jorge kept his word, and supplied Daquan with all the dope he needed to cover his spots in the N.O. and Baton Rouge. Money was coming in fast, too fast, fast enough for Mandi and Daquan to have to yawn over money counters. Daquan was definitely on the come-up, but he tried to balance it out with the time he spent with Vanessa. School saw less and less of him, until they wrote him off as just another lost ghetto child, but Vanessa kept him not only grounded, but hopeful that tomorrow could be a better day. He was too young to be facing such grown problems, and the game was taking its toll on him.

By the time the ball dropped in '93, Daquan was at a crossroads.

"Daquan," Mandi called out, as she knocked softly on the bathroom door.

"Yeah," he answered, soaking in a bath full of bubbles.

"Can I come in?"

He found the question strange because of the way things had been between them lately. After catching attitudes with

him over petty shit and prancing naked in front of him, her demeanor had iced over and she went back to a business-type relationship, like when they first met. She had stopped letting
him in when she showered, even going so far as to make him
move back into the guest room, which he redecorated to his
own taste. Her request really caught him off guard.

"Yeah, yo, come on," he replied.

Mandi entered the bathroom wearing a stylish black camel-
hair turtleneck that was oversized enough to hang past her ass
and conceal her tight stretch stirrup pants. Her brown leather
boots came up to her knees, which she crossed right over left
as she sat on the edge of the tub.

"What you gonna do tonight?" she asked. Since it was New
Year's Eve, Mandi figured he had plans.

Daquan shrugged. "I don't know. Nessa mama drug her
down to Mississippi to see they great-aunt or some shit, and
Nut an' 'em probably goin' to Club Whispers like they always
fuckin' do, so . . ."

She cut him off. "Good. You can drop the ball with me tonight." Then she stood up, like it was decided, looking in the
mirror and messing with her hair.

"And do what?" Daquan wanted to know.

She glanced over her shoulder at him. "You say that like it's
a problem?"

"No, girl, I'm just . . . curious," Daquan replied, trying to
figure out this mystery he called Mandi.

She turned around, crossing her arms, and leaned on the
sink. "I just figure, since we're always riding and running, we
could just go somewhere and relax. Have dinner or something.
New Year's doesn't always have to be a wild party, does it?"

"Naw."

"So," she smirked, "you 'bout it?"

Daquan chuckled, sinking neck-deep into the bubbles.
"I'm 'bout it, 'bout it."

Mandi walked out, leaving Daquan to finish bathing.

Daquan knew hanging with Mandi meant slacks and gators, so around eight he began getting dressed to impress. He threw on a pair of navy blue Ralph Lauren pleated dress slacks, a multicolored, hand-knitted Coogi sweater, and a pair of soft-bottom navy blue alligator shoes that were tailor-made in the Clarks style of cut. He wore a modest Movado watch and only one ring, which was on his right pinky. Daquan looked like he was twenty-five, not almost fifteen. It wasn't only the fancy clothes; the lifestyle had aged him a year for every day. He stepped out of his guest room and had to do a double take when he saw Mandi. She always looked her best regardless of what she wore, but he had never seen her quite like this.

Mandi had on a black backless silk dress, spaghetti laced around her neck from the front. It fit her just right, not hoochie tight or nun loose—it hugged her curves like a passionate lover. The slit up the side ran mid-thigh, showing off her smooth bronze skin, and her black sequined open-toe pumps accentuated her perfectly manicured nails. She wore her hair in a bun and diamond earrings that hung like miniature chandeliers swinging gently above her shoulders. When she saw him staring, she spun around, like, "What do you think?"

"Naw, it's what I'm thinking about," Daquan replied, dead ass.

Mandi giggled and grabbed her keys. "Come on . . . with your mannish self!"

They went to the world-famous Razzoo's Jazz Club in the French Quarter, sipping off the same drinks because Daquan was too young to order his own. After that, they went for a stroll down the Riverwalk and enjoyed mango daiquiris while mingling with the pre-midnight crowd. By ten, they were tipsy and hungry, so they went to Ralph & Kacoo's to eat.

They were seated in a booth near the rear, and Mandi ordered them stuffed bell peppers and a bottle of champagne. By the time the food came, they were halfway through the champagne, so Mandi ordered another bottle.

"So, are you enjoying yourself?" she asked, taking a bite of her peppers.

"Yeah, I am. I could get used to this type of shit," Daquan commented, looking around.

"What?" Mandi gasped sarcastically. "Even without loud, booming music and hoochies?"

He chuckled, "Well . . . maybe sometimes."

Mandi laughed. "I guess it's true—you can't take the 'hood out of the man."

"Fo' sho'," Daquan replied, "but that don't mean the man won't come out of the 'hood, though," he finished, pouring himself some more champagne.

"True, very true," Mandi said, wiping her mouth. "I'm glad you're enjoying yourself, but there's another reason that I wanted to hang out with you tonight."

"Which is?"

"I've been thinking about this for awhile, and . . . I think it's time for me to leave," Mandi told him, then sipped some champagne, eyeing his reaction over her glass.

Daquan sat up and sobered slightly. "Leave? Go where?"

"Home."

"Where is that?"

"Chicago," she replied truthfully.

Daquan played with his fork, pushing the morsels of bell pepper around. "For what?"

Mandi put down her glass. "Because I haven't been in a long time . . . When I left, I didn't go back. It's sort of like you and your grandmother, so I just feel that it's time. Try and close up some old wounds."

The mention of Grandma Mama put Daquan in a somber mood. He hadn't seen her since he got put out, either. Partly out of pride and partly out of shame. He wondered to himself how long it would go on like this.

"I mean," Mandi continued, seeing he wasn't going to speak, "everything is alright with you now. You can handle it from here. You don't need me as a go-between anymore, and Jerome is going to be away for a while. Hopefully not *long* long, but . . . for a while."

Daquan shook his head. "Still, though, it ain't the same."

Mandi slipped over next to him in the booth. "When we first started, it was just to get the rest of Jerome's lawyer money, remember?"

"Yeah, I remember."

"But then, you started doing so well, you even surprised me. Hell, I thought you were just a common street nigguh," she snickered, making him grin. "But you aren't, and I'm proud of you, Daquan. You may not be proud of everything you've done, but who can argue with success?"

"I guess you can't," he agreed. "But you ain't gotta leave, either."

Mandi smiled but did not reply. She reached for her glass and held it in front of him. "Let's have a toast, a toast to . . . *ahhh*, I got it, continued success in the new year."

They clinked crystal and threw their drinks back.

Once the sensation subsided, Mandi laughed and said, "Let's get out of here before we bring in the New Year passed out in a restaurant." Daquan paid the tab and tip, while Mandi got another bottle of champagne to go.

They staggered to the car, and Daquan asked, "You sure you aiight to drive?"

"No," she snickered, "but we'll soon find out."

Mandi definitely wasn't in any condition to drive. They almost had three accidents before making it back to her condo. Daquan got out like he had been on a roller coaster, while Mandi thought it was funny.

"That was fun. Let's do it again," she joked.

"*Shiiiit*," Daquan slurred. "Best believe I'll never ride wit' you fucked up again."

Mandi climbed out of the car and they made it inside, where she kicked off her shoes and reclined on the couch, breathing a sigh of relief. "What time is it?"

Daquan looked at his watch: "11:45."

"Fifteen minutes and it'll be a new year, huh?"

"Yeah, but the same ol' shit," Daquan commented, sitting down next to her on the couch.

"Got any resolutions?" she probed.

"Not really," he admitted.

Mandi sat up and looked at him. "Don't you want something else out of the new year that you didn't get in the old?"

Daquan shrugged.

"It's gotta be something," she persisted.

"To stay alive and free," he answered, grabbing the last bottle of champagne, about to open it, but Mandi stopped him.

"Wait until twelve. But, the way you do that is start thinking of your future. You're making a lot of money, and you need to find ways to clean it up. The game is to be *played*, not *lived*. What time is it?"

"It's 11:52. And I feel ya, lil' mama, I feel ya." He paused for a minute, then said, "There is one thing I wanna do. Start my own record label."

"Really?" she asked in a way that encouraged him to go on.

"Yeah, girl, 'cause I can rap for real. My shit is ten times—"

She cut him off again to ask the time.

"'Bout 11:56," he said. "I'm ten times better than most of them fools on the radio."

"I didn't know you could rap, Daquan," Mandi said, a hint of surprise in her voice.

He checked his watch. "It's 11:58, but yeah, ask anybody from the 'Nolia to the CP3 who the best is," he bragged, then added, "It's 11:59."

"Let me see your watch," Mandi requested excitedly. She held his arm in front of her, until there were ten seconds to go. "Ten . . . nine . . . get the bottle . . . *seven* . . ."

Daquan reached under his right arm and held the champagne bottle with his left.

"Five . . . four . . . you ready? Two . . . one . . . *Happy New Year*!" Mandi sang out, as Daquan popped the cork, and the agitated fizz bubbled out. It ran over his hand and onto the rug, so he put his mouth to it and guzzled some down, then handed the bottle to Mandi. After she took her swig, Daquan said, "Ain't you 'posed to kiss somebody now?"

Mandi smiled, shaking her head. "Yes, you can have a kiss, Daquan."

She leaned over and pecked him on the lips, and he could taste the sweetness of her mouth through the flavor of the champagne. "Now, rap."

"Rap?"

"Yes, rap. You said you were the best, didn't you?" she challenged.

Daquan thought for a minute, then rhymed:

Now it's New Year's—D.Q. won't shed no tears
Drink this champagne and toast to all my dead peers
Me and Mandi—she pretty, skin so sandy—and really
We diggin' this good time together, with good wine and good
weather
We chillin' and killin' and drug dealin' and I'm feelin' you,
shorty—
So let's pump the party!!!

Mandi's bottom lip protruded as she nodded. "I'm impressed. You do have a lot of talent."

"Thanks, yo," Daquan beamed.

Mandi cocked her head to the side and propped her hand under it on the top of the couch. "You have so many possibilities, so much potential, Daquan. Don't waste it. Especially in this life we're living. Really. Because there's no end to it, and once you're in it too long or too deep, there's no way out."

Daquan nodded, soaking in the lesson. "What's your story, Mandi? How you get involved in this heah?"

Mandi paused, then took another swig from the bottle. "I thought I knew, but I didn't," she shrugged, "so I had to learn fast." She wiped her mouth with the back of her hand, and sat the bottle on the coffee table. "I was your age, maybe fifteen, when I met this guy. He was smooth, you know, Chicago slick," Mandi chuckled, "and I was green. The type of green you don't know you've got. Anyway, he talked me into leaving home and moving in with him, and I jumped out of my skin to do it. Well, it wasn't long after I moved in, I had to jump back in my skin because he only wanted a piece of young pussy in his stable."

Her face soured at the memory, but she curled her legs under her and continued, "Don't get me wrong, you know. A woman would do anything for her man if the situation calls for it—but a stable? A pimp? Naw, I just couldn't get with that, but I couldn't go home, either. So I ended up in Vegas, doing exactly what he wanted me to do, but for myself, just to survive, basically. I met a few big spenders, a few high rollers, and I learned a lot and I've been applying it ever since. Now, basically, I am who I am, you know? No regrets, just . . . a lot of what ifs, you know?"

Mandi picked up the bottle and hit it again, then put it in Daquan's outstretched hand.

"Like, what if I go home? Or, what if I stay?"

"Well, what *if* you stay?"

She looked at him wistfully. "Daquan, how old do you think I am?"

He studied her a minute, cocked his neck back for a better view, and replied, "'Bout 25, 26."

Mandi chuckled hard. "Thanks for the compliment. No, I'm 36. Now, how old are you?"

"'Bout 25, 26," he joked, and made her laugh until her shoulders shook. The laughter subsided and the wistful look returned as she caressed his cheek.

"If only you were."

Her hand continued to caress his face until he turned and kissed her palm. Her body twitched subtly, but she pulled it back when Daquan did it again.

"Don't do that," she whispered, but he put her hand back on his face, and she caressed it again. Mandi kept shaking her head, but then she leaned over and kissed him gently on the lips . . . and then again, until Daquan felt her silky tongue meet his. He pulled her close, tickling her thigh, then ran his hand up her dress, trying to push her panties aside. Mandi broke the kiss and said, "No, baby, not like that. You've never made love to a woman, have you?"

Daquan looked into her eyes and shook his head.

"Then let me teach you."

Mandi reached up and untied her strings, then stood up and peeled the dress from her body. Underneath she wore no bra, only a pair of black lace panties. She took his hand and stood him up, slowly unbuttoning his shirt, kissing him on his mouth, sucking his lip and along his neck. Then she unzipped his pants and pulled them down where he could step out of them. Their two naked bodies wrapped around each other, touching and exploring, until Daquan pulled her to the floor.

"Lick my nipples," Mandi whispered, and Daquan sensually replied.

He licked and nibbled the brown nubs until they both stood as erect as the muscle between his legs. Daquan sucked and massaged Mandi's breasts, sending shivers through her that she expressed in soft whimpers. Feeling his dick up against her thigh made her start to grind her hips involuntarily. "*Put it in*," she urged, licking her lips and looking into his eyes.

Daquan didn't even have to use his hand—he just spread her legs with his and slipped inside, slow and creamy, making Mandi suck in her breath and wrap her left leg around his back. She met him thrust for thrust and grind for grind, arching her back to angle her pelvis so Daquan could hit her spot. When he did, she gasped and shot her head back like a pleasure deeper than pain had jolted through her body. She couldn't hold her juices back, releasing a flood of ecstasy.

Mandi pushed him over softly, then straddled him, using her hand to guide him in. "Oh, Daquan," she moaned. "Don't move, baby, just let me ride you."

Daquan lay still while Mandi worked him from every angle, flexing her inner muscles and leaning back, bracing herself with her hand and gripping his ankle.

"Damn . . . I can feel you in my stomach," she groaned, and he just watched her beautiful body wind up and down in smooth, fluid strokes like she was riding the ocean's waves.

"You're beautiful, Mandi. You're beautiful," Daquan whispered, reaching up to palm both her breasts. The compliment made her open up even more.

"Cum with me this time, baby," she urged, quickening her rhythm and tightening the contraction of her walls.

He could feel her body jerking, so he grabbed her ass, grinding deeper until they both came and she leaned down and covered his face with kisses.

"Take a shower with me. I want to bathe you now," Mandi said.

They went into the shower, where they made love again, then took it back to the bed, where they kept at it until they both fell asleep, satisfied.

Daquan didn't wake up until three o'clock on New Year's Day 1994. And he would've slept longer if Mandi hadn't whispered in his ear, "Happy New Year, baby," then kissed him on the cheek.

He opened his eyes to see she was already dressed in a baby blue velour suit, with her hair in a ponytail. "Happy New Year to you, too, lil' mama," he replied, still a little groggy.

"You hungry? I made you something to eat. Then we gotta go, because I have someone I want you to meet."

"Tell 'em I'll holla later," Daquan told her, turning over on his side.

"*Nooo*," Mandi whined, pulling him up by his arm. "Come on. You really need to meet them now."

Daquan rubbed his eyes. "Who is they?"

"It's a surprise."

18

Q93 was one of the hottest radio stations in New Orleans when it came to rap and R&B. The offices were located in mid-city on Gravier Street. It was the station Daquan grew up listening to, where he heard all the newest releases for as long as he could remember. So when Mandi said that was where they were going, he was excited but skeptical at the same time.

"Man, these nigguhs be fuckin' wit' stars and shit. They ain't fuckin' wit' no nigguh out the hood."

"You're already a star, baby," Mandi assured him. "Now, let's go in and prove it."

They entered the red brick building, and Mandi told the receptionist she had an appointment with Wild Wayne. While the lady got on the phone, Daquan looked around at all the promotional posters, past and future. Every act that had ever come through N'awlins had some kind of representation on those walls.

"You can go on in the back," the receptionist said, "Wayne's waiting."

Mandi thanked her, then she and Daquan walked through the doors into the hub of the radio station. Wild Wayne came out of a door down the hall and called, "Mandi, what's up, mama? Come on down."

Daquan passed door after door, half expecting to see some big stars just sitting in one of the rooms, but he didn't. Instead, he saw regular offices and an employee lounge. It wasn't until he got to the rear that it become obvious that this was a radio station. They walked past a room with plate-glass windows, and inside he saw a woman sitting on a stool surrounded by electronic panels. When she spoke into the microphone, he could hear her voice through the speakers along the wall. He recognized the voice of the female radio personality, Uptown Angela. Daquan had never seen Angela before, but he wasn't disappointed because shorty was definitely a cutie.

Wild Wayne was in the room behind the control panel, in a booth-like cubicle, rewinding two large twelve-inch reels. When they walked in, he hugged Mandi and shook Daquan's hand.

"Happy New Year, mama—where you been? I ain't seen you in a minute!" Wild Wayne commented.

"You know me, Wayne. I try to stay off the radar as much as possible," Mandi answered.

"I heard that, low key in '93."He chuckled, then looked at Daquan. "This the dude you was tellin' me about?"

"It is," Mandi confirmed proudly.

"What up, lil' whody? Mandi say you a rapper."

"Fo' sho', whody, the best theah is, ya heard me?" Daquan boasted, remembering what Mandi told him about being a star.

"Then let me hear something," Wild Wayne requested, as he completed the reel and put it back in the box. He was expecting another average wanna-be, and the only reason he had agreed to see him was because he'd get a chance to see Mandi. So Wayne was only listening with one ear until he heard Daquan spit the joint nigguhs in the Calliope always asked for, "The Calliope Code." Suddenly Wild Wayne stopped what he was doing and turned to Daquan, entranced.

When Daquan finished, Wild Wayne went wild. "Whody! Aw, man, this is gonna sound crazy, but the other day I heard some cat spitting that same verse. So I said, man, you hard, kick something else. But when he did, I could tell the first one *couldn't* have been his, because the second one was trash, ya heard me?" Wild Wayne laughed. "But I've been wondering who wrote that shit, 'cause I knew he was wit' the Cutt Boyz, and I *definitely* heard of them." Wild Wayne gestured to Daquan's medallion.

He was flattered to hear people were walking around rapping his shit like it was already a record. "Well, you know," said Daquan, "that theah is some shit nigguhs wanna heah ere'day, so it's already ghetto gold."

"Ghetto gold," Wild Wayne echoed. "I like that."

"And the Cutt Boyz," Daquan continued, "we tryin' to take the game to another level. We tryin' to start a label."

"A label," Wild Wayne thought pensively. "Well, Daquan, you definitely got a good idea, but you ever heard of Master P?"

"Master P? Seem like I have. Somebody said he from the CP3, but he went out west or somethin'," Daquan answered.

"He did, but he back and he got it goin' on. The nigguh is, like you say, ghetto gold."

Daquan nodded.

"Matter of fact," Wild Wayne went in his pocket and pulled out his wallet, "I got his studio number." He extracted a card from his wallet, picked up the phone, and dialed.

"Hello? May I speak to P, please? Okay . . ." he looked at Daquan. "They goin' to get him."

Daquan looked at Mandi, who only shrugged.

"P," he said into the phone, "this is Wild Wayne over at Q93 . . . Yeah, you busy? I wanna drop by, and believe me, it's worth your while." Wayne smiled, and winked at Daquan. "Okay, we'll be right there."

Twenty minutes later, Daquan was at Master P's studio on Jefferson Davis Street. Daquan had never been in a recording studio before, but he could tell this had to be an expensive one. A tall, brown-skin dude in a brown Dickie's outfit and a T-shirt with a tank and the words "No Limit" on it, shook Wild Wayne's hand. "Daquan," said Wild Wayne, "this is Master P."

Master P shook Daquan's hand, but his eyes danced on Mandi. "What up, whody?"

Then he turned to Mandi. "And you are?" he charmed, shaking her hand a little too long for Daquan. P and Wayne didn't see it, but Mandi did, and politely extracted her hand. "I'm Mandi."

"Okay, nice to meet you, Mandi," Master P replied, then went to Wild Wayne. "What's happenin', Wayne?"

Wayne pointed at Daquan. "That's what's happenin'," he grinned, feeling like this was history in the making and proud to be the initiator. Master P looked Daquan up and down, then asked Wild Wayne, "Whody, this ain't another one of your cousins, is it?'

"Nah, baby. Daquan, do that joint everybody in the Calliope feenin' fo'," Wild Wayne told him with a smile.

"You from the CP3, whody?" Master P asked, eyebrows raised.

"Fo' sho'," Daquan replied, then wasted no time in hitting Master P with that Calliope Code.

Master P was a true hustler who understood the benefits of keeping a poker face even when you're looking at four aces, but even he had to crack a golden grin when he heard what Daquan could do.

"Damn, whody, yo' shit is crucial, ya heard? What you tryin' to do wit' yo'self?" Master P inquired, ready to put him on the team immediately.

"Tryin' to start my own label, big homey, switch the game up," Daquan replied.

"Well, dig, come on in the back. Let's talk a little bit mo'," Master P offered, then all four of them went into his office. When they entered, Daquan saw two dudes playing Sega. One he didn't recognize, but the other he knew instantly.

"Yo, Cee! C. Miller, that you, whody?" Daquan asked excitedly.

Cee looked around and he smiled from ear to ear. "My nigguh Daquan," he beamed, getting up to shake his hand and give him a hug.

"What up, whody?" Daquan said.

"Y'all know each other?" P asked.

Cee turned to his brother, like, "Yeah, nigguh, 'member that dude I told you about I was locked up wit'? This him!" He turned to Daquan and said, "Nigguh, why the fuck you ain't call me? I told you what was goin' down."

Daquan shrugged. "Man, I lost yo' number, then them streets had a nigguh, ya heard?"

"Yeah, but I see it's all gravy, though," Cee remarked, observing Quan's medallion and gear. He looked at Master P and said, "P, what you think about Daquan performing wit' us tonight? Me and Silkk?"

Master P eyed Daquan. "You 'bout it, lil' whody?"

"Hell, *yeah*, I'm 'bout it!" Daquan exclaimed, and everyone laughed at his obvious enthusiasm.

"Riverboat Hallelujah, tonight at nine. We got a sound check in about an hour. Can you be ready?" P questioned.

"I'm ready now."

"Then I know I'll see you in an hour."

Daquan hung out with Cee in his Lincoln Town Car rental, catching up on one another's lives.

"Yeah, whody, Cali is aiight, but you know a nigguh had to bring it back home," Cee stated.

"Fo' sho'," Daquan replied.

"So what's poppin' in the CP3? Ere' since I been back, all I been hearin' is the Cutt Boyz. Hear y'all got shit on smash," Cee said, glancing over at him.

Daquan shrugged. "You know how it is, whody. A muh-fucka ain't tryin' to go to school twelve yeahs just to graduate to a McDonald's job, ya dig?"

"Fo' sho', but I'm tellin' you, D, this rap shit . . . it's sweeter than the dope game. A muhfucka ain't gotta worry 'bout no feds and snitches and shit. And wit' the deal my brother got, we 'bout to blow, whody!"

"Deal?" Daquan quizzed. "I thought your brother had his own label."

"He do, but you gotta have distribution. That's what I'm talkin' about, but the way P got it, ain't naan nigguh ever had a deal this sweet. He got a major distributing him but he keeps his masters."

"Masters?" Daquan quizzed again. He thought having a label was just making records and selling 'em. But every time Cee spoke, he said something else Daquan didn't know about.

Cee described the deal P had with his distributor, and how it was usually done, so that he could see how good a deal it was. "Most labels keep the artist's master tapes and pay them a royalty" Cee explained. "But as an independent label, we own our own masters and collect 85% off every record sold." Everything he said had Daquan's head spinning with all the ins and outs of the record business.

They went out to the Calliope and found Nut playing ball with Red and a few other dudes. When Nut saw Cee, he stopped the game and they greeted each other at center court.

"My nigguh!" Nut exclaimed, "Where you been, bruh? Locked up again?"

"Hell, naw, Nut—from the Calliope to Cali, baby," Cee replied. "But I'm back now, and we 'bout to show ya nigguhs how to stunt fo' sho'," Cee boasted, knocking the ball out of

Nut's hand and dribbling it, then putting up a three-pointer that swooshed—all net.

"Yo, I got a show tonight," Daquan told Nut proudly.

"A show? Where?"

"Riverboat Hallelujah," Cee answered. "Me and my brothers performing, so we asked Daquan to get it, too."

Nut gave Daquan dap, like, "Hell, *yeah*, whody! Let's bring the Calliope thang to these muhfuckas fo' sho'."

"Where's Rosco?"

"Out Baton Rouge. But he'll be theah. All us will," Nut assured him.

"Fo' sho'. Nine o'clock," Daquan informed him, then he and Cee bounced to get ready for the sound check.

They drove to Tulane Avenue in the Seventeenth Ward, where the Riverboat Hallelujah was located. Master P and Silkk the Shocker were already onstage, making sure the sound system was correct. The music of *The Ghetto's Tryin' to Kill Me!* boomed through the gigantic building. Cee explained the sound check to Daquan, and he absorbed it all. When it was his turn, he stepped on stage with Cee and took up the microphone. "Yo," he spoke into the mic, and heard his own voice booming. Daquan looked out over the empty room, imagined it full of people, and he felt his first case of butterflies. But the more he flowed, and heard C. Miller, a.k.a. C-Murder, flow, the stage felt more like the block and his nervousness went away.

When the sound check was over, they went back to Cee's suite to get dressed, and Daquan called Vanessa.

"Hey, baby, Happy New Year," she giggled. "We just got back from Mississippi like an hour ago."

"That's good, 'cause you right on time to go wit' me to a show," Daquan invited her.

"I don't know, Daquan. My mama might not let me go since we just got home," Vanessa answered.

"Even if it's me that's performin'?" he smirked, letting her know the good news in a slick way.

"Performin'? You mean on stage? Rapping?!" Vanessa was so excited, she asked obvious questions.

He laughed. "Yeah, lil' mama, me and my nigguh C-Murder."

"Hold on," she huffed, and he could hear her in the background yell for her mama.

A few moments later, Vanessa picked up the phone. "Where's the show, Daquan?"

"Riverboat Hallelujah."

"What time?"

"Nine."

She yelled all the information to her mother, then excitedly told him, "We'll be there, baby!"

"We?" he chuckled. "I didn't think this was yo' mama type of party."

"Please, boy, my mama cool. Besides, she won't let me go if she don't."

"Aiight, just don't say I ain't warn ya."

"I'll be there. And Daquan . . . I missed you."

"I missed you, too. See you later," he smiled, then hung up and went to get ready for the show.

"Are y'all ready to party?!" DJ Blacknmild of Hot 104.5 bellowed into the microphone, and the whole crowd cheered loudly.

"I can't hear you. Let me hear you, Choppa City—Whootie *whoo*!"

"Whootie *whoo*!" the packed house responded in exuberant unison.

"Are y'all ready for Master P and the No Limit Soldiers?!" Blacknmild yelled.

"Hell, yeah!"

"Then make some noise! Make some noise for New Orleans' own Master P!" The crowd went crazy as the beat to

"Time To Check My Crackhouse" vibrated the walls. Master P performed first, then Silkk the Shocker, who did his "No Limit Party."

"You nervous, baby?" Mandi leaned over and asked Daquan as they stood offstage.

"Naw, I'm ready," he assured her.

"I know you're going to do well," she encouraged him, kissing him softly. Cee walked up. He, Daquan, P, and Silkk were all dressed in fatigue outfits. "You ready, whody?"

"Hell, yeah."

Cee and Daquan took the stage, Daquan playing hype-man to Cee's "Ain't No Glock," even though he didn't know the words. He just fed off the energy of the crowd. Then Cee gave him the floor and he rocked "The Calliope Code" over Cee's track. He could see Nut, Rosco, Red, and the rest of the Cutt Boyz going wild in the front row, and Daquan even heard a lot of people singing along, amazed that they knew the words. He knew then what he wanted to do. He wanted to rap, and now that the crowd confirmed what he already knew, he gave it his all until he was exhausted and hoarse.

After the show, Quan and Cee celebrated with the Cutt Boyz backstage.

"My nigguh D.Q.! The Cutt Boyz is in heah, ya *heard*?!" Rosco boomed, amped up and throwing his massive arms like tree trunks.

"That shit was fire, whody, straight fire!" Nut propped him.

Daquan searched the departing crowd for Vanessa's face, and he was about to give up until he heard, "There he is, Mama."

He looked up and saw Vanessa and her mother and father approaching, so he moved forward to meet them. He hugged Vanessa and her mother, then shook her father's hand.

"Daquan, you sho' got a dirty mouth," her mother snickered, "but I'm proud of you, baby—you did good tonight."

"Thank you, Mrs. Phillips," Daquan replied.

"Yeah, Daquan, it was a good show," her father added, then said to Vanessa, "We're leaving in ten minutes."

"Okay, Daddy."

Her parents walked a little ways away, to give Vanessa and Daquan some privacy.

"So . . . how you like the show, lil' mama?" Daquan grinned.

"I loved it, Daquan. I'm so proud of you," she gushed, eyes full of infatuation and admiration.

"So when me and you gonna get together again, boo?"

Before she could answer, Mandi walked up and said, "Oh, hi, you must be Vanessa."

Vanessa nodded. "Mandi, right?"

"Yes, it's good to meet you," Mandi greeted, shaking Vanessa's hand. Then she put her arms around Daquan's neck and said, "Great show, baby," then kissed him on his mouth, keeping her eyes open with a cold stare.

Out of the corner of his eye, he could see confusion and hurt on Vanessa's face. When Mandi broke the kiss, he could see the anger on Mrs. Phillips' face and the astounded admiration on Mr. Phillips'.

"I'll see you in the car," Mandi said, adding a flippant, "'Bye, Vanessa."

Cee saw the whole thing, but didn't say anything.

"Vanessa, come on here, girl," her mother huffed, mumbling obscenities under her breath.

"Yo, Nessa, hold on a minute," Daquan started to say.

Vanessa's bottom lip trembled, on the verge of tears. The sound of Daquan's voice made her turn and walk away without looking back.

Cee came over and said, "Everything okay, whody?"

Daquan just stared at Vanessa's back. "Yeah, Cee."

"I'll see you at the after-party."

When Daquan got to his Caddy, Mandi was already in the passenger seat with the key turned back, listening to Jodeci's

"Come and Talk to Me," filing her nails without a care in the world. Daquan slid under the wheel, started the engine, and began to speak, but Mandi cut him off. "Go ahead and say something stupid, so I can curse your ass out for telling her to come in the first place."

Her words were spoken in a normal tone, but Daquan could tell she was vexed.

"Man, just chill out. I invited a lot of people," Daquan tried to reason as he pulled off.

"Yeah, whatever, just take me home. I'm tired."

"For what? We 'bout to go to this after-party wit' Cee and them," Daquan answered.

"No, *you're* going. I'm going home," Mandi insisted.

"You ain't heah what I said? I said, we go, girl. Why you gonna let some bullshit fuck up a beautiful day? These muh-fuckas helpin' me plan my future, and you sayin' you ain't gonna be there?" Daquan asked.

Mandi propped her elbow on the windowsill and didn't respond.

The after-party was held at Whispers, and the place was packed with people happy to see Master P bring his success home. While Nut, Rosco, and the Cutt boyz wilded, bringing the rah-rah to the party, Cee, Daquan, and Mandi mingled, but Mandi remained distant, although polite. They found a booth in VIP to kick back and politic.

"So what you think, D.Q.? You ready to bring your hustle to the rap game?" Cee questioned, sparking a blunt.

"Yeah, whody. But havin' my own label is a lot deeper than I thought," Daquan admitted.

"Well," Cee inhaled, offering the blunt to Daquan, who declined, as did Mandi. "Don't shit come easy if it's worth havin', lil' Daddy," he philosophized, exhaling a stream of smoke.

"I hear ya, Cee."

"Why don't you roll wit' No Limit? Sign wit' P for an album or two, and learn the ropes before you spread your wings. Believe me, we all about seeing nigguhs establish they own," Cee offered.

Daquan nodded, sipping on his gin and juice.

"How far you got wit' startin' yo' shit? You got a lawyer or a manager?'

"Naw, I ain't got no lawyer, but I got a manager, though. Mandi my manager," he told Cee, smirking at Mandi. "Yeah, whody, she believe in a nigguh, so she said she'd ride wit' a nigguh as long as I stay focused—ain't that right, Mama?" Daquan quipped, thinly veiling his apology in a commitment to keep it real.

She laughed lightly, shaking her head subtly. "*If* I can manage you," she quipped. "I'll be back—I'm going to the bathroom."

Mandi got up and walked, leaving Daquan and Cee watching her ass sway through the crowd.

"Lil' Daddy, you hittin' that?" Cee asked.

Daquan lit up a Camel. "Sumthin' like that."

"Get the fuck outta heah," Cee replied incredulously. "Damn, lil' Daddy, you dipped in gravy," he joked.

Nut and Rosco came through, both carrying bottles of Dom, and already pissy.

"What up, whody? This party live as a muhfucka," Nut commented, sitting next to Daquan while Rosco slid into the other side.

"What up wit' these bitches is what I'm 'bout to find out," Cee said, handing Nut the half blunt in the ashtray.

By the time Mandi came back a few minutes later, weed smoke filled the air and Daquan, Cee, Red, and Rosco were bugging together, passing the Dom.

"You ready, baby?" Mandi questioned softly.

Nut knew he was in her seat, but he ignored her. Daquan

looked at his watch. "Yeah, Mama, we can breeze." He turned to Cee and said, "I'll call you tomorrow."

"Aiight," Cee replied, then added jokingly, "Don't lose the number this time."

"Fo' sho', nigguh. This heah the combination to my future, ya heard me?"

Daquan dapped up Nut, Red, and Rosco, then got out of the booth, never noticing how Nut was grilling Mandi.

There was no doubt that Mandi and Daquan had chemistry between them—not just sexual, but a mutual understanding that came from shared experiences. Because of her past, his circumstance had endeared him to her, but it was his style and ways that attracted her.

They lay in her bed naked, Mandi resting her head on his chest, caressing the area between his stomach and pelvis.

"I want you to know I'm proud of you. You did your thing tonight."

"When? Just now?" he quipped, and she playfully hit him.

"On stage," Mandi emphasized, thinking to herself, *That, too*. She lifted her head off his chest and looked him in the eyes. "And I know how it feels to be young, but I'm tellin' you, Daquan, you're not gonna have me twisted over you, playing me to my face. Because I do know a few tricks I haven't taught you."

"What you mean, playing you?" he probed, running his hand through her hair. "I told you I—"

She put her finger to his lips like, "Shhh, don't even lie. I know you like her, and that's cool, but if I'ma play my position, she damn sure gonna play hers."

"Yeah? Well, what position Jerome play in all this?" he asked.

"Jerome already knows, because I told him how I felt a while ago. That's why I wanted to leave, so we wouldn't end up doing what we're doing now," she explained. "Because one of us . . . is going to get hurt. Somebody has to pay the price."

Mandi maintained eye contact a little longer, making sure he understood, then laid her head back on his chest and continued to rub his stomach.

19

The next couple of months, Daquan and C. Miller got tighter, as Cee schooled Quan to the rules of the music game. He helped Cee move into his new apartment on Napoleon Street and set up the miniature studio that they spent hours recording in. Daquan had signed a development deal with No Limit Records, so while Cee schooled him to the hustle side of the music game, Master P hipped him to the business side of the industry.

If he wasn't with Cee, Daquan was with Mandi. She began opening up his world to much more than just street life and love—she turned him onto books, jazz, politics, and how to read between political lines. Mandi had Daquan listening to Miles Davis and reading *The Autobiography of Malcolm X*. She schooled him to the role crime played in the dance of democracy—she even taught him her opinion of religion. He learned her viewpoints when he suggested they go to church one Sunday.

"For what?" she asked while feeding more drug money into the money counter. "Just tell 'em to send us a bill, because that's what most preachers is after anyway."

"I'm sayin' we goin' to pray to Jesus," Daquan retorted. "Shit, we need it."

Mandi cut off the counter. "Let me ask you this . . . you believe Jesus died for your sins?"

"Fo' sho'—yours, too. Ere'body," he stated firmly.

"Everybody?"

"Fo' sho'."

"Then what about the people who lived before Jesus? How could He die for *their* sins if they never had a chance to believe?" she asked pointedly, and Daquan couldn't answer, so she continued. "If God, who so loved the world, as they say, sent His son, I just can't buy that He sent Him for only us and not everyone who ever lived."

With all this schooling going on, Daquan almost never saw Vanessa. He had called her a few times, but she either hung up or flat told him not to call again. So he didn't, even though he wanted to.

It was the same with Nut, but for different reasons. His life was moving forward, but Nut's wasn't, so the separation was inevitable. It got to the point that Mandi started dropping the weight off to him and Rosco, because Daquan was in the studio, doing a show somewhere, or just chilling with Cee. It wasn't out of disrespect, but Nut harbored envy in his heart because he felt Daquan wasn't trying to fuck with him now that he was hanging out with rappers. The money was too sweet to let petty shit upset the flow. But Daquan heard about it in a strange way.

He had decided it had been long enough since he'd seen Grandma Mama, and he didn't want his situation to get out of hand like Mandi's. So he took his No Limit contract and went to the Calliope. He made sure he didn't wear his jewelry and he kept his gear simple.

Daquan walked up to her door, took a deep breath, and knocked.

"Just a minute," he heard Grandma Mama say from the interior of the house that he once called home. A few moments later, she opened the door. Neither one said anything at first. They were both savoring the moment but hating the hovering tension. Daquan saw how old his grandma was getting. Her hair was almost completely gray, and her wrinkles had deepened considerably. Meanwhile, she was admiring how old he was getting. At 15, Daquan's shoulders were broadening, and his height and weight had increased. He reminded her of Daryl so much.

"Hey, Mama," he greeted timidly.

"Hello, Daquan," Grandma Mama replied, her facial expression stoic.

"Can I come in? I need to talk to you."

She paused, then opened the door wide enough for him to enter. "I ain't cooked yet," she informed him as she closed the door, "but you can wait till I do if you want."

"No, ma'am, I'm okay," Daquan replied.

He sat on the couch and she sat in her favorite worn armchair, picking at the exposed padding.

"How you been doin'?" he inquired, trying to spark the conversation, but Grandma Mama, not being one to mince words, went straight to the point. "Not as well as you. Hear tell you some big shot 'round heah. That true?"

Daquan just dropped his head.

"Mm-hmm, it's true," she confirmed for herself. "Just like Jerome, huh? You see where he at, don't ya?"

"Yes'm, I do, but . . ."

"What?" she cut him off. "You don't think it could happen to you? You think you're smarter or somethin'? Done got yo' self one of them chicken bones?"

"I'm tryin' to do better, Grandma Mama—I'm tryin' to do something with myself and . . . " he took a deep breath, "and I wanna do somethin' for you, too."

"Do fo' me like what?" she asked, her tone pitched as if he had just accused her of a crime.

"I wanna buy you a house."

"A *house*!?" she echoed. "With who money? I hope you don't think I'ma do it with your'n."

Daquan pulled the contract out of his hoody pocket and handed it to her.

"I'ma do it with that," he stated proudly.

She looked at the paper. "Chile, you know I can't read nothing without my glasses. What is it?"

"It's like a record contract. I'm in development now, but when I sign to the label, I told them all I want is a house for you," he explained. Daquan could afford to do it, because he wasn't hurting for nothing.

"Contract? Development? Label? Chile, what is you talkin' 'bout?" Grandma Mama asked.

"I'ma be a rapper, Grandma Mama. The money's legitimate and maybe I can get out these streets," Daquan said.

"A rapper? Like on the radio?"

"Yes'm."

"And they's gonna buy me a house fo' that?" she probed incredulously.

"Yep."

Grandma Mama chuckled. "Lord, this' worl' done gone crazy. Rappin' for houses." She shook her head, then looked at him. "Well, I may not understand it, but it sounds a whole lot betta than what you doin' now."

Daquan's spirits were lifted just to hear her say that.

"What about Kimoko? Have you talked to her?"

The mention of her name brought his street element right back.

"For what?"

"What you mean, for what? That baby is what. If'n it is yours and you lettin' her run 'round like that, stealin' her mama money and whatnot, you could buy me a thousand houses and it still won't make it right," Grandma Mama preached.

He had set himself to tune her out, until she said something about *stealing*.

"Stealing?"

"Stole her mama food stamps just last week, so she put her out," Mama informed him.

If Kimoko was stealing, Daquan could only think of one reason for it.

"Where she stayin'?"

"Wit' some girl named Penny. That's what folks say, anyway."

Daquan was sick. He knew exactly who Penny was. An old dope fiend that took young fresh ones in so she could get high off the dicks they sucked. His conscience wouldn't allow him to disregard the chance that it could be his baby, so he kissed Grandma and said, "I'ma talk to her."

She nodded approvingly. "You do that."

Daquan went straight over to Penny's apartment and knocked hard until Penny's scrawny, two-tooth-having ass opened the door, flipping. "Goddammit, *who*—" she started to say in her gravelly voice, but when she saw it was Daquan, her whole tone changed. "Oh, D.Q.? What—"

He pushed right past her, like, "Where Kimoko?"

Penny took a pull on her cigarette. "She in the back." When he headed in that direction, Penny yelled after him, "D.Q., hol' up! She busy!"

Daquan barged through the bedroom door to find Kimoko on her knees, sucking some young, fat nigguh's dick. Her eyes got big and the fat nigguh didn't know what to think. He knew who Daquan was, and the fear his sudden appearance caused made his dick shrivel instantly.

"Get the fuck outta heah," Daquan ordered him.

The fat nigguh pulled up his pants and shuffled out the door—then Daquan turned his fury on Kimoko. He back-smacked her off her knees down to the floor. Standing over her, he hissed, "Get up and let's go."

She lay on her side, sobbing, "I ain't goin' nowhere wit' you!"

"Bitch, either get yo' ass up or I'll stomp that baby out yo' ass now!" he warned her, ready to set it off.

"This baby?! How you gonna speak on this baby?! You don't give a fuck about it! You wanna kill it, *kill* it!" she screamed, then hit herself hard in the stomach. She was about to do it again, but he grabbed her arm. Kimoko swung at him with the other, but he pinned both her arms across her chest, criss-crossed, like the straps of a straightjacket.

"Get *off* of me!" she cried, trying to wiggle free. "You don't care about this baby—just let me kill it . . . let me kill it . . . *let me kill it*," she begged, like its burden was killing her inside.

"Naw, Kimoko, I can't let you do that," Daquan replied, and he knew right then that the baby was his, because its life was already just like his had been. "Come on, we leavin'."

Daquan pulled her up slowly, and this time, Kimoko showed no resistance. He walked her up front, where Penny and another dope fiend were sitting on her broken-down couch.

"Oh, you a hero now, ha? Gonna save the world, ha? I'm surprised to even see you 'round heah. Heah yo' boy tell it, you too good for the CP3 these days," Penny remarked snidely, mad because he was taking away her money-maker.

Daquan ignored her, but he heard every word. He knew she was talking about Nut, but his mind was elsewhere, so he didn't even recognize the trace of a larcenous heart. After he shut the door, Penny prophesized, "She'll come back," then blew out a stream of smoke. "They always do."

As soon as Kimoko and Daquan walked in the house, Mandi knew what it meant.

"She gonna stay wit' us for a few days, till I get her a place," Daquan said, like he was exhausted emotionally.

"Okay, baby, I understand," Mandi replied.

He turned to Kimoko. "Go get yourself cleaned up."

"I didn't leave you."

"I called you, but you didn't answer."

"I couldn't."

"Why?"

They were in a field. The breeze was blowing and a stream ran a few feet away from where they sat, side by side. Diana looked at him with a mixture of love and pity in her eyes.

"Because you couldn't hear me."

He understood.

"I speak to your heart, Daquan," Diana explained, "but you haven't been listening to your heart, have you?"

Daquan shook his head. "Sometimes, I don't want to feel, because then I'll know I'm wrong. If I cared about Black, about Pepper, Pam, Mikey, then how could I live with myself?" he asked sincerely, looking into his sister's eyes for the ultimate answer.

Diana took his hands in both of hers. "I want you to do what's *right*, Daquan. The right you know in your heart so you don't have to be afraid. You can't change the mistakes you made in the past, but you can make sure you don't make them again. The life you're living now, you're bound to make them over and over, until they're no longer mistakes . . . They'll be your *life*."

Daquan knew what he had to do, and his sister's embrace gave him the courage to do it.

*   *   *

Kimoko's withdrawal wasn't as traumatic as it could've been, because her monkey hadn't had enough time to fester and grow, but it was painful to watch just the same. Her vomiting, her bodily convulsions, the way she'd shiver from cold sweats in the midst of fever, showed Daquan the other side of the game not many got to see. Daquan did what he could, but it was Mandi who really brought Kimoko through it. She was the one who cleaned up the vomit and changed the sheets. Mandi fed Kimoko even when she didn't want to eat, and it was Mandi who talked the pregnant mother-to-be back down when she wanted to give up.

A few days after that ordeal, Daquan and Cee sat in his living room watching *Rap City*. Redman's "Time for some Akshun," was playing, and Cee puffed a fat one, nodding to the beat.

"Yo, Cee, you ever seen a muhfucka quittin' dope?"

"Too many times, whody, too many to count," Cee answered.

Daquan shook his head. "Yeah, well, I don't never wanna see it again."

"How she doin'?" Cee inquired, because Daquan had already told him the situation.

"She betta. Her and Mandi went shoppin' and then to the doctor. Make sure everything aiight wit' the baby," Daquan explained.

Cee tapped the ashes off the blunt into the ashtray, and shook his head. "You gotta helluva broad on your team, lil' daddy. Most shorties, ain't no way they woulda let no chick stay wit' them, baby or no baby. Females cold-blooded when it come to each other, then on top of that, she brought lil' mama back? Mandi a soldier."

The conversation lulled while Redman rapped, then Daquan said, "I'm gettin' out the game."

"Yeah?"

Daquan looked at him and said, simply, "I got to."

Cee understood. He muted the sound of the TV and turned his full attention to Daquan. "I hear you, baby, and I been meanin' to rap wit' you on that. This thing heah is gonna be bigger than dope for a nigguh. Watch what I tell you. And straight up, you don't need nothin' to hold you back. But it ain't easy, whody, 'cause you breakin' a lot of bread, so a muh-fucka might not bite the hand that feed him, but they'll damn sure bite the hand that stop."

20

Nut had been spending a lot of time in Baton Rouge. It was a new place, the money was sweet, and his face was only known to those who feared it, or were too dead to talk. He felt like the man out there, instead of just being Daquan's man in the Calliope.

Daquan drove out and met Nut at a barbershop near Southern University, where Nut loved to hang out, because the females were close enough to flock through. Nut had copped a new drop-top gold Porsche for his fifteenth birthday, and he was sitting on it talking to three redbone chicks when Daquan pulled up in Mandi's BMW. The girls eyed him because of the whip, but when he got out, he wasn't jeweled up like Nut, and his Karl Kani was basic, so they gave their attention back to Nut.

Nut hadn't seen his old friend in a while, but he knew he was coming because they had already talked. "What's happenin', whody?" Nut greeted, sliding off the hood and giving Daquan a hug. "What you think?" he asked, gesturing to his new car.

"It's fire, bruh," Daquan answered in a lackluster tone.

Nut sensed his mood, and told the chicks he'd holler at them later. When they left, he lit a Camel. "I heard you went

Rambo up by dope feen Penny's lookin' for Kimoko," Nut chuckled. "Damn, whody, you been away too long. Lil' mama *been* out there."

Daquan was upset that he knew and didn't tell him, but he didn't let it show.

"How much it run you?" Daquan asked, referring to the Porsche.

"Seventy-five. But I ain't finished yet. By the time I'm through, it'll be about a buck, buck and a quarter," Nut bragged.

"Lot of money for a car," Daquan remarked.

"You know what they say—it ain't trickin' if you got it," Nut shrugged.

"But the sun don't shine forever, either."

"Then enjoy it while it lasts," Nut smirked, blowing a cloud of smoke straight up into the air.

Daquan nodded. "You know I'm 'bout to sign wit' No Limit, right? We 'bout to do a tour, go hard in this rap shit."

"Yeah?" Nut replied, thunking his cigarette away in an arc. "Good luck, whody. But that rap thang . . . it's shaky, you know? Ain't nothin' guaranteed. But dope? It's always gonna be feens," Nut reasoned.

"That may be true, but I'm tryin' to take my game to the next level, Nut. The game is to be played, not lived," Daquan told him, using Mandi's words.

"So what you sayin', whody?" Nut asked, perking up. He already felt it coming, but he needed to hear it to be sure.

"I'm sayin', I'm out. I'm done. If I'ma be a—"

Nut cut him off and spat, "You what? You *what*?! Fuck you mean you *out*?!" Nut was fuming so much he couldn't keep still. "What about me?! Rosco and all the homies? What we 'posed to do?"

"Come on, bruh, look at you! Your jewels, this car, your crib. You got your mama out the projects and everything, plus you still sittin' pretty. Nigguh, you ain't hurtin' for shit!" Daquan hollered back.

"This ain't shit! Fuck that," Nut huffed. "Aiight, gimme the connect. You wanna fuckin' rap, then rap. I can't rap, I can't dance, I can't do none of that shit. I *hustle*, I bang, I grind—nigguh, I *kill* fo' mine. That's all I know. So gimme the connect!"

Daquan looked at Nut, and he felt sorry for his friend. He was pacing back and forth like a caged panther. Trapped in a cage that he couldn't see his way out of, even though the door was always wide open and never locked.

"I can't."

"Why?"

"'Cause Mandi my connect and you know she—"

"Don't fuck wit' me, right?" Nut completed his sentence. "Right? Ain't that what you was gonna say? Man, fuck that bitch," Nut spat.

Daquan sighed. "It's over, Nut. After this last drop, it's over. We split fifty-fifty, then—"

Nut's laughing in his face made him stop talking.

"I shoulda seen this shit comin', whody. You ridin' around wit' stars, connectin' big and fuckin' that bitch, while we out heah, sleet or snow! Look at you. Where yo' Cutt Boyz chain? You don't even wear it no more, ha?"

"I'ma *always* be a Cutt Boy. A chain don't make me," Daquan answered with attitude.

"Yeah," Nut chuckled, "just like I thought. You probably lettin' Mandi wear it—shit, she wearin' the pants. She might as well wear the chain, too."

Daquan saw where the situation could go, so he turned and started walking away. "One mo' run, Nut. Then, you take it from there."

As Daquan pulled off, Nut had already made up his mind where he was going to take it.

*   *   *

The next person Daquan told his news to had a totally different reaction.

"I respect that, whody," Jerome told him over the prison phone. He had taken a plea deal for seven years. Although Jerome knew the feds had nothing on him, he still didn't want to fight the odds of taking the case to trial. Especially since the feds had an 85 percent winning average, and were known to do almost anything to keep it that way.

"You had a sweet run, so get out while you can."

Daquan was relieved to hear that Jerome felt that way, in spite of the fact that Daquan was stacking Jerome's cut off of everything he did.

"But it don't stop," Daquan assured him, "'cause No Limit 'bout to put N.O. on the map fo' sho', ya heard me?"

Jerome laughed. "I hear you, lil' cuz, I hear you. It's good you changing—that proves you growing. And yo, I respect what you did for Kimoko. That there was some real shit."

Daquan glanced over at Kimoko sitting on the couch, eating everything in sight.

"And yo, I'm changin' and growin' a little bit myself . . . I'm Muslim now."

"You what?" Daquan asked, not recognizing the word.

"Muslim. I became a Muslim," Jerome announced proudly.

"That's good, whody. I'm glad you doin' good," Daquan replied. He didn't know what becoming Muslim meant, but Jerome sounded proud of it.

The phone was about to cut off, so Jerome said, "Tell Mandi I'ma call right back. I love you, lil' cuz."

"I love you, too, Rome."

Daquan hung up and yelled to Mandi in the bedroom, "Jerome 'bout to call back! I'm takin' Kimoko to the doctor!"

"Okay!" she hollered back just as the phone rang.

Daquan helped Kimoko up and joked, "Come on, bring yo' big ass heah."

Kimoko sucked her teeth, "Shut up, 'cause it's your fault I'm like this." She smiled and Daquan admired her glow.

As they got in the car he never knew he was being watched. Nut and Rosco sat across the street in a blue Chevy Nova, waiting for Daquan to leave. They had been patient because they knew his schedule. Now, all they had to do was wait until he pulled off.

It wasn't hard for Nut to convince them to ride out. Faced with losing his meal ticket, Rosco was down for whatever. Besides, neither one of them saw themselves as crossing Daquan. He was out of the game, as they saw it. Their target was Mandi. She was the one with the connect, and since he didn't fuck with them, they were definitely going to fuck with her.

The only thing was, they had to keep Daquan out of the house long enough to snatch Mandi up, make her take them to the connect, and leave her body behind. After that, nothing else mattered. If Daquan was truly out of the game, he couldn't get mad. But if he flipped on his boys over a broad, then it proved they really wasn't boys, so it was whatever.

As Daquan rode, his beeper went off back to back with Nut's code. It was so persistent, he finally pulled over and called back.

"Nut, what up?" Daquan asked when the phone picked up.

"Naw, whody, this Lil' Red."

"Oh, what up, Red? Where Nut?"

Lil' Red was a Cutt Boy, too. He was just the dough boy. "Man, you need to come out to the CP3 soon as you can."

"What up?"

"I can't talk on this heah," Lil' Red replied, just as he had been told to say.

"Is it them peoples?" Daquan asked, looking around, checking his own surroundings.

"Naw, but you need to come through."

Daquan sighed. Regardless of everything, Nut was still his

man. "Aiight, I'll be through soon as I can," he told Red, then hung up.

A few minutes later, Red beeped Nut with the code for, *It's done.*

There was no way for Daquan to know that Nut and Rosco were at Mandi's door. She came and looked through the peephole, sucking her teeth when she saw them standing there. She opened the door, asking, "What is—"

Mandi never got a chance to finish her sentence, because Rosco shoved the door open so hard, it knocked her off balance and she fell to the floor. Before she could get up, Nut had his .38 in her face. "Close the door, Rosco," he told his partner.

"Nigguh, have you lost your mind?!" Mandi asked from the floor. She knew what it was, but she wasn't ready to accept the fact that Nut had caught her slipping so easily.

Nut kicked her in the face hard enough to bring blood gushing from her nose. "Damn! You just don't know how *long* I wanted to do that, you stupid bitch!" Nut hissed, keeping the gun in her face.

Rosco snatched Mandi off the floor and pulled her head back by her hair.

"You know what it is, Mama, so do yourself a favor and tell us what we wanna know," Rosco advised her ominously.

Mandi saw murder in both men's eyes.

"I-I don't have anything," she told Rosco truthfully.

"Fuck what you got, bitch, you gonna take us to your connect!" Nut ordered, grabbing her around the throat and squeezing until she got lightheaded. When he let go, she fell to the floor, gasping for air.

Nut snatched her up and dragged her into the bedroom, then flung her on the waterbed violently, making it shake and roll. He grabbed the cordless and threw it on her chest. Mandi was just regaining the ability to breathe freely, so she spoke hoarsely when she said, "I ain't calling nobody. Call 'em your-self."

Rosco snickered, "Then you really do wanna die, ha?"

Nut was waiting for her to resist, so he wasted no time in dragging her body to the edge of the bed by her ankles and yanking her sweatpants off. She tried to grab the elastic top to keep them up, but Rosco punched her in the stomach with a massive blow, knocking all the fight out of her.

"Yeah, Mandi," Nut licked his lips. "I knew you liked it rough. So I'm gonna give it to you rough." Nut leered once she was naked from the waist down. Rosco got bone-hard just looking at her juicy thighs and shaved pussy. Nut looked around the room furiously. He went into the bathroom, then came back out. He knocked everything off the dresser, search-ing back and forth.

"Fuck is you doin', whody?" Rosco wanted to know.

Nut threw a drawer open and began snatching out bras— then he grabbed a longer, lower drawer and looked through there. Finally, he ransacked her panty drawer, and when he got to the bottom, what he saw froze him instantly. Nut didn't find what he was looking for, but what he found was even more valuable to him.

Pepper's Cutt Boyz chain.

He couldn't believe his eyes, and in the first few seconds, he was too numb to feel. Rosco was getting impatient. "Yo, Nut," he called him, but Nut didn't respond. The tears flowed from his eyes as he slowly turned around, holding the chain in his hand.

"This . . . bitch . . . this . . . *bitch* . . . killed my *brother*." Every word sent pure hate through his veins. When Rosco saw the chain, he shook his head, enraged as well.

As soon as Mandi saw what he had, her eyes got as big as saucers and she tried to scramble away. Her movements in-censed Nut and he caught her coming off the bed and kicked her to the floor, where he kept kicking her until two of her ribs cracked.

"This bitch killed my brother!" he bellowed, still kicking until Rosco had to pull him off of her.

"Nut, chill! *Chill*! We gonna handle it, but first, make this bitch talk!" Rosco advised him. He had love for Pepper, too, but his mind was on robbing the connect.

Nut stared down at Mandi, moaning in agony. He knew after finding the chain in her house, not only did Mandi have to die, but Daquan as well. If he didn't kill Pepper, at least he knew, and that was the ultimate treachery, justifying everything he was doing.

"I'ma kill that nigguh," he growled, imagining Daquan's face when he felt the hot lead cut through him.

Nut dropped down on Mandi, grabbed her left hand, and blew a hole clean through it, all in one motion. The pain was so great, she damn near passed out.

"Pl-Please," she blubbered. "I'll tell you what you want to know."

"Naw, bitch, now you gonna suffer," Nut promised her, then spotted what he had been looking for on the nightstand.

The curling iron.

He flipped the switch and smiled when he saw the red light pop on. He put it between Mandi's legs, cocking them wide, then slid the iron in. She winced from the metallic intrusion, then Nut began to pull it in and out, fucking her with the rod.

"This pussy hot, lil' mama, ha? I'ma set it on fire," he chuckled mockingly.

It didn't take long for the metal to get hot and begin to slowly sizzle between Mandi's inner walls, and she finally blacked out. The room smelled like fried rotten fish, and Mandi's flesh was puckered dry and pussed. Nut let it get completely hot then inserted it again, waking Mandi up as she let out a high-pitched scream of pure agony. Even Rosco finally said, "Aiight, Nut. Take it out. She said she was gonna talk."

Nut slid the curling iron out, and blood seeped from her womb.

"Now," Nut announced triumphantly, "take us to the connect."

There was no fight left in Mandi. The pain they had inflicted had taken every ounce of will out of her, except the will to die. She would tell them the truth, then pray Nut would kill her swiftly.

Mandi took them to the Slidell suburbs. She lay on the floor in the backseat, her hand wrapped in a towel, still naked from the waist down. She could barely speak above a whisper but she explained the whole layout. Jorge's spot was in a residential area—a man and his wife lived there with a small child. The neighbors never knew that they lived next to a major Louisiana dope distribution center, because no one did anything out of the ordinary there.

Nut and Rosco pulled up on the block and saw the yellow house near the cul de sac. They parked, watching the house for activity. The neighborhood was peaceful. They got out, leaving Mandi in the car, knowing they didn't have to worry about her going anywhere. They walked around to the side of the house where the man was watching TV. They went to the rear and saw the patio door, just like Mandi told them. They squatted on either side, listening intently. Nut cocked the Mac 11 and nodded to Rosco.

He stood up and shattered the patio glass with a short burst of automatic gunfire. They rushed in and saw the woman scream and try to run in the kitchen, but Nut cut her down in the doorway. The child was small and Rosco grabbed him up, just as the man came out firing a nine. Nut got low and aimed for the man's knees, crippling him instantly. Rosco ran over and took the gun from him, then put it to his son's head.

"Please don't kill him," the Spanish man said. "I'll give you whatever you want!"

"Where the dope?" Nut demanded.

He and Rosco drug the man in the back. "It's in the mattress," the man said, pointing.

Rosco snatched the mattress up, looking for a hidden zipper. He found it and unzipped the whole mattress, flipping it open like a suitcase. Neither he nor Nut had ever seen that much dope at one time in their lives. There was close to fifty bricks of heroin, lined neatly along the hidden compartment that looked like it could easily hold three times as much.

Rosco snatched up the bedsheet and started putting the bricks in it. Once they were all in the sheet, he tied it into one big sack, turned to Nut, and said, "I got it! Let's go!"

But the sight of that much dope made Nut have a change of plans. He spit flame into Rosco's chest, killing him right where he stood; then Rosco dropped to the floor with a thud. When the man saw Nut kill his own partner, he knew he and his son were next. He mumbled a Spanish prayer right before the slugs of the Mac tore open his skull, then his son's right behind him. Nut snatched up the heavy sheet and flung it over his shoulder. He exited the way he came and ran as fast as he could with over a hundred pounds on his back. He put the bag in the backseat and drug Mandi out by her heels, banging her head on the pavement. When she saw the Mac aimed at her head, she breathed, "Thank you." The shots ended her pain forever. Nut had gotten what he came for, but the job was only half done. He turned the car around and headed straight for Daquan.

Daquan looked at his watch again, having already checked it a few minutes before that, and again before that. Nut was keeping him from a lot of stuff he had to do. It had been dark, but it was full-blown night when he said to Red, "Man, where the fuck he at?"

They were standing outside of the spot, and it was booming as usual. The other Cutt Boyz were serving the fiends, while Red responded, "He comin', bruh. He said he'd be heah."

Red had given Daquan the story Nut had given him, telling Daquan how Rosco had gotten into an argument with his girl, and he hit her. She had called the police without his knowing, and when they came they had smelled weed. Since the apartment Rosco had in Baton Rouge was in his girl's name, she let them search it and they had found a gun—a gun Nut thought he may've used in a murder up there. He needed Daquan to meet him in the Calliope because he might have to bounce.

Nut knew Daquan would believe the story, because he had no reason not to. He knew Daquan wouldn't turn his back on him, so Nut used his sense of loyalty to keep him away from Mandi's long enough to complete the job.

Daquan knew Kimoko would be finished at the doctor's by now, and he had to pick her up. Plus, he and Mandi were supposed to be meeting Master P to discuss the final touches of his contract, and P was the "P" in punctuality—he called it "being on *point*." Now, Daquan was already late.

But there was another reason why Daquan waited. It felt like this was some kind of sign that he was doing the right thing. He didn't wish any bad on Nut or Rosco, but if they were out of the way, his life would be less complicated. With Nut on the run, or Rosco locked up, there would be nobody expecting to be supplied, and his exit from the game would be that much smoother. That was worth waiting for.

"Say, whody, I'ma go to the store. If Nut come, tell 'im I'll be right back," Daquan instructed Red.

Daquan didn't take his car, opting to walk instead. It had been a while since he'd walked through the CP3, and the nostalgia attracted him. It was a pleasant spring evening, his favorite time of year. He looked around at the place he called home, remembering how they used to play football in the grassy area that separated the entrances of the project buildings. He strolled past the basketball court, and remembered the time Desiree beat up Pam. The thought made him wonder what happened to Desiree. She had moved out to Baton Rouge and they had lost contact. Daquan remembered the crush she once had on him, and it made him smile. Then he remembered the way he crushed *her*, because he had fucked Pam. She never spoke to him after that. He wondered if he ever did see her, would she still be mad, or would she be over it?

He approached the store and entered it about the same time Nut's gold Porsche skidded up on Red. Nut jumped out the car and ran straight up on Daquan's car with his nine drawn. When Red saw that, he didn't know what to think. Nut walked up on Red and demanded to know, "Where that nigguh at?"

Red was shook. This hadn't been a part of the plan, but from the look on Nut's tear-stained face, he knew something had changed drastically.

"He went to the store," Red replied.

"Go get them thangs! I'ma kill that nigguh!" Nut's voice boomed.

When the two other Cutt Boyz heard Nut raving, they came over to see what he was yelling about.

"Kill *who*? Daquan?" Red asked. Shit was really serious, he thought.

"Who else? That nigguh killed Pepper!" Nut accused him, and all three Cutt Boyz who heard him stood there, shocked.

"Killed Pepper?" Red echoed, not believing his ears. "Naw, Nut. How you know? You sho'?"

"'Cause I know, muhfucka. You think I'd lie on my dead brother?! Go get them goddamn things—whody finna die tonight!" Nut promised.

The other two ran off to the stash to follow orders, while

Red still couldn't believe it was true. Either way, he knew how Nut was, so there was no way he'd question him further. And there was no way he wasn't gonna ride with Nut, because to go against him would make him look like he was on Daquan's side. This certainly wasn't the time to be the voice of reason. Red just hoped Nut was right, and that Daquan was guilty, because either way the verdict had been passed, and court was about to be held in the streets.

Daquan came out of the store, and his beeper went off. He looked and saw it was Kimoko. He figured she was just telling him she was ready, and he started not to call, but he wanted to make sure there wasn't anything wrong with the baby. Daquan was still worried how her addiction would affect the pregnancy, so he decided to call her.

Daquan walked down the street to a Superman-style phone booth at the edge of an abandoned corner store. He slid open the rusty door with a squeak, and deposited a quarter. The clink of the metal being digested by the phone came at the same time four AKs were being clipped and cocked.

Nut looked from face to face for any sign of fear or reluctance on the Cutt Boyz' behalf. If there was any, they hid it well.

"What store he go to, Red?" Nut asked, gripping the AK.

"Probably Rose Tavern. I told you he left walking," Red reminded him.

Nut tossed the keys to Red. "You drive."

Daquan waited out the three rings before Kimoko answered.

"Where you at, Daquan? I'm ready to go."

"Everything alright?" he questioned her.

"Yeah—wit' the baby, that is. But I'm about to starve, boy," she giggled.

Daquan smiled. "Lil' mama, you always 'bout to starve . . . You okay, though?"

"I'm fine."

Daquan paused, not knowing how to phrase his feelings, so he began slowly.

"Kimoko . . . I, um . . . I'm sorry for the way I treated you at first. I ain't know how to take you or the situation."

Kimoko was silent, but he could hear the soft rustle of her breathing.

"And um . . . I want you to know that I believe the baby is mine. I do, and even if it ain't, believe me, I'ma take care of it like it was, fo' sho'." He could hear Kimoko sniffle and say, "Daquan, you don't have to . . ."

Daquan cut her off smoothly, like, "No, Ki, I *do* have to . . . you not only the mother of my child, but you good peoples, and you don't deserve nothin' less than that same goodness. So if I can give it to you, then I will."

Kimoko's sobs smothered her words, so she whispered through her exhaled breath, "Thank you, D. Thank you for saying that. I really needed to hear that."

Red pulled up in front of Rose Tavern, and one of the Cutt Boyz went inside. He dashed right back out and announced, "He ain't in there!"

"Go back to the spot," Nut ordered, thinking Daquan was on his way back. If he hadn't just then glanced to his right as they passed Tonti Street, he wouldn't have been able to holler, "There he go! At the phone booth!"

Daquan had his back turned to the street, with one finger in his ear. The phone was old, making it hard to hear. With the passing cars it was almost impossible.

"But look, don't get it twisted, lil' mama—I can't carry you like that, you know, like me *and* you. It's me *got* you, ya dig?" Daquan clarified, so there'd be no misconceptions.

"And me got you, too," Kimoko flirted, happy to know she had someone to at least count on, if not truly love, in this world.

Nut, Red, and the other Cutt Boyz pulled up across the

street, the sounds of their closing doors and approaching foot-steps muffled by the traffic.

"Okay, girl, gimme about twenty minutes, and I'll be there to get you," Daquan assured her.

The sound of metal tapping on the outside of the booth got Daquan's attention. As he turned around, he got the feeling of déjà vu, like he had done this before. He didn't know when or where until he saw the four faces of death, and the AKs aimed at his chest. Then he remembered.

It was his dream, literally coming true.

"Game over, nigguh," Nut said, and Daquan's mental lip synch was only a split second behind the actual words.

The AKs raised and the last thing he saw was flame leaping from their muzzles. Then . . .

He blacked out. When he opened his eyes he could hear things as if they were coming from the other end of a vacuum. The gunshots, Kimoko's screams over the phone, his own heartbeat. If they were shooting him, he didn't feel it, because the first shot mercifully pierced his heart, severing his connection with physical life forever. The rest of the slugs were just mutilating an empty shell.

Behind Nut and the Cutt Boyz, he saw Diana appear, walk-ing toward him. She strolled right through them and into the booth, extending her hand to Daquan.

"Come with me, Daquan. We can finally be free."

He took Diana's hand and allowed her to lead him out of the booth. He walked through Red, the two other Cutt Boyz, and past Nut. He could see the look of pure hatred, deep hurt, and mental confusion in the eyes of his best friend, and he understood exactly what had happened. Daquan knew what this was for, and he accepted it.

He whispered to Nut, "I ain't mad atcha, whody." But Nut couldn't hear him, because his heart had died long ago. Daquan looked back at his own body, jerking and twisting, as blood squirted and smeared the inside of the shattered phone booth. When the shooting stopped, his corpse finally dropped, falling face-down on the pavement. Then he and Diana disappeared together into the cool Louisiana night.

Epilogue

Kimoko had a little boy, whom she named Daquan, Jr. She did her best for a while, but gradually she succumbed to the lure of the streets, eventually ending up right back at Penny's, like Penny knew she would.

Grandma Mama took Daquan, Jr. and spent the last years of her life raising him in the house that we bought him on the strength of the contract D.Q. never got a chance to sign. Melissa took over the house and raising Daquan, Jr. until Jerome came home and took him from a boy to a true man.

Nut blew up off the lick, going O.T. as far as Atlanta and picking Lil' Red as his right-hand man. He had a strong run, but Lil' Red ended up snitching him out, just like Pepper had done Jerome.

Me? Well . . . y'all heard of me . . . I survived, and stayed true to my man's memory, 'cause I thought y'all oughta know, ya dig? Just in case there's any young Daquans and Nuts out there, always remember—no matter where you go or how far you get, death is always . . . right around the corner.

Trust no muhfuckin' body!!

Holla!!!

DEATH AROUND THE CORNER

C-MURDER

The following questions are intended to enhance
your group's discussion of
this book.

DISCUSSION QUESTIONS

1. How does Diana help Daquan throughout the book? What would her life have been like if she had lived longer?

2. Is there anything Grandma Mama could have done to keep Daquan off the streets? What would have made a difference in his life? More money? A father? A different environment?

3. How does Daquan justify his actions? Does Daquan truly believe it when he tells himself that drugs took his life away, so they owe him a living?

4. When Daquan goes to jail, the narrator says, "The worst kind of heart is a young, bitter one." What is the meaning of this statement?

5. Why does G-Money attack the prison guard when he knows that he will be beaten? What effect does his beating have on the other prisoners, and on Daquan?

6. What does Diana mean when she tells Daquan, "You can't change the mistakes you made in the past, but you can make sure you don't make them again." Does Daquan heed her advice? Why or why not?

7. What examples can you think of when Daquan made decisions based on emotion rather than having a thought-out plan. How did those decisions work out for him?

8. How does Mikey, the boy who is kidnapped, differ from young Daquan?

9. How does Nut's relationship with Daquan change from the time they first meet until the end of the book? Are there any clues early in the story that predict how things will turn out in the end?

10. When Melissa tells her son Jerome to stop selling drugs, but spends his drug money anyway, what message does she send him?

11. What does Daquan's father mean when he says "You got to be more than good. You got to be smart." Is he? Is Daquan? Why or why not?

12. Is Mandi a good or a bad person? Does she deserve what happens to her at the end? Who is she thinking about when she tells Daquan that "very rarely is there honor among thieves, which means, if someone is a thief, then he'll steal from anyone. It's hard to trust people, Daquan, even if you want to." Does she listen to her own advice? Does Daquan? How is Daquan's relationship with her different than his relationship with Vanessa?

13. Is Nut a good or bad person? What do you think will happen to him at book's end?

14. In the end does Daquan make good on all the mistakes he's made? Does he deserve what happens to him at the end?

Post your thoughts on these and other questions at www.deatharoundthecorner.com

AUTHOR'S NOTE

People always ask me what made me want to become an author. First of all, I was behind bars facing a life sentence, so I didn't know what the future held. But I knew one thing: I had to get on my grind. I had to get my hustle on. Plus, I like to express myself and put my words out there. Since I couldn't do it in music, I said let me do it with a book. I had been doing a lot of studying and reading. A lot of people don't know I was an honor student in school. I read about 500 books since I've been locked up, so I felt like it was time for me to get started to become an author.

The first thing I did was I started reading a lot. Sometimes I read a book in one day. So I started getting real interested in everything about books, and I just started feeling the flow and how different authors express themselves. I learned a lot by just hands-on experience. Whatever I'm doing, I learn quick. So that was the first process, just reading and getting interested.

Then I'm like, All right, let me just try writing. But I'm my harshest critic. So then I said, I need some info on this. I need a book that can teach me how to write a book and write a novel, and all about publishing. I wanna know everything about the game, ya heard me? So I got all that information through the library. So then I'm sitting down, reading it all and getting the game in my head. One of my favorite authors, Dean Koontz, even wrote a book on how to write a novel. His was crucial 'cause I liked how he put his words together. But I still wanted the urban crowd. So it's me mixed with Koontz—that's how I feel. And that's how it all started.

Writing *Death Around the Corner* from prison took me two years. I wrote everything out by hand in notebooks and then mailed them out to be typed up on a computer. It could have been done before that, but sometimes there's so much happening on the tier and so much going on in your case and your personal life that you just have to chill. And then Katrina hit— the storm. I sent out a lot of chapters that were lost when all the mail got shut down. So once we came back from Katrina, and the mail started rolling, I called and said to look for the mail! The post office said to call this number and go on this Web site, 'cause it's all just sitting in crates out in the sun. So four months later I got all the chapters back. Then I just finished the last of them right then and there. And that was it.

I chose the title *Death Around the Corner* because every day I was locked up I kept hearing about people getting killed— young dudes. Three murders one day, four murders, five murders. There was just a lot of brothers getting killed. So I said it looks like everybody has to watch their back. It's serious out there. Death is so close—right around the corner. Everybody can relate to it, from my hood to your hood. Anywhere. So that was the theme of the whole book.

Daquan starts out how we all start out—innocent. Just a little boy happy for the little things in life: going to school, playing in the grass, having fun on the seesaws at the park. Then at five years old, he has his first sight of tragedy, and it all goes downhill from there. This is a story for all those people that society gives up on. There's millions and millions of Daquans out there. You can just drive through the hood to see a snotty nose with a Pamper, no parents at home, no parks to play in, abandoned. There's millions and millions of Daquans in the world. Not just black, but white and everything else—South American, Asian, African.

Once you read the book you will understand where I'm coming from. It's just the life of a young black man growing up in the hood with the odds against him. So anybody can get it. Death is always right around the corner. And with all my books that I write, I'm gonna make sure they have a crucial, crucial twist that nobody would think about. 'Cause I be thinkin' about some *other* things sometimes. You'll just have to keep reading to learn more about that.

And if you love this book, get ready for Tru Publishing, 'cause we got a lot more heat coming for ya. So peep game.

Peace
Corey Miller, a.k.a. C-Murder

The following excerpt is from
Kenji Jasper's powerful book
SNOW,
another VIBE Street Lit book.
Available from Kensington
in March 2007.

I traveled the stretch of hallway like a ninja, listening for the loud sounds of young Black men with money to lose. It wasn't long before I heard them, behind the last door on the left, 7H. Mike Mike had told just enough of a lie to cover his ass. And I had to keep loving him for that.

Standing in front of the door, I wasn't worried about what I was gonna say, or how many people I was going to have to lay to an early rest. All I wanted was the money so I could leave, make my final walk home and sleep for the few hours I had left before breakfast. I wasn't preoccupied with inflicting pain. I didn't care about what the action would do for my reputation in the streets. It was just another job, just what I *had* to do in order to survive.

I kicked the door in the perfect spot and it flung open, splintering the inside edge of the wooden frame. There were six of them that I could see. I didn't take note of their size or color, only their hands, several of which were already in laps and waistbands. That was a mistake.

#1 wounded one in the arm, another in the thigh and a third through what sounded like his right lung. A bullet screamed by my ear and three more lodged in the doorframe just inches away from me. Too close. I darted into the hallway and rolled to the right, barely fast enough to evade the spray of bullets that punched through the outside wall.

Apparently they needed me to liven up the party. So I pulled out something special I'd snagged from my hiding place in the sewer tunnel, to oblige them. I didn't have time for the OK Corral. I had a family to get back to.

I pitched the pipe bomb low and fast, aiming for it to hit the opposite wall so that it'd stop far away from the money on the table. I counted to four and covered my ears. It blew and I was back inside, gunning down everything that had the nerve to still be moving.

The glass in all of the windows had been blown out and an orange flame was quickly crawling across the dingy brown drapes, pushing clouds of smoke toward me. But I could still see my prize.

The money was all over the table, crisp 20s, 50s and 100s. I salivated. But I was too fixated on the pie. That was my mistake.

A bullet exploded through my right shoulder. I couldn't believe it. I wasn't supposed to get hit. I let off in the direction the shot came from, even before I had the chance to see who it was. I twisted around to see blood gushing from her belly as she fell to her knees and then to the floor.

She couldn't have been more then seventeen, short and pretty with round hips and high cheekbones. She was the kind of girl I would have pulled back in high school, if I had ever gone. She dropped to the floor like a bag of bricks. That was unfortunate.

There was a shoulder bag on the back of one of the chairs at the table, and I went for it, tucking #2 back in my pocket to free a hand up. I broomed the money in and zipped it closed, knowing that the fire department would care about the fire before the cops bothered with the murders.

"I guess I won the hand," I said as I turned my back to the

room of corpses. I was almost through the open door when I heard crying from the back room. Was it my baby?

No, it wasn't Kayi. But it was a kid nonetheless, something too undeveloped to move on its own. And through its ears, that kid became a living witness to my merciless mayhem. I thought about smiling little Kayi and I almost dropped #1 on the ground. And I never dropped my heat.

I tucked the pistol away as I went to the back room and put the child in her stroller. Then I rolled her out into the hall, away from the growing inferno. Doors would start opening and I wasn't going to run the risk of being ID'd.

I took the back stairs down to the basement, where I crept out of the broken emergency exit that led to the alley in the back of the building. As always, the night had kept things in my favor. I barely felt the cold, or the wind, or the profuse sweat on my brow as I trudged though the twelve snowy blocks that got me to our house. Adele's Acura was in the driveway, my '78 Buick Regal parked in front of it. I'd have to cut the treads off the boots and dump them, just in case.

I dropped my keys trying to get inside. My hands twitched more violently each time I struggled to pick them up off the ground. On the other side of the door I figured the shaking meant that I was coming down with something. So I made my way across the living room to the kitchen, where I gave light to the dark house. And then I put on the water for some tea.

#1 and #2 and the cash were on the couch in the other room when I hung my coat over one of the metal chairs surrounding the kitchen table. The pain in my shoulder worsened, then I noticed the blood. The right side of my sweatshirt (and even the longjohns underneath) were soaked with the sticky redness. But I wasn't light-headed so the blood loss couldn't have been too bad.

I got the paramedic's kit out from the bottom of the pantry as I prepared to dress my own wound. The bullet had luckily gone straight through. But I taped gauze on both ends so it would clot. I was finishing up when Kayi came alive upstairs, her cries as shrill as a soprano's. I raced up the two short flights to find the cause of her late night madness.

On the way I heard Adele snoring in our bedroom. It made me happy to know that I'd been there to answer our baby, and to give Mommy a break after what had more than likely been a very long day at the office. The wound clotted on its own in the hours that followed after I brought my sweetie down to the kitchen, got her a fresh bottle of pumped breastmilk from the fridge and warmed it in a pan. My right arm was stained brown in places from the drying life fluid. But my baby didn't care. All she wanted was some time with her Daddy, just like that little one back in 7H. I put *my* little girl down in her crib and put another strip of tape on my shoulder.